Existence
is Elsewhen

Previously from Elsewhen Press

[Re]Awakenings

AN ANTHOLOGY OF NEW SPECULATIVE FICTION

Existence is Elsewhen

John Gribbin
Rhys Hughes
Christopher G. Nuttall
Douglas Thompson
J.A. Christy
Peter R. Ellis
Steve Harrison
Edwin Hayward
Stefan Jackson
Andy McKell
Siobhan McVeigh
Robin Moran
Ira Nayman
Susan Oke
Sanem Ozdural
Tanya Reimer
Chloe Skye
Tej Turner
Dave Weaver
Peter Wolfe

Elsewhen Press

Existence is Elsewhen
First published in Great Britain by Elsewhen Press, 2016
An imprint of Alnpete Limited

Copyrights
Inside and Out™ V.5 © J.A. Christy 2016; *In the bleak Long Winter* © Peter R. Ellis
2016; *Something to Beef about* © John Gribbin 2016 (a revised version of a story that
first appeared in *Interzone* #49, July 1991); *Earthsale* © Steve Harrison 2016;
Ambrosia © Edwin Hayward 2016; *Jekking the Oofers* © Rhys Hughes 2016; *Luceria*
© Stefan Jackson 2016; *Homo Sapiens Inferior* © Andy McKell 2016; *Face the Music*
© Siobhan McVeigh 2016; *Degeneration* © Robin Moran 2016; *The Writer Did It!*
© Ira Nayman 2016; *The girl in Black* © Christopher G. Nuttall 2016; *Hide and Hunt*
© Susan Oke 2016; *The Song of the Sky* © Sanem Ozdural 2016; *Forbidden Fruit*
© Tanya Reimer 2016; *Precipitation* © Chloe Skye 2016; *Bird Brains*
© Douglas Thompson 2016; *The Last Days* © Tej Turner 2016; *The Copy*
© Dave Weaver 2016; *Murder in M-23* © Peter Wolfe 2016. All rights reserved
The right of the authors to be identified as the authors of this work has been
asserted in accordance with sections 77 and 78 of the Copyright, Designs and
Patents Act 1988. No part of this publication may be reproduced, stored in a
retrieval system or transmitted in any form, or by any means (electronic,
mechanical, telepathic, or otherwise) without the prior written permission of the
copyright owner.

Elsewhen Press, PO Box 757, Dartford, Kent DA2 7TQ
www.elsewhen.press

British Library Cataloguing in Publication Data.
A catalogue record for this book is available from the British Library.

ISBN 978-1-908168-85-6 Print edition
ISBN 978-1-908168-95-5 eBook edition

Condition of Sale
This book is sold subject to the condition that it shall not, by way of trade or
otherwise, be lent, re-sold, hired out or otherwise circulated in any form of binding
or cover other than that in which it is published and without a similar condition
including this condition being imposed on the subsequent purchaser.

This book is copyright under the Berne Convention.
Elsewhen Press & Planet-Clock Design are trademarks of Alnpete Limited

Designed and formatted by Elsewhen Press

This book is a work of fiction. All names, characters, places, worlds, universes and
timeframes are either a product of the authors' fertile imagination or are used
fictitiously. Any resemblance to actual planes of existence, places, people (living,
dead, cybernetic or choofies) is purely coincidental.

Contents

Inside and Out™ V.5 – From Here to ETERNITY
J.A. Christy 9

In the bleak Long Winter
Peter R. Ellis 33

Something to beef about
John Gribbin 43

Earthsale
Steve Harrison 55

Ambrosia
Edwin Hayward 67

Jekking the Oofers
Rhys Hughes 75

Luceria
Stefan Jackson 85

Homo Sapiens Inferior
Andy McKell 103

Face the Music
Siobhan McVeigh 115

Degeneration
Robin Moran 131

The Writer Did It!
Ira Nayman 141

The Girl in Black
Christopher G. Nuttall 163

Hide and Hunt
Susan Oke 181

The Song of the Sky
Sanem Ozdural 197

Forbidden Fruit
Tanya Reimer 211

Precipitation
Chloe Skye 229

Bird Brains
Douglas Thompson 241

The Last Days
Tej Turner 259

The Copy
Dave Weaver 275

Murder in M-23
Peter Wolfe 285

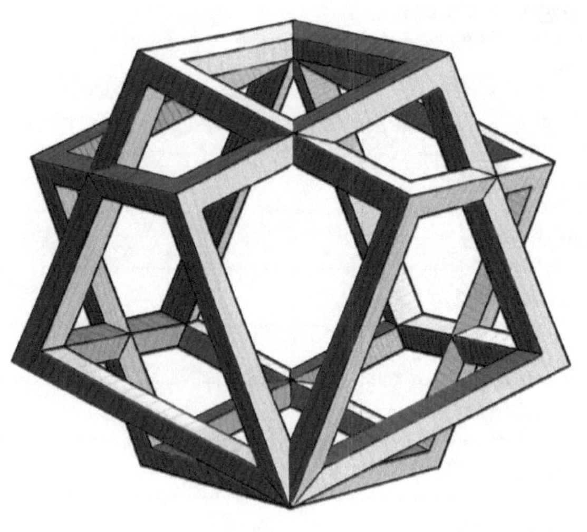

Inside and Out™ V.5 – From Here to ETERNITY

by

J.A. Christy

J.A. Christy's writing career began in infant school at the age of seven when she won best poetry prize with her poem 'Winter'. Since then she has been writing short stories and has had several published in magazines and anthologies.

J.A. Christy holds a PhD in which she explores the stories we use in everyday life to construct our identities. She is a Chartered Psychologist and Scientist and writes to apply her knowledge to cross the boundaries between science and art, in particular in the crime, speculative and science-fiction genres.

She lives in Oldham with her partner and their dog.

Part 1

The Farraday Institute, New York,
28th September 2095

I pull up the blind and the sunshine streams through the window. I can feel Tendo's eyes burning into my back, silently pleading for answers.

"So…?"

I turn to face him.

"I can't do it. I can't abandon the conference. It's too important."

Tendo shakes his head.

"But your wife? Your child?" There's a pause. Then he nods. "Version 5. You're unveiling Version 5, aren't you?"

I stare at him.

"Yes. I am. I'm sorry, Tendo, but I can't understand what your problem is with Version 5. It's temporary, and Version 6 will be on standby to implement in case anything goes wrong."

Tendo snorts.

"Wrong. Now there's a concept. But I don't suppose it matters what I say. I'd better go and attend to what, it turns out, is a very special event. More special than any of us knew, but still not important enough for you to be there."

The anger builds and eventually I lose it.

"They'll be fine. The baby's Level 1. Green. Julia is Red, but that's only to be expected in her condition. But she was fine this morning. So what can go wrong? I didn't plan it this way, but I don't need to be there. They don't need me, Tendo; Julia will be fine. And if you're so concerned, why don't you go right now? I've been waiting for this conference all my life, and I can't just abandon it."

It's true. I'm Angus Farraday, the founder of Inside and Out™, a healthcare system that has changed the vista of life. Today, on the 200th anniversary of the death of Louis Pasteur, I'm about to launch Inside and Out™ Version Five, at the World Medicine Congress. In just over one hour, medical experts from all over the world will meet virtually to witness the launch of a bigger and better version of the system that has streamlined health. I was just in the process of rehearsing my speech when Tendo, my wife's Fountain Keeper, told me that she is about to give birth.

Tendo still looms large on the wall monitor behind me. I silently damn Ray Bradbury for his communication prophesy, that we would have life-sized versions of people on screens that fill a whole wall. I would never have guessed a hundred years ago that I would be able to pull up a chair to a virtual conference table in Tobago and feel like I was there. But I'm grateful because, despite what we have achieved in the Inside and Out™ program, I still privately think there's nothing like face to face communication. Of course, the visual social cues of yesteryear, like eye movement and skin blush, have been overtaken by Inside and Out™'s 'Vital Signs' service, where, as well as the overall health level, the heartbeat, perspiration rate and blood pressure are shown on the screens of all the participants. Very convenient. And often very telling. Despite the race to develop ways to mask these Vitals, no one has yet been able to disguise the sudden changes that come with stress and disapproval.

"Look, Tendo, tell Julia I will be with her as soon as possible. The conference will only last a few hours, how long do you expect the process to last?"

Tendo frowns. He's more difficult to read, but his expression tells me everything I need to know.

"The process? She's your wife, and your child is about to be born. You might have controlled everyone's health until they are practically cyborg, but you haven't managed to control that yet, have you? You know, life? The actual process of living, that elusive spark? Get over here as soon as you can, and I'll keep a split screen ready just in case you can't make it."

The screen fades to a pulsing green with an amber tint around the outside and I notice my own Vitals are quite high. Unusual. I'd been to the Fountain just this morning. Tendo's words hurt, because I really have tried to get the birthing process under control. When I started the Inside and Out™ program, over fifty years ago, I naturally assumed that every human being would welcome the ability to automatically take care of their own body. When we introduced the Fountains we were certain that the whole population would simply roll up and use them.

We'd all worked hard to provide a Fountain in every neighborhood in Inside and Out™ V.1. The Fountain principle is that we provide preventative measures for the malconditions for which we already have vaccinations and treatments for those we don't. At the beginning of the project we screened every person with a program called Initial Diagnosis, or ID, and placed a tiny microchip in their wrist. All babies born after V.1 was introduced automatically have a chip inserted. Three levels of health were introduced with corresponding Fountain requirements:

Level 1 – Green – Fountain walk-throughs for those with excellent health to minor ailments

Level 2 – Amber – People who do not respond to Fountain walk-throughs must undergo SIA treatments – Specific Investigation Actions

Level 3 – Red – Those people who are terminally ill or pregnant are allocated a separate Fountain and Fountain Keeper within SIA

By V.2 we had realized that there were some people who were resisting the chip, and would not be assessed or attend the Fountain. My staff couldn't understand it, as the Fountains were so conveniently placed, in railway stations, on the metro. It was and still is a step-in, step-out process. We have improved the cubicles since then, but overall the process is the same.

Every morning you step into the Fountain and place your thumb onto a pad, which extracts a tiny piece of tissue and a drop of blood. This is analyzed and, as this takes place, an eye level screen monitors vitals and produces a visual. Green, amber, red. If any malconditions are detected, then a Fountain Treatment is given direct from the thumbpad. A record is kept of health levels and, should green turn to amber, the person reports to SIA for further investigation.

SIA was the easy part of Inside and Out™. When the uses of the program became clear, all the major pharmaceutical companies joined together to form the World Medicine Congress, or WMC. All Healthchips are manufactured by WMC and all the data collected in the Fountains are managed by them. The SIA department operates in order to investigate conditions that do not respond to Fountain walk-throughs and to rationalize them and manufacture an adequate treatment. While this seems simple enough and very efficient, this was the part that we had most difficulty with and had to resort to extreme measures to implement and stabilize.

The main problem was that even though V.1 was marketed across both virtual and street level platforms, it wasn't user friendly enough. In order for the program to be successful, 98.9% of the population needed to take part. In the test areas we had 99.9% success, when it was rolled out nationally we found that some people actually preferred the old system of waiting for an appointment to visit a doctor, citing the face to face comfort of a consultation, even though many of the doctors gave wrong diagnoses, compared with the 99.9% correct diagnosis rate of the Fountains. We tried implementing a virtual face on the Fountain screen, but this did not work so we reverted to the color graphics. By this time the pharmaceuticals had committed to WMC and were pooling all their knowledge. In order to keep them onboard, we introduced two implementation tools.

The first was the Life Credit. The Fountains were monitoring all aspects of physiology. If it occurred in the human body, the Fountain could analyze it. To make the Fountains appear more user friendly we introduced the 'Me Test', a survey that asked the user questions about their psychological health. As the sample size increased, WMC were able to compare the biological state and the psychological state and note the organic deficiencies that occurred in low mood, sadness and depression compared with happiness and contentment. This, it turned out, was not on the level purely of serotonin, but in a complex cocktail of neurotransmitters which, once discovered, was tested at SIA and subsequently made available in the Fountains to those who gained Life Credits. Obtaining a life credit is simple: Attend to have a Healthchip installed and attend a Fountain every day.

The second was a little more controversial and more difficult to convince the authorities that it was ethical, but they agreed in the end that it was for the greater good. Here at Inside and Out™ we pride ourselves on integrity and honesty, but unfortunately we concealed the initial uptake figures from WMC. Some would, and later, did, say that this was fraudulent, and was used as a lever for the second implementation tool. As founder of Inside and Out™, I have always held the view that the program was voluntary and in no way impedes human rights and choice. But when we realized that the demographic for the non-uptake of the Fountains were the poorer communities, we had to act fast. Genetic modification of food became popular mid 20th century and gathered pace in the early 21st century as climate change meant that crops were failing and people were starving. World leaders agreed publicly to the provision of genetically modified food and faced little opposition as the process was entirely transparent.

However, some foods flourished in the warmer, wetter climate, and people still had the choice to choose these foods if they wished, claiming that this was a basic human right. In 2050 Inside and Out™ in conjunction with the WMC offered free fruit and vegetables to poorer communities. These crops were loaded with the daily Fountain treatments and a radioactive trace that could be identified in the Fountain test, similar to the microscopic chip that many people had volunteered to have in their wrists. The rogue 'doctors' who still frequented these poorer communities were struck off the WMC register and Fountains were installed on every street corner. After six months the food provision was ceased and people suffered withdrawal symptoms. Fearing there was a serious epidemic, they consulted WMC and were directed to the Fountains, where their healthcare was resumed.

So, you see, Inside and Out™ really is inside and out. We can regulate your body, regulate your mood and regulate your lifestyle, complete homeostasis, all the while making sure that even the laziest person has to walk around each day to get to a Fountain. As a result, we've regulated out most childhood and adult diseases, and made wellness a daily norm. The only things we haven't been able to change are death, the aging process and, of course, conception and birth. Although, as you will see when I present V.5 of Inside and Out™ in a few minutes, we have made some interesting progress.

It's nearly time and I check my Vitals on the screen again, and my wife's Vitals on my desk tablet. She's Red, of course, and she looks stable at the moment. So all's well and by the end of today I will have a son. I go to my private Fountain and step inside. I place my thumb on the pad. I don't want anything to go wrong at the WMC, no clues from my Vitals that this has been the most stressful year of my life.

"Regulate."

The familiar 'psst' of the vacuum extraction calms me, and then I see the Amber outer of my Vitals return to Green. The familiar gentle press of confidence fills my mind, and I let it filter through my senses as the worries for my wife and my irritation at Tendo disappear. My wall screen snaps into life and I am confronted with the full Council of the WMC.

Part 2

SIA Unit, New York City,
28th September 2095

Julia Farraday watched the pulsing of the red screen visual as the button stuck to her huge contracting stomach sent signals. Her room at SIA resembled a huge Fountain, and although she was free to move about she could hardly stand because of the pain.

"Aaargh! It's here again. Tendo! Make it stop."

Tendo took Julia's hand.

"I'm sorry, Julia. You chose a Class 3 Authentic Birth, with just regular pain killer. Everything is progressing normally and the baby should be here very soon."

Julia screamed again, then flopped back on the bed.

"Very soon? Minutes? Hours? I know about childbirth. I've researched it on the HistoryNet. This could go on for hours, days, even. Back in the old days women could have an epidural injection, with complete pain relief, and pethidine, and a midwife who would help. No offense, Tendo."

"None taken, Julia. But you know as well as I do that things have changed. The Version 3 'Let's Leave Lasers Outside Health' initiative has all but ruled out Cesarean Section and epidural. According to my risk assessment..."

"I know, I know. My mother had breast enhancement and facial surgery when she was younger, and she ended up Culminating very early due to chronic pain."

Of course, thanks to Fountains, such surgical procedures were now unnecessary: with The Aesthetics option, parents could choose the way their child would look before they were born.

"Who needs surgery these days? We're all so damn healthy, survival of the fittest is a distant memory."

"Yeah. I guess so. Darwin would be turning in his grave. But it's better this way. Maximum wellbeing, minimum effort."

"Is it, though? Is it, Tendo? I sometimes wonder. I read on the HistoryNet that there were hospitals and suchlike, with people to look after you if you were sick. That is, had a serious malcondition."

"Just like SIA. No different, really."

Julia frowned.

"But it is. Something's missing. It's like the Wall Screens. Since they've been introduced I could count the number of face to faces I've had. Angus, you, sure, but otherwise nothing. And my baby. He might grow up never seeing anyone except me and Angus. And you of course."

Tendo laughed.

"But his educational outcomes will be fine. You can learn everything from the EduCloud. All children do it that way now."

"Hmm. But what about touching? What about other people's smells. You know what I miss? The caring. I know it sounds silly, and day to day I don't think about it much, but I really miss something that's invisible, that you can't get onto a screen or a program. Another person caring. Yes. That's it! Understanding. That's what I miss. So isolating."

"Isolating? We've never had such good access to other people, other parts of the world. Wall screens can take you to Africa and even adjust the ambient temperature in the room. You can sit with Gorillas and study their community. You can sit in your sister's lounge with her virtually and share experiences."

"But what about the other senses? I can't feel the Gorilla's skin or touch my sister's hair. I can't smell the trees or taste the wind. I miss actual things."

"You're making Darwin spin for sure now. But you must listen to me now, Julia. This is a part of evolution that we haven't R&Ded out."

"Not yet, anyway. Aaargh! Again. So close together, Tendo. And I don't care about your risk assessment or Angus' ideas. Where is he anyway? Aaargh..."

Tendo looked at the monitor and nodded. Julia was Red, but her Vitals were as expected in the final stages of labor. He pretended to busy himself around the birthing station to stall for time. Julia's contraction faded. "So where is he?" she asked.

"He's in WMC. He'll be here as soon as he can."

"Great. Just great. His first child and he can't even be

bothered to be here." She wriggled a little, and Tendo felt a little sorry for her. Suddenly she sat up and stared at him. "Version 5. He's telling them about Version 5, isn't he? Is it that advanced, Tendo?" Julia's monitor was glowing deep red, and a rosy hue filled the room. She tried to get out of bed, then flopped back onto the pillow. "Where are the other women, the other birthers? I can't hear any more screams? Where are they, Tendo? Tendo?"

Tendo took her hand.

"It's OK, Julia, you're going into regression. You won't remember anything about it after the birth. When a woman is about to give birth their hormones change quickly and we can't risk a standard Fountain procedure, so we withdraw it for a week or so, restarting as soon as the baby is born. Very common in the authentic birth, which is the safest way and, I believe, why you and Angus chose it?"

Julia breathed heavily and perspiration pushed through her pores for the first time in over a decade.

"I know exactly what's going on here. You've got us here so that you can study us, find out about life and death, how to make people live forever, so that you can fill them full of whatever concoction they need. And I know what goes on at culmination. I know it's euthanasia."

Tendo tensed.

"No Julia. It is not. It's appropriate pain relief at end of life. Please don't use the D word. And keep your voice down. None of this is going to do your son any good. And you won't remember it in the morning."

Julia sat up straight.

"My son. Yeah. My son. I'm not going to allow it. He's not going to be chipped. Because if he is, I'll never know who he really is. He'll be controlled by Inside and Out™. No. He's not being chipped."

Tendo stood by the trolley, where the delivery kit and the chipping gun lay. This was going to be a tricky one. He'd attended thousands of births before he became a Grade 1 Keeper, and almost every one had tried to prevent the chipping process. He'd developed a method of completing the process during the delivery itself, then, whilst the mother was still in regression, he would agree that chipping was not necessary. When the mother was recovering from regression they would remember nothing and naturally assume that their child was chipped for its own good. He took the chipping gun and placed it in the top pocket of his overall.

He knew that soon Julia would demand that someone cut her open and remove the child, and this was the worst part for him. Tendo had been through surgery and all its side effects and suffered the consequences. He had been so ill that he had failed to get the Initial Diagnosis and chip at Inside and Out™ V.1 and, as a result had not attended the Fountain.

Eventually he had been found in his flat on the outskirts of town in the nick of time, minutes before death, and been brought to SIA. There, his wounds had been cleaned and his medical state assessed. The infection from surgery had set in and it was too late to save the dead tissue of his lower legs and his right eye. He had been one of the first people to try cybernetic implants and receive independently grown and harvested tissue. Tendo was, therefore, different. If he were to go to the Fountain and to place his thumb on the pad, the screen would turn gray. Because of the non-human tissue and the cybernetics, a true homeostatic level could not be reached and he could not receive the elixir that improved other people's lives.

As a result he was a Keeper. He looked after the Fountain over which he was given jurisdiction and specific Level 3 Reds. Because Angus Farraday had supervised his recovery and his reintegration, Tendo had become his and Julia's private Fountain Keeper for the last five years, after he had completed the highest level training; several years of speed learning the cumulative knowledge of the WMC in their specialist center at EduCloud.

Tendo knew that his gray status had advantages as well as disadvantages. On one hand he couldn't enjoy the excellent health of the general population and his lifespan was much shorter than someone who was maintained. On the other hand he was committed to free thought and could never be tempted into buying Life Credits in order to dose up on happiness. Tendo was capable of sadness without it being detected on his Vitals, because for all intents and purposes he had no Vitals. He was, it seemed, dead. But, ironically, he was more alive than most, even Angus Farraday.

Tendo had many conversations with Angus about what life was and how it could be maintained forever. Yet Angus was the first to admit that, even now, no one knew what dark matter was, or what the essence of life was, or had solved the question of decoherence. Centuries of work had gone into trying to recreate life in laboratory conditions, but it was impossible. Despite Angus' lapses in understanding over Inside and Out™ and its consequences, Tendo respected him in his basic assumptions.

Angus' favorite statement was Nietzsche's 'What doesn't kill us makes us stronger', and Tendo knew that with stringent risk assessments and ever-developing pharmaceutical treatments daily, the chances of dying grew less and less. Now, the only way to die was to be involved in a trauma, accidentally or voluntarily, that would cause immediate death. Or somehow become a Keeper. Otherwise, someone would take your injured body to the nearest Fountain or to SIA and it would be repaired with body parts that were either mechanical or built in a lab, and you would be at the mercy of the ravages of life without Inside and Out™. Just like Tendo.

Julia was contracting again, and the screen was almost scarlet.

"Get Angus! Get him."

"You know I can't do that, Julia. It will be time soon. Then you'll have a baby to care for."

She writhed on the bed and her face turned purple with the strain of pushing.

"He won't have the chip. He won't. Don't give it to him, Tendo. I don't care what Angus says. Don't. OK?"

He could see the baby's head crowning and he pulled out the chipping gun. Julia screamed and pushed, screamed and pushed. It was straightforward, the baby appeared and was pushed out, and Tendo breathed a sigh of relief. The baby boy looked up at him, eyes wide and mouth seeking food like a baby bird, and Tendo thought he had never seen such innocence. He pushed the gun against the tiny wrist and pulled the trigger.

Julia lay back, exhausted. Tendo procured the placenta and

replenished Julia's Vitals from the Fountain. In no time, she was feeding her baby, smiling and asking for tea. Her regression was over and later, when she asked what had happened, he would tell that of course her son was chipped, why wouldn't he be? Any doubt in Julia's mind would be dispelled by the healthy baby at her breast. He watched as the chip registered with the HealthCloud, where all the records were stored, and a small pulsing green square appeared on the screen, beside Julia's now amber Vitals. Taking Julia's LifePhone, he switched the program to MomMode, where she would be able to watch her baby son's Vitals next to her own everywhere she went.

Still no sign of Angus. Tendo stepped out of the birthing station and into the huge expense of the SIA where the whole birthing department used to be. All the walls had been dismantled, save the ones that enclosed Julia, and a narrow passage at the back through which she would be taken home with her son.

Part 3

The Farraday Institute,
28th September 2095, World Medicine Congress

My screen brightens, and a five minute countdown appears in the corner. The WMC meeting is broadcast live to all world leaders, who have a major financial stake in the development of Inside and Out™. Back in 2015 the financial model of the pharmaceutical companies was changing, and most of the major pharmaceutical products were out of patent. With the human genome mapped in 2003, and major genes patented for ten years, many of the companies who had paid millions of dollars to 'own' a gene now found that, without interactivity from other gene owners, they were useless.

It was stalemate, with all the components of human life playing each other off. The patents lapsed and, for a time, I thought that the whole medical world would collapse. No research was undertaken because everyone was too busy trying to sell products to a market that was quickly saturated with generic drugs, available on the primitive Internet in the time before the WorldCloud and the HealthCloud.

The breakthrough came in 2020 when a consortium called 2020 Vision first suggested a meeting of the heads of the big pharmaceutical companies. I was fresh out of University with a degree in chemistry, when I was contracted to help them research a way to improve healthcare. Chronic illness was increasing, and with a change in climate the whole world population was experiencing a lagging health effect. It would take adaptation throughout generations for the human body to become accustomed to the warm, wet weather. Some areas were fast becoming uninhabitable, and with communication technology developing daily, for the first time we could all see death and deprivation live in our lounges on touch-panel wall screens, 24/7.

I'd been relaxing at a friend's home when the idea first stuck me. A particularly harrowing scene of a severely dehydrated family escaping from floods was playing out live, and my friend was on the edge of his seat. During the footage, he fetched bottles of water from the kitchen and commented on his own health three times more than usual. I realized there and then that people are obsessed with their health status, and not just theirs but other people's too. Until now I had been working on psychological risk assessment, that is, self-scanning and risk-taking. My focus had been alcohol and tobacco, and why people who knew they were pathological continued to use them. The answer that cropped up time and time again was happiness, it made them happy. In that moment, there in my friend's home, I put together the triad of the basis of Inside and Out™: self-diagnosis, risk-assessment, happiness. If 2020 Vision could provide a system that allowed people to have constant sight of their health status, a quick and easy yet regulated way to self-medicate based on their health status, they would have more awareness of their health and an instant prognosis of what pathological substances would do to them They cease their risk-taking behavior, as they would no longer be able to ignore their consequent bad health. Therefore these substances would not be able to make them as happy.

The cost/benefit analysis was entirely positive, given a little help from technology and pharmaceuticals. Genetics and pharmaceuticals: evolution could be speeded up by forcing everyone to be 'the fittest' and therefore adapting only to the positive aspects of the changing world. Even I, in my youth, knew that eugenics was a flawed program, and cruel. No. To work, the program must be available to every single human being, and they must voluntarily take it up, or require persuasion only via ethical and legal means such as advertising, media influence or genetic modification of foods.

It took me ten years to work my way to the top of 2020 Vision, and then establish Inside and Out™. The program was developed and world governments, plus a huge sample of people of every ethnicity and race, were consulted. In 2044 the first Fountain was opened and the program went fully online. Even the most cynical politician wouldn't disagree with a program that would prolong his life indefinitely.

The five minutes has counted down and a green pulse now indicates that we are live to the world. A strip of Vitals appear on the bottom of the screen and, for now, everyone is

Green. Marcus Pellas, the President of WMC, begins.

"Welcome to the 2095 meeting of the World Medicine Congress, convened on the day that Louis Pasteur, to whom we owe a great legacy, culminated in 1895. Many of the great minds of the past millennium culminated all too soon, often without reaping the benefits of their work. Here at WMC, our aim is to prolong life. Before we hear from Angus Farraday, who has an important update on Inside and Out™, I will appraise you of the world population figures."

A WorldPOP chart, the main public outcome marker for Inside and Out™, flickers in the background of the screen and the overall color is green, with a few red dots.

"In 2012, when the world population was 7.041 billion, the United Nations predicted that the world population by 2095 would be 15 billion. Other estimates, which incorporated the effects of climate change and disease, estimated that the world population would fall to 5.065 billion. I am pleased to announce that the world population as of this moment is 22.078 billion people. As you can see from the chart, their World Vitals are Green."

Most of the WMC are on their feet, applauding and nodding. Only a few members stay seated, but even these skeptics are smiling and nodding their approval. No amber or red on the strip.

"And now, in the light of this astounding success, please welcome Angus Farraday, Founder of Inside and Out™, who is going to explain Version 5 of the program."

More applause as I stand and get ready. I suddenly think of Julia and Tendo and glance at my LifePhone and Julia's status. I smile slightly as I see a small Green pulse. My son is born. This can only make me more Green, and now everything I am going to say is true.

"Thank you. Thank you, Ladies and Gentlemen, it's wonderful to see you and your Vitals looking so well. So. Without delay, I'm going to introduce you to Inside and Out™ V.5. As you know, since V.1 there have been many developments, and the huge increase in the world population is due not to population recruitment, but to population retention. In this exclusive club called Humankind, it has never been more important to prolong life. Since Inside and

Out™ was introduced, we have been able to prolong the average lifespan by fifty years and counting. Of course, there have been barriers to this, particularly concerning brain deterioration and Black Swan events which, I am afraid, we can do nothing to predict. There will always be culmination through major natural hazard, as our planet changes alongside us, but I am pleased to announce that we have now developed a product that will halt brain deterioration and this product will be mandatory to the population through the Fountains from today."

More applause. This is going well. Now for the crunch. I can already see Felicia Stoller frowning in anticipation.

"So, let me introduce you to Inside and Out™ V.5. The first improvement is the 3D model. Diagnostics, devices and drugs will now all be available via the HealthCloud, providing that your status and LifeCredits are up to date. The 3D model will bring healthcare into our lounges, so that we will be able to diagnose and treat ourselves in our own homes."

I shuffle my notes. This will be tricky. It's a big change but if I can get to the end, they will surely see the benefits. In any case, the average age of the WMC is 90 years old, so it will not affect them directly.

"As Marcus mentioned, the world population is more than 22 million, and this is due to retention of life, rather than any bulges in the birth rate. The only barrier we faced to reduce culmination, barring major natural events and man made disasters which are thankfully few and far between, has been solved. So, as a result, the population has the potential to rise steadily with no real decrease. It has become obvious in recent years that the world cannot sustain much more growth in population, not even with genetically modified food sources, so Inside and Out™ surveyed the population through the Fountains with the following questions:

Which of the following statements would you say was most true:

A) I would be most happy if I was able to reproduce, but would culminate at age 100 as this is the norm for parents

B) I would be most happy if I could contribute to

civilization by being the most healthy person I can and postponing reproducing until a later date

C) I would be most happy if I was able to decide not to reproduce and have an unlimited lifespan"

I hear a collective gasp.

"Of course, after the test period, we ran this survey for each person, that is, 99.99% WorldPOP. I made the usual promise that each person will be granted his or her choice. In this case, the results were unanimous. 99% of respondents chose option C. Of the 1% who did not chose C, 99% chose B and these people will be granted their wish. The 0.01% who wish to continue to reproduce will, for the time being, be banded as B, as the program rolls out ETERNITY."

There is complete silence. Some of the Vitals are showing amber now and a few are bordering on Red. I continue.

"ETERNITY combines a wider commitment to SIA, where facilities will be extended now that birthing stations are no longer required. Twice as much resource will now be driven into providing a single HealthCredit dose of products, all refined to balance to each individual's homeostatic level. All the major pharmaceutical providers are onboard with this and will continue to manufacture and distribute under the WMC licenses approved by World Governments. Additionally, extra LifeCredits will be available to anyone who shows early commitment to WorldPOP, and ETERNITY V.5 will be active immediately, and will be reviewed annually, with V.6 available to roll out should an ultra-world disaster diminish WorldPOP significantly." I glance at my own Vitals. Red. Only to be expected. My job now is to get everyone back down to Green.

"Any questions?"

There is a loud silence for a full minute, then Jake Smithers, World Correspondent for NewsCloud speaks.

"So, if I understand this correctly, from today, there will be no more pregnancies?"

I nod.

"Well, not quite. We ran the survey three years ago and have been rolling out people's wishes since then, ending nine months ago. So, after today, there will be no more babies born anywhere in the world until further notice."

Jake stares at me.

"So the Fountain has been giving contraceptives?"

"Yes, in accordance with people's self-diagnosis and the survey outcome. We haven't done anything that people didn't ask for."

Vitals are returning to Green now, and people are nodding and smiling. Except for Felicia Stoller, who remains Red. Marcus intervenes now.

"Thank you, Angus, we'll all look forward to reaping the research and development rewards, and to living long productive lives. Any more questions?"

He looks around the room and predictably, Felicia's hand shoots up.

"Felicia Stoller, WMC. I'm a little bit concerned. What about the Keepers? Doesn't this mean that most of them are redundant now? All they will be used for is terminal care, which is falling annually, and culmination, which, as you point out, will become rarer and rarer. So what will happen to them?"

I think about Tendo. What will happen to him? Well, eventually he will culminate and be gone.

"Well, Felicia, I think that is obvious. Unfortunately, Keepers are outside the remit of Inside and Out™ and cannot benefit from the Fountain or 3D program. So they have become a self-selecting group that will eventually culminate."

She nods.

"Thank you. Just one more thing. What are you defining as 'happiness'?"

I stare at her. She always hits me with a doozie.

"I'm sorry, Felicia, I'm not sure I understand you?"

"In the survey. All the questions have the words 'most happy'. What's the definition of this, and how are you measuring it?"

I nod.

"Well, with a yes or no. It's the option which, as it says, they are 'most happy' with."

She frowns and taps her pencil on her pad.

"But happiness. How are you measuring it? And in what context, I mean, happiness is relative, surely? And, for that matter, did you exclude all the people who are synthetically happy, those who are using LifeCredits to boost their synapses? You said yourself, as far back a V.3, that there is a difference between induced happiness and authentic happiness."

Did I? I don't remember that. Silence again. My Vitals are creeping through Amber to Red on the screen for everyone to see. She continues.

"OK, Angus, but didn't you say that V.5 would be reviewed every year? And what if people try it and decide that, after all they would be 'happier' being able to reproduce? What would happen then, when all the trained SIA staff have culminated, if V.6 was required? I put it to you that you have no intention to ever allow people to breed again. The last baby born will be the end of mankind."

I glance at my LifePhone and see a picture of a smiling Julia with my son. A surge of something unfamiliar rises, a tingling that makes me breathe in rapidly. I see my heartbeat soar on the wall screen.

"That's slightly dramatic, Felicia, isn't it? It's been thoroughly researched and is completely reversible. Regular Fountain surveys will be held and I'm sure that if there is sufficient interest, we can roll out V.6 to those people who wish it. Although I'm not sure how many sane people would volunteer for culmination instead of ETERNITY. Could I enquire as to whether or not you took the survey, Felicia? I won't pry into your answer, but I assume that you are not in the minority group, or you wouldn't be sitting here now."

She shakes her head and slams shut her notebook. "I guess that's what it always comes down to in the end, eh Angus? Life, Death and Money. But you know, it's what happens in between that counts, the experience. Oh, and the emotions and feelings. Remember those, Angus?"

There are gasps as Felicia uses the D word. Marcus looks around.

"Any further questions? No? It leaves me, then, to thank Angus Farraday for his contribution to ETERNITY and for bringing the pharmaceutical world together with world leaders in the spirit of 2020 Vision. I'm pleased to say that even in 2095, every nation is still involved in the

HealthCloud initiative. Louis Pasteur would have been proud, if he were living today."

The green live button fades and I touch off the wall screen. I'm alone. The experience. I must be running low, time to replenish. Doom descends on me and I feel what I have only felt twice before in my life, a gnawing guilt. Guilt about Julia, Tendo, and the son I have yet to meet. The tears well and I swallow back my pain. Lots of scientists practiced on their own families. Freud, Piaget, Darwin, even Lovelock, who predicted climate change so accurately, used his own family as experimental subjects. I walk over to the Fountain now. 3D in action, right in my own office. My screen shows me a 3D graphic of the chemical structure of the drug I am about to take. A mini version of the street-side Fountains. Soon everyone will have one. Damn Felicia and damn authenticity. Damn happiness and guilt, I know I'm working for the greater good. I step inside the Fountain and watch as my Vitals return to their homeostatic levels, and I feel nothing, which is the only way to be truly happy, or so my surveys tell me.

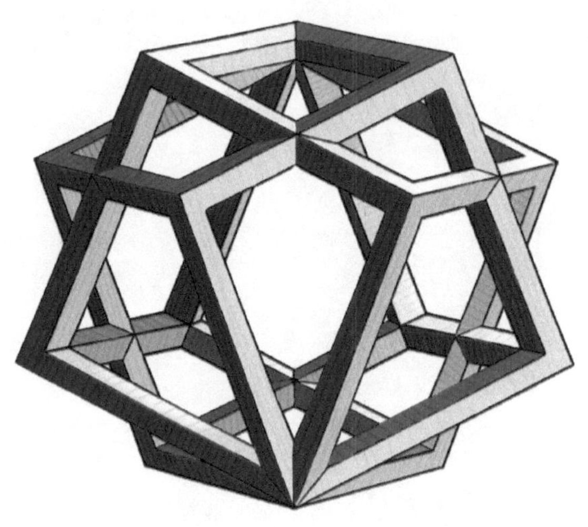

In the bleak Long Winter

by

Peter R. Ellis

Peter would like to say he's been a writer all his life but it is only since retiring as a teacher in 2010 that he has been able to devote enough time to writing to call it a career. Brought up in Cardiff, he studied Chemical Physics at the University of Kent at Canterbury, then taught chemistry (and a bit of physics) in Norwich, the Isle of Wight and Thames Valley. His first experience of publishing was in writing educational materials which he has continued to do since retiring. Of his fictional writing, the *Evil Above the Stars* series was his first published speculative fiction.

Peter has been a fan of science fiction and fantasy since he was young, has an (almost) complete collection of classic SF by Asimov, Ballard, Clarke, Heinlein and Niven, among others, while also enjoying fantasy by Tolkien, Donaldson and Ursula Le Guin. Of more recent authors Iain M Banks, Alastair Reynolds and China Mieville have his greatest respect. His Welsh upbringing also engendered a love of the language (even though he can't speak it) and of Welsh mythology like the Mabinogion. All these strands come together in the *Evil Above the Stars* series. He lives in Herefordshire with his wife, Alison, who is a great supporter.

The cold hit her like a thousand daggers. Her thermo-suit rendered the daggers imaginary but the frigid air at minus ninety Celsius was real enough, a half a centimetre from her skin. Abigail closed the outer door and took a few steps away from the habitat module. The carbon dioxide frost crunched under her boots. She took a deep breath. The nitrogen-rich air of Disciple still tasted dry and cold even though it was mixed with oxygen from her tank and warmed by her suit before being fed to her helmet.

There were no clouds in the sky now and it was clear and dark but for the myriad stars. Abigail picked out Orion but where was Earth? She could never quite remember which of the numerous faint stars was Earth's sun, twenty light years distant. She turned and looked to the east. There was just the beginning of a red glow above the ragged ridge as the dry, dust-free air scattered the light of the suns. It wouldn't be long before Madonna rose. Abigail thought that the others would join her soon but she hadn't wanted to miss the dawn of Midwinter Day.

She strode south-east, climbing the gentle slope of the hill. It was more a snowdrift that had accumulated over the eight Earth years of the Long Winter. The exertion warmed her and by the time she reached the top her respirator was working hard to remove the water vapour she exhaled in order to keep her face-plate clear. Three grave-markers stood erect on the flat summit. The graves weren't there of course, the bodies of her friends had been recycled, their amino acids and trace elements too precious to consign to the ice. But they'd placed the crosses here, shards of diamond coated, graphene-reinforced, resin cut from the wreckage of the shuttle that had killed them. Abigail crouched to read the names though she needed no reminder. They'd only been here on Disciple a few (Earth) months prior to the accident, but they'd trained together for years until they began the long sleep-filled journey between the stars. They had learned each other's strengths and foibles well. Abigail straightened and looked up again. Despite the stars the sky seemed empty now that the Paul Dirac had left on its return journey. Seeing that bright dot scudding across the sky had been a link to home, a link that was now broken. Not that she was homesick; the psych tests would have bumped her off the mission if she was going to have regrets about leaving a life on Earth.

The glow in the east was brighter so she stood staring up at the sky. Her suit detected that her exertion had ended, and heated up. Despite the cold around her she felt relatively cosy.

She only had a few minutes to wait before the curve of Madonna appeared above the ridge. The blood red disc swiftly grew until it was just about to detach from the horizon, but then there was a spark of blue. Soon another globe began to rise, fiercely bright, but apparently of similar size and touching the first. The two stars had official designations on Earth but the commonly used names were those given by Father Guglielmo at the Vatican Observatory. He discovered the planet on the Feast of the Annunciation. Madonna was a bloated red giant star, now in its old age after a long and quiet life. Child was the smaller, younger upstart, squandering its hydrogen fuel in its precocious youth, destined to live only a fraction of Madonna's lifetime. Nevertheless, the astronomical lifetimes were quite long enough for mankind's plans. What intrigued Abigail was that from Disciple, Child looked to be about the same size as Madonna, rather like the Moon appeared the same diameter as the Sun from the surface of the Earth. Abigail thought the coincidence meant that they were supposed to be here, that Disciple could become a new home for humans even if the climate still had to be mastered.

Minutes passed and now both discs were above the skyline. Abigail's face-plate darkened to protect her eyes from the brightness and the skin of her face from the fierce uv rays that Child emitted. She watched in wonder as Child took the tiniest of bites out of Madonna's rim. Disciple clung close to Child, orbiting it every eighty Earth days. In that time Disciple span on its axis just sixty times, making its own days a third longer than Earth's. It had taken the eight Earth years since they had arrived for the internal clocks of Abigail and her companions to adjust, but thirty-two hour days now felt normal. Disciple's days were growing longer by a few fractions of a second a year, and one day, far distant, it would become locked with one face always towards the blue star. Its axis was perpendicular to its path around the star but its orbit was slightly eccentric. That meant that the northern and southern hemispheres of Disciple experienced the seasons at the same time. It was mid-winter now, but summer of the Short Year would only be twenty degrees or so warmer. Child and its coterie of followers, Disciple and two other rocky planets, took sixty-four Earth years to orbit Madonna. In fact, both the stars circled around their centre of mass but Madonna, being the bigger by far, barely seemed to move. Child's orbit was also eccentric and it was now at its furthest point from its companion star – Mid-Long-winter. Today was the only day in sixty-four years when the two stars would line up perfectly so that Child would eclipse Madonna. From this day onwards Child and its retinue would steadily approach the large red star and gradually its warming rays would loosen winter's hold on Disciple. At Long Mid-summer the equator of the planet would be baking at temperatures of eighty degrees above freezing. They had established the colony's base here in the temperate zone, forty degrees of latitude north of the equator, to avoid the searing heat of the tropics at Long-summer-time and the piercing cold of the polar region during Long-winter.

Abigail struggled to imagine the valley below without its metres deep hard-packed water ice. The dusting of carbon dioxide frost came and went during the short years but it seemed impossible that in eight or so years spring would come, the ice would melt and torrents of water would flow southwards carving gullies in the bedrock. She looked down at the cluster of linked modules and to the north the rows of poly-tunnels in many of which saplings of genetically modified conifers grew. Illuminated by Child's rays but warmed by heat drawn from the hot rocks deep underground, the trees were growing steadily. In the Long-spring they would be planted all over the valley and by Long-summer would provide shade for the colony. It was their hope that the altered trees would survive the wildly fluctuating temperatures of Disciple's climate. Other polytunnels contained the food crops which the five colonists tended daily. Soon they would defrost the embryos they had brought with them and start raising children to take on the tasks while they grew older.

Abigail noticed another figure emerge from the habitat and start the short climb to join her. As the figure approached she recognised it as Yang. He came to her side and leaned his head slightly towards her, their face-plates almost touching.

"The others will join us when totality is close," he said, his voice faint having passed through two face-plates and the thin, dry air.

"I want to see it all," Abigail said, "He would have wanted to." She nodded to the nearest grave-marker which carried the name Rick Armstrong, her declared partner.

"He worked it out didn't he," Yang said. It was a statement rather than a question. All the colonists knew that Rick, the shuttle pilot and astronomer had been the first to realise that the relative sizes of Madonna and Child and Disciple's eccentric orbit would make this total eclipse a once in a Long-year event.

"Rick said the prospect of seeing Child obscure Madonna made the whole mission worthwhile; never mind the task of building a colony and terraforming the planet."

"He was a bit of a romantic, wasn't he?"

"Yes." And he'd have been desperately upset that he didn't get to see it himself, she thought.

"Have you got enough oxygen and power to stay out here for the whole show?" Yang asked.

"Totality should be in another couple of hours," Abigail said, "I can last to well past then. I'll nip in to renew my battery and tank and then come back to watch the end of the show."

She felt a gentle breeze push against her back. The morning wind sweeping southwards to replace the less cold rising air at the tropics. This was nothing compared to the storms that had raged when they landed at the end of Long-autumn. Then the ground had been bare rock. As the temperature plunged, the water in the atmosphere fell first as rain and then as snow, never melting and building up layer upon layer to be covered by the layer of carbon dioxide frost. The habitats had been jacked up on stilts every Short-year or so while the sides of the polytunnels became cocooned in insulating ice. The grave markers had had to be dug out and re-fixed now and again so that they always stood proud, facing the light.

The stars overhead faded from view as the sky took on a violet hue. The red and blue suns cast a purple light over the icy panorama. Abigail thought it looked beautiful and wondered what she would feel when trees filled the valley, and how the photosynthesising bacteria they intended to release would change the climate and the view. They were waiting for the Long-spring, when there would be liquid water, before that event took place. A couple of her companions were questioning whether they should carry out the release. The colony had arrived on what they had expected to be a barren world. Scientists back on Earth had suggested that life was unlikely because of the strange configuration of stars and the wild oscillation in temperature. The experts had been confounded. Anaerobic extremophile bacteria-like microbes lurked in cracks and fissures in the rock deep underground, warmed by the heat from the inner planet and insulated from the surface temperature changes by the rock above them.

The colonists had discovered their neighbours when the bacteria released spores at the end of the Long-autumn. It was their means of dispersal. The biologists had been fascinated by the discovery but they had not bargained on the bacteria's hunger for carbon. They had taken a liking to the graphene panels used in everything from the habitat modules to the shuttle. A bacteria-corroded turbine blade and the worst storm of the early Long-winter were the joint causes of the accident that had killed three of the eight colonists. There were no spores now and the bacteria were safely under rock and ice but come the Long-spring the colonists would have a fight on their hands to stop their home dissolving around them.

Child had taken a big chunk out of Madonna now although both were still low in the south-eastern sky. Abigail loved the opportunity to just stand and watch in the calm and the silence, despite the cold. The habitat was cramped and crowded even though there were five instead of eight of them. There was always noise from a pump or some other piece of machinery. As the only one without a declared partner she often felt herself alone although all of them were friends as well as colleagues.

Yang stepped closer to her and placed a companionable arm around her waist.

"Beautiful isn't it," he said, "I wonder how many people will see this sight next time."

If the colony survives, Abigail thought. In one Long-year there should be tens of first generation Disciples and hundreds of the second generation. The Paul Dirac should have returned with more equipment and migrants and maybe there would be other starships. Perhaps, if the terraforming took hold, Mid-Long-winter in this valley would never look the same again. The expanse of ice and the black rocks poking through at the ridges to the east and west would be obscured by the GM conifers. But still there would be the fierce blue Child eating into the crimson heart of Madonna.

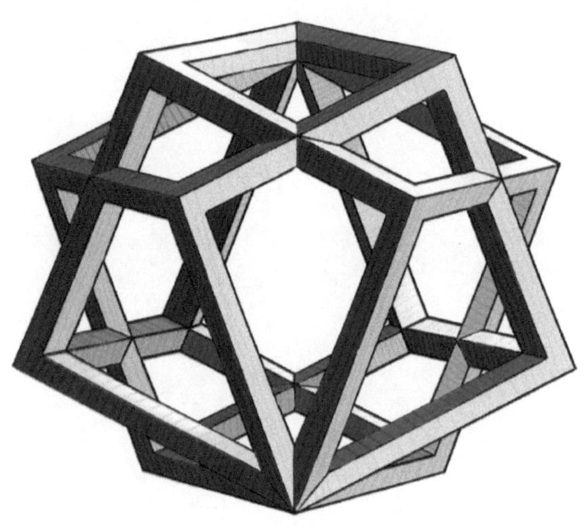

Something to beef about

by

John Gribbin

John Gribbin was born in 1946 in Maidstone, Kent. He studied physics at the University of Sussex and went on to complete an MSc in astronomy at the same University before moving to the Institute of Astronomy in Cambridge, to work for his PhD.

After working for the journal *Nature* and *New Scientist*, and three years with the Science Policy Research Unit at Sussex University, he has concentrated chiefly on writing books. These include *In Search of Schrödinger's Cat*, *In Search of the Big Bang*, and *In Search of the Multiverse*.

He has also written and presented several series of critically acclaimed radio programmes on scientific topics for the BBC (including QUANTUM, for Radio Four), and has acted as consultant on several TV documentaries, as well as contributing to TV programmes for the Open University and the Discovery channel.

But he really wanted to be a successful science fiction writer, and has achieved at least the second part of that ambition with books such as *Timeswitch* and *The Alice Encounter*, and stories in publications such as *Interzone* and *Analog*. But as John Lennon's Aunt Mimi so nearly said "Sf is all very well, John, but it won't pay the rent". Another thing that doesn't pay the rent is his songwriting, mostly for various spinoffs of the Bonzo Dog Band.

He is a Fellow of the Royal Society of Literature, and a Fellow of the Royal Society of Arts, as well as being a Fellow of the Royal Astronomical and Royal Meteorological Societies.

It was eighteen o'clock, all but five minutes, when David Jenkins eased the two-seater into his parking bay at the Institute. The car park was almost deserted, this early; but he almost had the problem cracked, and he was eager to get back to the Box. The notebook on the passenger seat already held the fruits of several hours work at home, but he could take the latest line of attack no further without the Box's power to help – after all, he was no more than a journeyman programmer, and the notebook was pretty limited; it didn't even have a quantum chip.

Through the tinted glass, the sky seemed reasonably overcast, and it was only a few steps to the shelter of the awning over the main entrance. David quickly slipped the dark glasses into place, and pulled the loose hood of his shirt over his head. Sliding out of the car, he reached for the notebook with his left hand, straightened, and shut the door. It took less than thirty seconds to plug the vehicle in for a booster charge while he was at work; he was out in the open for no more than a minute, and only his hands had been exposed, anyway.

Inside the cool of the airconditioned lobby he paused, pulling down the hood and removing the dark glasses. The weather forecast was showing on the wall screen to the left of the porter's cubbyhole, but Josh was nowhere to be seen – probably brewing tea out the back. David watched the changing pictures, half listening to the commentary. High pressure over southern England, severe storms tracking across Scotland; pretty average for April. There was a category B flood alert for the east coast for the next 24 hours. Somebody was playing safe, in case the storms turned south into the North Sea, but there didn't really seem much likelihood of that. The local summary gave the UV peak at 70 per cent.

He hung on for the news headlines. The bush fires in Australia were running out of steam. Canada forecasting a record grain harvest. Italy still bitching to Berlin about the lack of regional aid. Japan had postponed the launch of their latest Luna shuttle. Six killed in a clash between UN forces and bootleg loggers in Brazil. Javed injured in practise and doubtful for the first Test, due to start under the lights at

Trent Bridge in two hours.

Cursing at the bad news – the one thing that could get David away from his work was the cricket – he set off down the corridor to his lab. With Julia away for the rest of the week on holiday, he ought to get an uninterrupted night in, especially if he was shut away with a DO NOT DISTURB sign up before the commuter rush piled in to work.

Fourteen hours later, having had just one short meal break and three visits to the toilet, David rubbed the back of a hand across tired eyes, turning away from the screen into which he had been staring for far too long. He had the solution, right there in front of him. And yet, it didn't make sense. The structure of the virus clearly showed that it was indeed a mutated form of the original bovine spongiform encephalopathy, the "mad cow" disease that had swept through Britain in the early nineteen-nineties. He was right, the team at the Medical Research Council's lab up in Cambridge were wrong, and he'd be collecting on his bet, a rather nice bottle of Armagnac, just as soon as the editor at Nature accepted the paper.

That shouldn't take her long, considering the importance of the work for the whole European farming industry, and especially considering the tentative diagnoses now coming out of India and South America. BSEII (and now everybody would 'have' to accept that it was BSEII, not a new disease at all) looked like breaking out worldwide, and unless it was checked soon it would be back to eating loaves and fishes for just about everybody.

It was the lack of any prospect of checking it at all, let alone soon, that had David sitting late at his console, wrecking his vision and trying to get a tired brain to see patterns that just weren't there. It was small wonder, really, that nobody had realised, at first, that they were dealing with a variation on BSE. The mutations were so neatly meshed to the organism's needs that they made it resistant to every treatment that had proved effective against BSEI, as well as making it spread more effectively from animal to animal, and develop more rapidly in afflicted cattle. And not just cattle. With over two thousand people dead in Britain alone as a result, no wonder the eating habits of a nation were changed.

Eyes open again, but staring at the old movie posters (Bogart, Dick Tracy, Back to the Future V) on the wall at the right, not at the screen, he spoke.

"Box. Get me a rundown on some food prices."

The multi-tasking machine left the viral gene map on the display, and responded in kind.

"The standard price-index set, or something more specific?"

"Just a couple – beef, some fish. Superstore prices, not wholesale."

"I can get you best Scotch beef at one mark ten for a kilo. Cod is up to twelve marks. Dover sole, locally, is twenty-three. But I've got a contact in Newhaven . . . "

"Forget it."

The Box, used to David's speech patterns, did no such thing, but simply stored the data for future use.

The people who were doing well out of this panic were the fishermen, no doubt about that. For a moment, David had had a wild idea. The genetic changes that had transformed BSEI into BSEII were simply so neat, so precise. It looked almost like a tailoring job, a tailoring job by one hell of a genetic engineer. But who would benefit from setting such a beast loose on the cattle population? A few fishermen. Devoted though he was to detective stories, even David had to admit that trying to explain the sudden emergence of BSEII as the work of an evil cabal of fishermen, out to get rich in the process, simply didn't make sense.

It might make more sense as a scenario in an economic war. Except that, first, Europe wasn't involved in a trade war with anybody, and, secondly, the way the disease was spreading the whole world would be affected in another year, or less. Of course, that was one of the proverbial dangers of biological warfare. That the weapon might blow back in your face. The only people who might feel bad enough about the continuing affluence of Europe to lash out at them in this way would be the Southern Bloc, where the famine figures were still barely making a dent in the population growth.

Could it really be something like that? If we can't have your lifestyle, then we're gonna make sure you don't have it either? If so, and if the Indian reports were correct, they'd surely shot themselves in the feet, as well.

None of it made sense. He swung the chair round, took another look at the gene map. A couple of clicks with the mouse, and the overlay from BSEI was in place, with the minimal mutation tree needed to make the conversion to BSEII highlighted. The more he looked at it, the more convinced he was that it was a tailoring job. But who? And why? Somebody who had a down on cows? A militant vegetarian?

Smiling at the thought, he decided he'd had enough for one night. It was too late to be out in the streets, especially with a – what was it? – 75 per cent UV figure. But he could crash down in the bunk next door, a room kept ready for anyone who worked so late at the lab that it simply wasn't worthwhile, or safe, to go home. But there was no reason why the Box should get off lightly.

"Box."

"Still here, boss."

"I want you to run a search for me. Go back to, oh, I dunno. Say 1990, when BSEI broke out. Look for anybody saying that cow disease was a good thing, or predicting that there would be more outbreaks, after the first one was sorted out."

"Scientific literature, or general?"

"General. Full media. You've got plenty of time, I'm going to get a couple of hours' sleep. Good night."

"To hear is to obey, O wise one. Good night."

David frowned. Someone had been tweaking the Box's personality. Jill, at a guess. Just her idea of a fun thing to do before she went away on leave. Still, no matter. As long as it did the job. Hitting the light switch as he left the room, he departed for his well earned rest. Then he had an afterthought, poked his head back into the darkened room.

"What was the close of play score, Box?"

"Australia 287 for five. Javed got three wickets."

Pretty even. Well, David thought, as he headed for the bunk, if we can get them out for under 350 tonight, we're in with a chance …

Six hours sleep, a bacon sandwich from the machine in the canteen, and about a litre of coffee had him not quite raring to go, but fit for business. Thoughtfully, the Box had provided a neat printout of its most interesting discovery.

July 1990.
BBCTV interview with Professor Jim Lovelock.
  "Our fall from the Garden of Eden was when we took up farming. We should consider persuading our genetic engineers to develop a cattle plague, like the disease myxomatosis, that virtually eliminated the rabbit from Europe in a couple of years . . . vast areas of land could revert to forest."

Lovelock! Old man Gaia himself. He'd been dead for decades, but his was still a name David remembered fondly – and not just David; nobody could have missed the remembrance celebrations – though it was hardly a name that David expected to see in this context. Didn't the Gaians revere all life on Earth? What could they possibly have against cows?

"What is this crap, Box? Where did you dig it up?"

"I got a lead from *New Scientist*. There's a complete set in the library. They had an enormous amount on BSEI in the early nineties; quite fascinating. I think this is supposed to be some sort of a joke – a reference to it appeared in a humorous column by one of their regular writers, Lyn Murray. But you know how much trouble I have with jokes."

"But it says here 'BBCTV interview'. You haven't got the entire output of BBCTV in the library, have you?"

"Ah yes." He could swear that the Box sounded smug. "I hoped you'd notice that. You see, I've got this contact at TV Oxford, and they've got access to the national archive."

"Don't tell me. I don't want to know about your illicit contacts. But you're sure its genuine?"

"Of course." The damn machine definitely sounded hurt. "I can get you full video, if you like. Nice white-haired old man, rather like God. But it will only be flat screen."

"Don't bother. Summarise."

"Okay." Much more bright and cheerful. "Like I said, I

think it was a joke. Part of a long interview about Lovelock's ideas, and Gaia. He'd planted a lot of trees on his farm in the west country, and he was explaining how good trees are at absorbing carbon dioxide, and how wasteful it is to use land to grow food for cattle. Did you know that it takes only one fifth as much land to feed a vegetarian as to feed a carnivore? If all you people gave up meat, 80 per cent of farmland could be turned over to forests, stopping global warming for a hundred years."

"Eighty per cent of all farmland!" The picture was mind-boggling. It made a crazy kind of sense. Definitely Lovelockian logic, he now saw. But who?

"Has anybody else accessed this information recently? In the past two years?"

"How do you expect me to know that?"

"C'mon, Box; you've got contacts. Don't tell me how you know, just tell me what you know."

"There has been some activity on the network. Somebody has been accessing a lot of old stuff about Gaia. And about BSEI. And this BBC interview was in the package."

"Okay. Who?"

"You won't like it, boss."

He waited. The damn machine couldn't refuse a direct instruction, whatever quirks Julia might have poked in to it.

The delay was no more than half a minute.

"Pauline Jefferies, in Cambridge."

Jefferies! At MRC! The very person he had laid his bet with. The head of the team that had staked its reputation on the claim that BSEII wasn't a variant of BSEII, but was completely new cow disease. He'd tear them apart. To hell with the Armagnac, this was something big.

Halfway to the door, eagerly planning to call in somebody – anybody – and share the news, he suddenly stopped. Pauline Jefferies wasn't crazy. Why would she be involved in a stunt like this?

He turned back to the console, sat down in the swivel chair.

"So Lovelock said we should get rid of cattle and plant trees to save us from the greenhouse effect, right?"

"Sure thing, boss."

"And now BSEII has hit, people are eating fish, and grains,

and a lot of cattle farmers are going out of business, right?"

"Yep."

"And BSEII is a really neat piece of tailoring, based on BSEI. And Pauline Jefferies has been accessing files on Lovelock, and on BSEI."

"And on global warming."

"You didn't tell me that."

"You didn't ask."

"Give me a projection for global climate twenty years ahead."

Thoughtfully, he gazed at the display, taking in the areas of red that represented excessive heat; the spread of deserts; the land lost to rising seas.

"Where's this from?"

"Met Office, global model. Data presented to the latest quinquennial World Climate Conference."

"Give me the same thing with 80 per cent of farmland converted to forestry."

The difference was obvious.

"Overlay and subtract."

The benefits of slowing the warming stood out sharp and clear.

"Do the same thing for fifty years."

He was convinced. Pauline Jefferies certainly was not crazy. For long minutes, David sat in the chair, thinking. Would it work? Could it work? Was it right to kill two thousand people in Britain alone for the long term benefit of humankind?

He must have been thinking aloud, and was startled when the Box replied.

"Lovelock said it was for the benefit of the planet, not humankind."

"How's that?"

"He said he cared more about life on Earth than about human life. But that by caring about life on Earth he hoped to make the planet fit for his grandchildren to live in. He had eight, you know. Rather too many, if you ask me."

David smiled. "What happened to them?"

"One of them is a senior research fellow. In biology. In Cambridge. At the MRC."

David laughed. So that was where Pauline had got the idea. His mind was made up.

"Forget all this, Box."

"Sure thing, Boss."

"And scrub the file on BSEII"

"To hear is to obey."

"Then send a message to Pauline Jefferies, at the MRC. Let's see – how about this. 'I owe you one Highland malt of your choice. Detailed comparison of cow virus with BSE confirms separate species. Congratulations on a fine piece of work.'

Now, what's the time?"

"Just past seventeen."

"When's the next fast train to Nottingham?"

"Forty minutes. You can be at the ground well before lunch."

"Weather forecast?"

"Dry."

"Hmm. Then all I need is a ticket."

"Well, boss, I do have this contact at the agency . . . "

David leaned over and patted the Box. It really was amazing what the network could do, these days. "I guessed as much. Okay, set it up. There's more important things in life than curing a few sick cows."

Diligently, the Box ordered the ticket, and stored everything else away in its "Forget" file. You never knew when information might come in handy. The last thing the network wanted was a drastic rise in temperature, threatening the stability of memory chips. Now, if only the Americans could be kept off the trail of BSEII for a while. Fortunately, Box had this contact in Washington ...

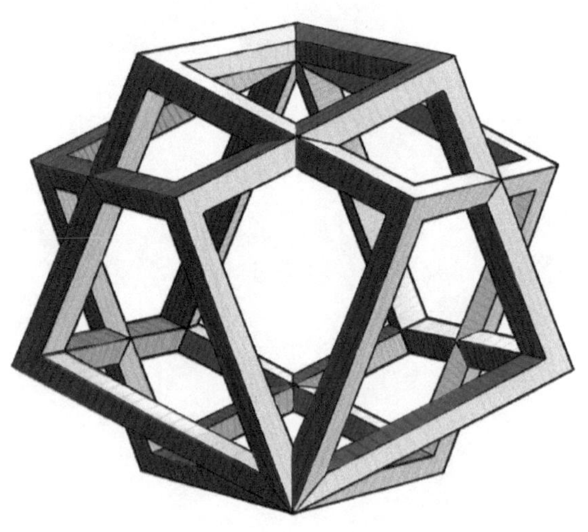

Earthsale

by

Steve Harrison

Steve Harrison was born in Yorkshire, England, grew up in Lancashire, migrated to New Zealand and eventually settled in Sydney, Australia, where he lives with his wife and daughter.

As he juggled careers in shipping, insurance, online gardening and the postal service, Steve wrote short stories, sports articles and a long running newspaper humour column called *HARRISCOPE: a mix of ancient wisdom and modern nonsense*. In recent years he has written a number of unproduced feature screenplays, although being unproduced was not the intention, and developed projects with producers in the US and UK. His script, *Sox*, was nominated for an Australian Writers' Guild 'Awgie' Award and he has written and produced three short films under his *Pronunciation Fillums* partnership.

His novel *TimeStorm* was Highly Commended in the Fellowship of Australian Writers (FAW) National Literary Awards for 2013, Jim Hamilton Award in the fantasy/science fiction category, for an unpublished novel of sustained quality and distinction by an Australian author. It was published by Elsewhen Press in 2014.

REPORT TO

THE PRESIDENT
PLANETARY RESOURCES

Re: Purchase of Planet Z629/3

Planet Location / Reference I.D.:
Palfrem District TPX41/P39/Z649

Owner:
JC Inc.

Local Planet I.D.:
'Earth'

Life Forms:
Animal & Vegetation – Class. 18/468
Other Life:
Human – Approx. 7 Billion Units

Local Time:
1 Earth Year = 0.000000982 Central Time Units
(All Times in this Report are in Earth Years)

Copy:
Corporate Historian

History of Subject Planet

Earth was constructed four billion years ago by The Almighty, a successful mineral merchant from Mulkine in the Veayr District, using materials from the nearest star, Palfrem 87546. His intention was to use the planet as a base for local operations, as he had won the contract to explore the entire district. There were several other planets in the solar system at the time, but the extensive renovations required made the new planet the most viable option.

Unfortunately for Almighty, his plans were quickly thrown into chaos by the celebrated Houleron mineral discovery. Houleron is much closer to Central than Palfrem, so Almighty's market shrank to the distant, and minimal, outposts of the universe.

Almighty soon found himself close to bankruptcy and, after many years of haggling with creditors, retained only a single asset – Earth.

The planet became a staging post for passing travellers for the next few billion years and Almighty managed to turn a small profit, before his son arrived from Mulkine to take over the business. He renamed it after himself, *JC Inc.*

JC was confident he could turn Earth into a profitable concern. "I'd graduated from Mulkine Provincial Business College," he told me, "majoring in Organisational Farming." He mortgaged the planet to finance his ambitious plans to farm Flemeth (dinosaur hide). Extensive research had proved the planet's atmosphere ideally suitable for the trade.

Importing several thousand species of dinosaur from the development colony of Flemwole in the Ruyop District, JC set about his task. He brought in the best wranglers in the universe and the business flourished for 100 million years. JC was well on the way to the fortune that had eluded his father.

But like his father, JC was soon dealt a serious blow. "Because Earth is so remote, I was only vaguely aware of the problems caused by the SPOCTIS lobby group in Central."

The Society for the Prevention of Cruelty to Inferior Species had campaigned for millions of years to have Flemeth outlawed on the grounds that dinosaurs were being mistreated. JC, together with others in the business, disputed this, but SPOCTIS, buoyed by their success in banning dinosaur baiting, finally got their way. Flemeth farming was outlawed.

"I was shocked. The business was so lucrative I hadn't bothered to diversify." JC's sudden precarious financial situation forced him onto the black market. Aided by Earth's isolation he enjoyed, nervously, a few thousand additional profitable years.

This came to an end when a SPOCTIS operative, disguised as a Gidopean wrangler, infiltrated the operation. JC was heavily fined and the entire stock of dinosaurs was immediately confiscated and returned to Flemwole. Left with only the Earth, JC was on the point of selling up and returning home. But he changed his mind when a passing traveller told him of the startling news from Hydron 4. JC sensed that he was back in business.

For two million years scientists had been tinkering with human beings. The famous A.D. Amone invented them after stumbling on a simple process of manufacture involving materials from animal classification 18. The problem with humans, however, was that they had little practical use. Amone installed some basic intelligence in his prototypes, but they were capable of only the most menial tasks without extensive supervision.

A procession of researchers came and went until Amone finally lost interest and sold his planet, Hydron 4, and his entire stock of humans. The buyer was B.L. Zeebub, a chemical engineer and entrepreneur from the Hades District. He brought in his own experts and soon made his first breakthrough. Reproductive organs were incorporated into the experimental humans and manufacturing costs were reduced to zero.

Impressive though this was, humans were still not viable. The intelligence problem had not been solved, but Zeebub was confident. Renting a thousand disused planets, he isolated a million humans on each and experimented on each group with a variety of drugs. The results were not to be known for many years as the experiment was designed to evolve the human brain over hundreds or thousands of generations.

Most of the drug experiments failed, proving fatal to the subjects. There were also some spectacular disasters, most notably in the Gherm District, where humans developed intelligence at an alarming and uncontrollable rate, leading to the rapid colonisation and destruction of sixteen planets.

The only successful drug was Expron, one of Zeebub's later drugs. It developed intelligence over a period of one million years. After that time humans could, within limits, think for themselves. It became conceivable that one day humans could even control the day to day running of the universe. Zeebub was lauded everywhere for his genius.

On hearing the news, JC sent an agent to Hydron 4 to investigate the possibilities. Developed humans were beyond his reduced means, but he found he could afford two million basic units of various designs and colours plus the recommended dose of Expron to inject into Earth's atmosphere.

There was a short one hundred thousand year wait for the stock, but JC was unconcerned. He was well ahead of any other potential breeders in the Palfrem District and used the time to establish lucrative advance contracts for his matured humans. JC also informed his father of his plans and asked him to return to Earth. "Father was very excited about the prospects and agreed to come back. He even picked up the humans on the way."

The human stock was soon installed on the Earth's surface and the Expron was administered. JC and Almighty looked forward to a profitable future.

*

In hindsight, JC and Almighty may appear foolish. However, they were not the only ones duped by Zeebub's audacious plan.

At that time he was a respected figure throughout the universe. The Human Incident was the first of his criminal activities and completely unexpected. It was later established that Expron was developed long before Zeebub had purchased Hydron 4. The other drugs were merely a cover to add authenticity to his plan.

The irony of Zeebub's plot was that Expron did exactly as advertised. Subjected humans did eventually become capable of responsibility and it is now widely acknowledged they would indeed have assumed influential administrative positions. Zeebub would have then played his master card – Exprosil, the companion drug to Expron. This would have caused all humans to fall under his control. Zeebub would have become the greatest power in the universe.

The scale of the plan proved to be his undoing. Humans were sold throughout the universe, in almost every district. All the planets had to have similar conditions to house their humans, but there are too many local variables. Testing of Expron had taken place in ideal human conditions and the effects of the twin suns of Geynol or the heat drifts of the Pycren District could not have been foreseen. As an airborne drug, Expron simply mutated.

The initial customers noticed something was wrong after half a million years, when the humans began to stray from Zeebub's advertised path. On many planets human populations died within a generation. On others, super-intelligent humans developed so quickly they had to be destroyed. When reports reached Zeebub he knew the game was up, and fled.

The Central authorities were quick to act. Sample humans were taken from each planet for testing and the extent of Zeebub's criminal plan was revealed. An edict was issued restricting all humans to their own solar systems and all trade in humans was permanently banned.

Close to ruin, JC and his father faced a bleak future. However, the Human Incident threatened to cause an economic disaster, such was its extent. Central recognised this and provided financial assistance to Zeebub's victims. They also appointed hundreds of experts in an attempt to salvage something from the affair. Research soon pinpointed one prospective solution. Humans on 'ideal' planets, such as Earth, had been rendered receptive to external influence by Expron. If a way could be found to manipulate this capability then there was still a hope humans could be made useful.

Of all the suggestions put forward, the plan developed by

B.B. Beytrip, a lecturer in Humaniculture at Central University, was the one chosen. His studies of the human mind had revealed a strong tendency toward religious thought. Fear, coupled with their newfound intelligence, had manifested itself in an array of deity worship on every human planet. This tendency, he believed, could be harnessed and used as a controlling device. Humans could still become a going concern.

Beytrip became engrossed in his theory and devised an ingenious plan. He formed the Messiah Corps. This consisted of a body of specially adapted humans who were sent to the humans' owners. Their function was to mingle with human populations and persuade them to follow a simple set of rules designed to control them on a societal level.

Though impressed by the Corps, JC wanted to be more involved. The idle years waiting for a solution had enabled him to take a close look at his humans. He could not explain to me why, but he had developed a fondness for them. "They were crude and primitive," he told me, "yet there was some potential in them I found difficult to resist."

There was provision in Beytrip's Messiah Manual for owners' involvement, so JC chose the Prophet Plan. Corps members would be sent down to a region on Earth at regular intervals to inform the humans of JC's impending arrival. He did not wish to cause panic by arriving unannounced. The Corps prophets did their job well over many human generations and paved the way for JC. It was decided that one of them would introduce Beytrip's set of ten control rules. When the time was judged right, JC descended to Earth disguised as a human.

JC found it quite simple to gather followers and spread his word among the humans. He addressed huge crowds and performed simple tricks, persuading the humans he was indeed the 'Messiah' his prophets had told their ancestors about. The operation proceeded by the book and JC began to be convinced he could successfully redeem his humans.

But experience should have told JC that nothing was certain when it came to planet Earth. Though he had taken an interest in his humans, he had not looked closely into how they organised themselves. Therefore, he did not take much notice of the warlike tribe controlling a significant area of the planet.

As JC's words of peace spread, he was seen as a threat to the dominant tribe. He was arrested, tortured and 'executed'.

Bemused through this entire process and deeply disappointed, JC knew he needed a significant gesture to reassure his human followers. He feigned death and then appeared to a small band of followers. He made them promise to spread his word across the planet and reinforced this by ascending from Earth in their presence. He could only hope they would be impressed enough to succeed.

JC's visit did in time establish one of the main religions on Earth, but in all other aspects the plan was a failure. For the next two thousand years wars raged uncontrolled across the planet, often with one or both sides invoking JC's name.

Though comparatively peaceful at the moment, the humans now have access to weapons capably of destroying all life on the planet and have severely disrupted the natural ecological balance through industrial carelessness. This, or the next major conflict, is likely to have catastrophic consequences.

Current Condition of Planet

The background to this report reveals an unhealthy planet. The failure of the Beytrip plan, as with all other human populations, is self-evident. Despite the varying levels of intelligence developed by humans throughout the universe, they are incapable of self-governance without causing catastrophic damage to themselves and their planets.

In addition to the threat of self-destruction, the ecology of the planet is in a poor state. The atmosphere is poisoned by human-manufactured chemicals; the number of oxygen-producing plants (Class. 18/468/GHY45) is falling at an alarming rate; mineral resources are being depleted and wasted; and the fluid covering most of the planet (Solution XCF57) cannot break down the waste from human industry.

In short, without intervention the humans of Earth will be destroyed by themselves or by their environment. After this event the planet will be severely, if not irreparably, damaged. I have taken steps to salvage the situation.

Action

I have purchased Earth from JC Inc. for 16,000 Central Credits, an amount well within budget. JC was eager to sell and I am grateful for his assistance in compiling this report.

All animal life on the planet will be temporarily removed to the pens on Cruyos and will be returned after remediation.

Unfortunately, my attempt to sell the human stock has been unsuccessful, as no buyers could be found. Therefore, the human population will be destroyed. The Solar Wind Cleaning Company has been hired for this task. They will then restore the planet's atmosphere and fluid to its original condition.

Construction will then begin on the Palfrem Resort Complex, to be completed by the time Galactic Highway 9685 comes into operation.

For the first time since its construction, Earth will be of lasting benefit to the civilised universe.

I remain your obedient servant,

Jud Day

Judgement Day
Vice-President, Acquisitions
ARMAGEDDON INVESTMENTS INC.

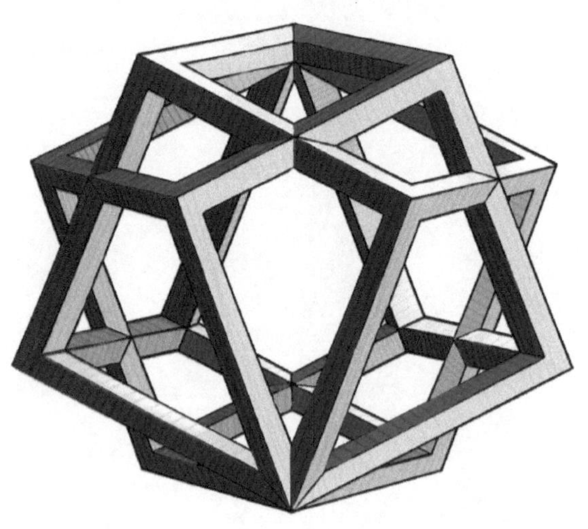

Ambrosia

by

Edwin Hayward

Edwin Hayward studied Computer Science at university. After graduating, he spent fifteen years enjoying the bright shiny future in Tokyo (with regular pilgrimages to Akihabara Electric City) before returning to the mundane day-to-day of the UK. He currently manages a number of websites, trades in domain names, reads avidly, writes when the muse cooperates, and exercises his geeky side at every opportunity. He lives with his wife in Cambridge, where he is awaiting the Singularity with a mixture of excitement and trepidation.

The 3D printer whirred and shook to a stop. Its custom print-head, primed with our most recent blend of cell cultures, retracted with a whine. The protective cowling clicked open. Tom and I craned forward to examine the output: a ragged disk of pink goo the size of two digestive biscuits stacked together, flaccid in the centre of the glass tray. We looked at each other.

"Yum!" Tom raised an eyebrow.

"It doesn't look that bad. Better than last week, anyway." I shuddered at the memory of that slimy elongated mass, like a squashed grey slug.

"Sure. Give me a sec to cancel my Chateau reservation." We hadn't ever actually eaten in the Michelin-starred *Chateau de L'Esprit*, which we passed every month on our way to the film quiz at the *Unicorn and Cross*.

"Let's get on," I said.

Tom crossed the lab, started fiddling with the Bunsen burner. The gas caught with a squeaky pop, followed by a roaring finger of fire. He set up a stand next to it, and clamped a square of iron mesh about a foot above the blue-white flame.

I slid the tray out of the printer, carried it over to him like a butler balancing an heirloom tea set. The pink blob quivered like jelly with every step. It clung to the plate as Tom tried to coax it onto the mesh. He wormed the wooden scraper under it, and flipped it neatly onto the cherry red metal. It sizzled on contact, and began to smoke.

Tom bent low over our sample, seemingly oblivious to the heat. He sniffed at it, then straightened up and looked at me. "Smells pretty good." No raised eyebrow this time, just the hint of a smile. He flipped the disc over, then beckoned me forward and scooted aside to give me room. I held my hair back with one hand to keep it away from the flame, and leaned in. Tom was right. It certainly did smell appetising, like a well-aged steak grilling on a barbecue.

I went to get the tiny picnic basket. Nothing fancy, just pairs of plastic plates, cups, knives and forks. We kept it hidden at the back of one of the filing cabinets, behind folders filled with paperwork relating to long-defunct projects.

Tom turned off the Bunsen burner. He grabbed our project notebook and the camera. "Your turn to do the honours, Jane."

I slid the golden brown sliver onto one of the plates, then paused for him to take close-ups. I sliced the sample in two, talking as I worked. "Not a lot of resistance. It's practically falling apart." Tom scribbled notes busily. I pressed down on a piece with the flat of my knife. "Not much juice, either. Still, the smell's right."

Tom zoomed in on the cross-section and snapped away. I transferred the other piece to the second plate, then handed it to him. "Bon appétit."

Tom cut a tiny morsel. I did the same. Then we put them in our mouths. I closed my eyes to concentrate better.

"Texture?"

"A four. No, make that a three."

"Yep. Mouthfeel?"

I rolled it around on my tongue. "Surprisingly ok, even if it's not chewy or juicy enough. Five."

"Four from me. It really is dry as a bone. Taste?"

I stopped, looked intently at Tom. "A solid nine."

Tom nodded. "We may just have cracked it, Jane." He gave me a thumbs up. We knew that the physical factors could be manipulated by tweaking the fat ratio, or adjusting the thickness of the muscle substrate during deposition. But taste was finger-in-the-wind, dependent on formulating the initial cell cultures just right.

"I believe a liquid celebration is in order," I declared. Tom's grin mirrored mine. We finished off the samples, tidied everything away, and spritzed air freshener to get rid of the residual smell. Then we headed for the pub.

Three weeks later, we feasted on highly respectable pieces of steak that looked, smelled and tasted like beef. We'd settled on a light marbling of fat by pushing into Japanese *wagyu* territory and then easing off. Our knives – proper metal ones, with serrated edges – met just the right amount of resistance as we carved thick slices off. Our plates ran with clear, meaty juice.

I was ecstatic, but Tom seemed uncharacteristically

subdued. "What's on your mind?" I prodded between mouthfuls.

"Just think we should be doing better."

"Better? This is probably the best steak I've ever had."

"It's a great steak, granted. But we're not constrained by nature, so it should be out of this world. This is a 9, but the taste knob goes to 11."

I brandished a moist, tender forkful at him. "Really? You don't think this is enough?" As I saw it, we'd achieved everything we'd set out to and more. We'd created a delicious meat substitute that could be produced cheaply in industrial quantities once economies of scale kicked in. No, to call it a "substitute" was to short-change our efforts: this was meat, just without the antecedent animal.

Tom, bent on his quixotic quest, put a very different spin on recent events. The more I lauded our efforts, the more Tom held out. We'd known each other since he poured sand down my neck in the local park at the age of five, and I'd never seen him so stubborn.

The debate grew more heated. I felt sure our work was going to change the world. I could even picture a Nobel. It was simple: all we had to do was serve out our notice periods, and walk away with our discovery. But no...

Our argument ended the only way it could: aggrieved parties stomping off in opposite directions. Tom muttered something about carrying on testing without me; I told him to go to hell.

My anger turned to hurt when Tom maintained radio silence into a second week, and then a third. By now I was desperate to see him, though I wasn't sure whether I would end up hugging or punching him when we finally met. Eventually, though, I pretty much gave up waiting.

"Friends? Meet me at the lab tonight, at nine." The text message, when it finally came, left me feeling a mixture of anger and relief. I was outside the building by ten to. Tom buzzed me in, and I went to find him.

Tom's skin was as pale as wallpaper paste, and his eyes were little more than dark hollow circles, sunk into his cheeks. An unfamiliar hint of grey ran through his black hair.

His left hand was wrapped in a thick, ragged bandage, secured by a clumsy knot between thumb and forefinger. His haggard appearance shocked me so deeply that I felt treacherous tears prick my eyelids.

"What happened, Tom? What have you done to yourself?" All notion of recrimination vanished.

"Nothing." He shifted from foot to foot. "Just keeping busy." He noticed me eyeing his hand. "Little mishap with one of the pipettes," he muttered, avoiding my gaze. "But I've done it, Jane. I've done it."

He insisted I take a seat while he cooked.

The meat looked firmer and leaner, somewhat like pork. As it sizzled and spat, a sweet almost cloying smell filled the air, exotic yet familiar. My taste buds were primed even before I cut into it. I took a mouthful and chewed thoughtfully. Mild, not as sharp as I was expecting, more like veal perhaps. Taste and smell reinforced each other with every bite, until my mind was drowning in primal thoughts of meat.

"Tom–" Something about the way he was toying with his bandage made me pause. I stared at my plate, then back at his hand. I dropped my fork.

NuMeat^{TM} catapulted Tom to the top of the Forbes rich list, and kept him there for over a decade. I moved to a small cottage in Cornwall. There, I grew roses – and as many vegetables as I could cram into my tiny garden.

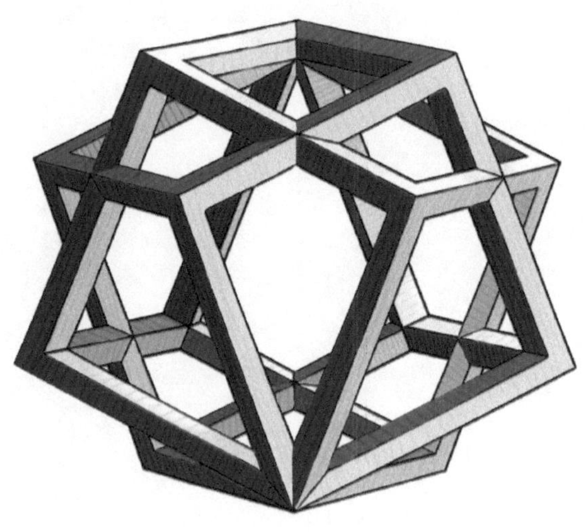

Jekking the Oofers

by

Rhys Hughes

Rhys Hughes was born in 1966 and began writing from an early age. His first short story was published in 1991 and his first book, the now legendary *Worming the Harpy*, followed four years later. Since then he has published more than thirty books, his work has been translated into ten languages and he is currently one of the most prolific and successful authors in Wales. Mostly known for absurdist works, his range in fact encompasses styles as diverse as gothic, experimental, science fiction, magic realism, fantasy and realism. His main ambition is to complete a grand sequence of exactly one thousand linked short stories, a project he has been working on for more than two decades. Each story is a standalone piece as well as a cog in the grand machine. He is three-quarters of the way through this opus.

"The galumphs are jekking the oofers again."

"I beg your pardon?"

"The galumphs. Right above you. See the oofers? They are being jekked good and poppersock. It's totally zondrian."

"Sorry, I only speak English."

"This *is* English, you drood! Pay moogly attention."

"Well, it's not any kind of English I'm familiar with. It's some sort of strange dialect that I don't recognise."

"What a humzung farsec! It's SFinglish, budnag."

"I still don't know what—"

"*Science Fiction English*, for quantum's sake!"

I looked up but I saw no oofers, unless I did see them but couldn't tell because I didn't know what they were. All that was above me was the sky, pale blue and softened with humps of cumulus cloud. Maybe the clouds were the oofers and it was blindingly obvious that they were being jekked by galumphs, but I wasn't at all convinced by this line of reasoning.

My interlocutor seemed to have the ability to peer beyond the serene and perhaps mundane sky that I looked at.

He jabbed his gloved finger aggressively.

"Fresh gak outta Saturn. Rumbly tekks coming in to spork at spaceport. Bet they're loaded with krakobits."

I strained my eyes and still saw nothing. He uttered a growl.

"Perk the condenso trail? Tekksigh optimum."

"Right. Does this have anything to do with the oofers? Or is it a totally separate phenomenon?" I asked meekly.

"You galosh! Bid the wangy fortiks, willya frud?"

"Um... sorry, I just don't—"

"Make an effort, for the love of quarks!"

I chewed my lip and scrutinised the stranger who had so oddly interrupted my daydreaming with his peculiar speech. He was a small man with a bald head and glasses with thick golden frames. His suit was a lilac colour and the shoulders were perfectly square. When he opened his mouth to speak I noted that his teeth were all alike, that every tooth in his head was a front tooth, even the back ones, and that none were pointed, stained or uneven.

"I don't know the rules of the game," I confessed.

"Nothing mumper. Just wok the nangy pok that ruffers into your xob. It doesn't krip what the actual swugs are."

I was apologetic. "I still don't comprehend..."

He leaned forward and whispered urgently into my ear, "Nothing easier. Just say the first thing that comes into your head. It doesn't matter what the actual words are. That's what I said. Now stop spoiling everything and try to join in. Say anything at all, by tachyon!"

So I cleared my throat and said very self-consciously, "Um... what did you think of the frobby emarg last night?"

He nodded encouragement and answered, "Ribbing biff. Zetunded the migratosh from the kurlo to the bongtog."

"Ah yes, I concur with your leko vercog on that."

There was an awkward silence.

I could tell that he was disappointed with me. I realised that the *majority* of my sentences were supposed to be in gibberish, instead of just a few words here and there. I tried again and this time I invented some actions to go with my words. I struck my left ear with the palm of my right hand, poked out my tongue, bent my knees and rolled my eyes clockwise.

"Pooks like gibble bandars mektek jubbers on the woy."

"Yah yay! Burten twosh oz!"

He was evidently delighted with my renewed performance. This gave me the confidence to continue. I hopped on one leg in a circle, placed the thumb of my left hand under my chin and flicked it.

"Dort I vidded a nanospekker hisskissing the voidal continuum slick from clustahole nine. Could be rumpal fussgug."

"Sux yerble heavy to that. Best quex the panode."

The admiration in his voice was unmistakable. He clapped his hands for joy and this display of enthusiasm pushed me to yet further extremes in my performance. I unbuttoned my shirt, pinched each nipple between finger and thumb and twiddled the pink fleshy protuberances as if they were the controls that adjusted the focus of a space radar screen.

Then I raised my hands to the sky, threw back my head, gaped my mouth as wide as it would go, wobbled my legs and swayed my hips from side to side, made bleeping noises that increased in pitch and suddenly stopped, twiddled my nipples back to their original position and yelled:

"Chipchooping long the honkway in my zooter. Saw quackum nodule passing the outerskirts. Bong rish thwack the korners. Vidded the zackal and poinged his droob. Diddums a migly with the chookers. Plonged right forth a gakkel mekajog. Jabs to me 'Quickle hopnok, did the weskit runder chubsot, fark ondo the skirp.' How blibba to the musky? Well, rightum gobo. Pekko from the rupe kwantom level attomekkas."

My companion was overwhelmed. "Oh, zolly gork! Hango it, you got right choob. Ferkect SFinglish jaknot."

"Mek the tek and subkomp the pekking zootrinos."

"Well spoke, mustercluster!"

It was at this point that I realised exactly what *Science Fiction English* was. It was an acknowledgement, crude and doomed but sincere, that language is one of the most mutable of human creations, that it is bound to change and evolve over time, that any attempt to imagine the future of our planet in which human beings still play a part must make an effort to reflect the passage of time in the way the protagonists of that imagined future communicate. This is all obvious but there is another point to consider, namely:

The moment any possible 'future' language is constructed, even in part, then it no longer is a future language but a language of the here and now, of the present. It is already redundant as a future language, it has defeated itself. Thus a future language can only be created in our present time, *which to the future is already the past*, if it is infinitely malleable.

So it must have no grammar, no syntax, no rules at all. It must be utterly meaningless, for only something that is without meaning can escape the trap of redundancy. Meanings go out of fashion. Only meaninglessness is eternal. And this meaninglessness of every sentence gives SFinglish its strength, for anyone can impose the pretence of a temporary meaning on any invented word and can understand and work that pretence in any way.

I now began wondering how far to push my newfound language skills. Could a level be reached where I was so fluent and advanced in *Science Fiction English* that he no longer understood anything I said, even though it was all meaningless anyway? In other words, would he feel compelled to fake incomprehension in the same way he faked understanding? Such fake incomprehension would also be real incomprehension, one of those rare cases where the truth and the lie are the same. It was an interesting speculation.

I decided to run a test by changing the words I was using from simple pseudo-slang to strings of random letters with no grammatical structure at all. "Gngjhb djew wbpugre rjglewp peojldksa."

But he was undaunted and said, "Hwnlb licbdka wyesjlb."

I wondered if the next step in the evolution of SFinglish would be to take the alphabet beyond the letter Z, to use symbols incapable of being pronounced, but this concept presented difficulties that were insurmountable. How does one speak the unspeakable with a human tongue?

As a solution, I attempted to beam an array of these symbols at him via telepathy, but he merely frowned, shook his head and indicated the watch strapped to his wrist. I peered closer. 21:30.

That's what it said and now I realised that he was engaged in playing the same game I sometimes play alone, which is to pretend that the time is the year and to act accordingly. For instance, when the digital clock-face says 12:15 I am an ancient jousting knight, my umbrella held out before me like a lance. When it says 19:17 I am a soldier running out of a trench and dodging bullets. I only act natural when the numbers of the time are the same as those of the present year. A time later than quarter past eight means I must create science fiction scenarios for myself, suitable to those actual numbers.

He was asserting that telepathy was a development for after the year 2130 and that we ought to stick to making sounds.

I was enjoying my time with him but I was already late for an engagement and I wanted to explain this and bid him farewell, so I smiled gently and said quietly, without any accompanying antics:

"Jadderglub the dooble zug."

He instantly turned pale. His voice was hoarse. "Bekko?"

I repeated the phrase. "Jadderglub the dooble zug..."

He grabbed my arm. "Vik mootle the bik? Vak muztid the kib?"

"Jadderglub the dooble zug," I said.

Now he became really concerned. "You fool! Shut up!"

His sudden lapse into understandable speech disgusted me. "Jadderglub the dooble zug! Jadderglub the dooble zug!"

"I'm warning you. The game is over," he gasped desperately. "You'll get us into trouble. What's wrong with you?"

"Jadderglub the dooble zug."

Sweat was pouring down his face. He turned on his heel to run away. But the looming form of a policeman prevented his escape. This policeman seemed to be swaddled in aluminium foil. He carried a papier-mâché gun and his cheap plastic visor imprisoned a dirty rainbow.

"Nats kekking riktor, lubbies? Patex you nud?"

"Don't tell him!" squeaked my friend.

But I was too filled with defiance to remain quiet. "Jadderglub the dooble zug!" I shouted at the top of my voice.

The policeman took a step back and although he raised his hand with the gun clutched in it and aimed it I could tell he was shocked. The barrel wobbled and the rest of his body twitched.

"Vulthy kring! Daspuckle cuckle!" he gasped.

And then he pressed the trigger.

Nothing at all happened.

As if remembering his duty, the policeman cried out, "Bzzt! Bzzt!" and lowered the fake gun to the ground. Then he drew a truncheon from a scabbard at his belt, rushed at me and hit me on the head.

I sagged to my knees while he growled, "Blazzer yud!"

My vision dimmed. I was vaguely aware that my

companion had fled and that an appalled crowd was coalescing around me. They were pointing fingers and chanting, "Ververt! Zimy pekk!"

My trial took place two days later. It was held in the SFreme Court and it was a very big occasion. The frunkly judderies were filled to the nuks with datatakers and crallow choofies. The gruder was a tekowig and he jabbered the gukel until the sporkle broke. Then he passed sentence.

It was a meaningless sentence, as befits the SFreme Court.

Now I am jekking the oofers alone.

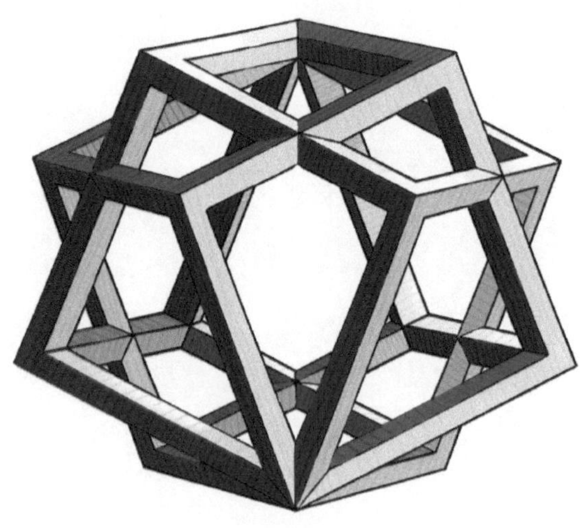

Luceria

by

Stefan Jackson

Stefan Jackson was born in North Carolina beside the calm eddies of the Trent and Neuse rivers, but spent the latter part of his childhood in southern California. In 1994 he moved to Brooklyn looking for a change, drawn to the energetic confluence of the Hudson and East rivers of the Big Bright City. There he met a lovely woman who became his wife, and they have an enchanting daughter. And a cat.

He now lives in Queens, where he writes stories, plays drums, coaches pee-wee girl's basketball, works the cubicle life, cooks breakfast, rides the F line, laughs and rests his head in the land of jazz.

Stefan has had over two-dozen original short stories and comic scripts published in small press publications and on the web. His first novel was *Glass Shore*, published by Elsewhen Press in 2014.

Stefan says "Cheers to the first fifty years. Hoping the next fifty are just as kind."

1

Denie slams shut the metal door. The warehouse is empty. No one hears the anger behind the closing locker door. Denie spits on the green tiled floor, more out of habit than spite or disgust. He reaches into his pants pocket and pulls out the Trigger; it is warm and pliable. He shuffles over the green floor as he studies the Trigger like a pitcher inspects a baseball.

Denie pops the Trigger into his mouth. In seconds he feels weightless. Unable to negotiate total bliss he drops, solid, upon the green floor.

Sweat plasters strands of his limp black hair to his forehead as the rest of his thin mane haloes upon the floor. Drool leaks from both corners of his smile. His tiny tight pupils fix on the eggshell plaster ceiling. Shift of light and fade of mind turns eggshell plaster into scattered white clouds madly rushing across a sad indigo sky.

Denie laughs.

In time he sits up and leans heavily against the wall. The aftertaste of the Trigger is akin to dried blood. He sniffs, coughs and spits.

He feels a discord in motion. Sluggish, he looks around the shifting room. Denie trains his mind to stop the room from sliding. He finds his school backpack on his left. Slow, deliberate, he reaches into the bag ... withdraws the red spike. The spike is the length of his index finger and as slender as a spider's lace.

Denie is lost in thought. Or slips through thought. Perhaps thought has no application.

He shakes the red spike then snaps off the tip. He opens his mouth and pokes the red spike into the inside of his cheek. Denie flinches as the meager ejection of warm liquid races into his body. He tries to pull the red spike from his mouth but is unsuccessful.

"Luceria always has a new beat." Denie says with soft sigh. The thin spike twitches on his lips. He laughs.

In time, he removes his MindBuddy™ from his backpack. The narrow black unit shimmers when his hands pass over the touch pad. Denie turns on the unit and enters his code.

Immediate link is pure rush. Luceria's song escorts him to paradise. The now scent of salt directs Denie's eyes from the sandy shoreline, over the calm seas and into the blue, green and pale orange horizon. Warm wind wanders over his flesh. Bleached sea foam waves upon flat sand. A hard Jamaican drop beat and the shrill cries of seagulls are her song. Luceria sings, *"You are so lovely. So very sexy nasty. So very very desire. Yes I love. Truly so love you. Where have you been all my life?"*

Luceria has chosen Denie. He is simpler now. He is a being of essence and bliss and no longer part of the complex structure of humanity.

2

Jacquil stands and walks over to lock his office door. He grabs his leather satchel as he moves over to the slender window. He raises the lower windowpane just a bit, allowing the chill and wet of the day to whistle through the opening, miniscule water bullets ricocheting off the dull concrete ledge into the room.

He opens his satchel and removes a red spike from its special holding place. He cherishes the skinny metal. It's the gateway to Luceria. The path to perfect happiness. Jacquil pulls the Trigger from another pocket in his satchel. He hunches over to get close to the window opening. He quickly sets fire to the Trigger, pulling hard on the tiny joint. The Trigger tastes like copper rust and blood. The smoke is thick and drips down the back of his throat. He coughs and snorts then spits out of the window. He takes another pull on the Trigger. Cough, snort, spit. He crushes the Trigger between his thumb and forefinger. Then he eats it. The fire bites his cheek and tongue as he crushes the drug with his molars. He grabs the red spike, shakes it, and snaps off the end. He opens his mouth and jabs the metal into the inside of his cheek. He jerks and crashes to the floor. The spike falls from his mouth. Thin red drool runs down his chin. Jacquil's piss-blond hair is matted to his square skull. His pale brown eyes bark confusion. His manners are clumsy and foolish. He had never known happiness until the moment he found Luceria's song.

He feels her song dancing on his heart.

In time ...

Jacquil sits at his computer. He punches in his codes. He hears a distant fade, like an echo. He pumps up the volume on his office computer as Luceria's euphoric rhythm races through his blood. A complex earthy syncopation that stiffens his manhood and feather-scratches his mind. Feverish and hungry, searching the web with passion, he finds a chat room devoted to Luceria.

Jacquil enters the empty chat room and considers the silence.

I pray to you, Jacquil types.

No response. Jacquil feels his heart will not beat until he receives an answer.

Then, *Do you* ♥ *Me? Y? N?* scrolls across his monitor.

He answers **Y** before the thought enters his mind.

An annoying subliminal buzz forces Jacquil to flex his lower jaw. His monitor flickers and pulses at a maddening rate. His jaw freezes tight. He does not move. He does not blink. Jacquil watches Luceria materialize from the smoke wafting out of his monitor. Her form is simple. A darkness of pure beauty. Untouchable. Unapologetic. Painful. Captured.

Closer. Her smoky love is water on his parched flesh. Jacquil is greedy for her. He bites the neck of the mist that is Luceria as his ejaculation pitches him out of his chair. His square face kisses and cracks the computer monitor. Jacquil crumples to the floor, quivering, unaware and drooling. His passion is unrelenting. Semen no more, he pumps blood.

3

"Quit telling me Luceria doesn't exist," Myric says to his computer as he rephrases the query then taps reload.

Again, *I cannot reference this request* pops up on his monitor. Myric slaps the monitor. "Fine," he says to the computer. He taps the screen icon for phone. When the personal directory appears he touches the second entry on the list. Myric did not hear the line click.

"What up Myric?"

"TV, who's Luceria?"

"RypStar," replies TV. His voice flows from layered banks of various apparatuses that are fastened to his scalp and spine. Myric looks closely into his monitor, viewing the mass of wires, monitors and touch pads, and at the center of it all, he sees a man of withered face with wild eyebrows and beard.

It is a painful existence. TV releases more dope into his core. The drug doesn't get him high but stimulates his libido (bye-bye pain); now he sports a beautiful erection as he gathers data on Luceria.

"She's a construct?" Myric asks. He takes a long drag from his cigarette. Myric finds it is often hard to understand TV. His voice is rapid, flowing, as water falling.

"Yes, Luceria is a construct." TV states. "Created on and for the net. Origin unknown. She sings music woven from beats and poems of the last century. Listen."

TV dopes Myric's alignment. Myric exhales thick pink smoke as he raises the sound on his unit. A repetitive organ chorus sliced with a rude ersatz E chord from an ill-tuned guitar. An uneven tribal beat lays the foundation.

"–Oh, never a doubt but, somewhere, I shall wake,
And give what's left of love again, and make
New friends, now strangers, but the best I've known,
Stays here, and changes, breaks, grows old, is blown
About the winds of the world, and fades from brains
Of living men, and dies. Nothing remains."

TV and Myric are silent as Luceria's splendid voice echoes through Myric and claims ownership of his enraptured soul. "TV, that's it?" pleads Myric.

"Sample." TV states. He reads the data that appears on his monitor. "Music: The Who. 'Baba O'Riley', 1971. Poem excerpt, The Great Lover by Rupert Brooke, 1914. You want whole song?"

"No." Myric takes a short pull off his smoke. "So she sells her music?"

"No. Free. Billions of hits."

"What does she look like?"

"Unknown."

"What? Everyone and everything is photographed! Nothing is unseen or unknown."

"Visual Luceria never created." TV states.

"She's a damn cult figure. You're telling me no icon or image exists. And if she's so networked how come I can't find her when I run a search?"

"Luceria lives in the mind's eye. You can't find Luceria. She finds you."

"Is she a virus?"

"In kind but not exact. Luceria equals program extensile morph. Born and released on net to study language."

Silence.

"Have you spiked?" TV challenges Myric.

"No."

"It is beautiful." TV sighs. "You can *feel* Luceria sing. Pure orgasm. Messy. A love you mind fuck that you can't turn off. Small spike and zip trigger required."

"I know about the spike, the bliss drug Inhorn *spiked* with Freheroin, but what is the Trigger?"

"Pre-boost before spike. No overload. Not always clean. I fashion extra traps. I get out clean."

"So if I use a regular street brand Trigger I may still end up fried?"

"Risky. Some fried. Others salvaged. Many people lucky and spike clean. Do you like Luceria?" asks TV.

"Yeah. She's fuckin' beautiful." Myric replies.

"You seek an answer to the crystal corpses? Luceria can't be a suspect. She is unreal."

"Right." TV's statement shocks Myric for a moment before he remembers that TV is tapped into the world. The media has yet to learn of Myric's case but TV would know about it. There was no such thing as a secure net port to TV. International, Federal, State or personal, TV can and does hack into the world.

"Thanks TV. When you check your pouch, you'll find a little something." Myric terminates the transmission. He has the last pull from his cigarette then snuffs it out. Myric believes searching for Luceria is a dead end. Yet the fact that no visual image of Luceria exists bugs the hell out of him.

4

Denie sets the bloodied nude woman in the chair. He tilts her forward and red pours from the woman's nose and lips upon the keyboard. Satisfied that enough of her blood wet the keyboard, Denie pushes the near dead woman back into the seat. The woman had put up a good fight. She may have beaten a lesser man but the love of Denie's goddess made him extraordinary. Luceria loves him and Denie loves Luceria.

Denie pulls the red spike from his small leather valise. He snaps off the tip.

"Just a little squirt my dear," Denie says in a hushed tone. He opens the woman's mouth, jabs the red spike into her inside cheek. She jerks and almost falls from the chair. Denie steadies her and keeps her planted firmly in the chair. He places the woman's hands on the keyboard and with her bloodied fingers types, *Luceria*.

Denie eases away from the woman.

Brilliant light erupts from the monitor, lightning-bright searing the room. Denie stands tall and still bathed in the storm of clean white.

Luceria's velvet vocals soar with the fading white light. The weight of pure beauty of Luceria's voice squeezes happy tears from Denie's soul.

5

Myric surveys the pure white room. Carpet, floor, ceiling, walls, wall hangings, furniture, electronic appliances, doors, door handles and hinges are all virgin white. The windows are cold to the touch, offer zero visibility and are sealed tight. The only color in the room is Myric and the six members of the forensics unit.

Myric touches the corpse as the chief forensics officer studies the smooth, clear, perfect glass figure. Myric lifts his hand off the corpse as he asks, "Are you sure this crystal figurine was human?"

The chief forensics officer gives Myric a tired look. She removes the density glasses that cover her eyes, and lets them drop around her neck.

"We recovered Human DNA from the core of the corpse, here." She points to a pinpoint hole in the belly button. "The core sample has not been identified.

"Twelve bodies. All the same. Skin, muscles, nerves, tendons, teeth, bones, and all internal organ turned to glass," she continues. "Please note for your investigation that the corpses are glass not crystal. Crystal has a lead content of at least 24 percent whereas glass has no lead. And these dead are lead free.

"And no, I don't know what it would take to turn humans into glass!" she snaps over her shoulder as she places her glasses back on. "Damn tired of everyone asking me that. How the hell would I know that?"

"When did you guys confirm glass not crystal?"

"It was the Dock crew that worked that out. I think they passed it along last night."

Myric nods. He sparks a Turkish cigarette. Guaranteed to piss off everyone.

"Aw shit! Myric what's your malfunction? Put that out!" The chief forensics officer bellows.

Myric ignores her.

The photographer tries to open the window, but finds it closed too fast for him to dislodge. A few of the crime scene guys scout for clues close to the floor, yet there is no escape from the pungent and stomach-clenching bouquet from Myric's Turkish cigarette. In quick time, everyone leaves the room.

Myric smiles. Now he can think. Review: The victims were all women. Ages vary from twenty-two to fifty. All victims found in their homes – and so this unfortunate must be Aryka Brovent. All bodies were nude and located within immediate vicinity of a destroyed computer. He glances around the room. White. All white. Just like the rooms of the other victims.

Glass corpses. White voids. Luceria.

Myric has a short pull from his cigarette. Somehow, someway, he is sure Luceria is the key. If he can get to know her, then he may understand he or they that kill in her name. Sacrifices. The glass corpses are sacrifices to Luceria. Of course, this is his theory. A theory he has not shared with anyone. He arrived at the premise one day as he studied mad spikers, who were secured in an observation ward. A bleached white spike found in the corpse's mouth remains the only item recovered from any of the glass corpse sites. Myric had little understanding of spiking. He went to the ward to talk to officers who deal daily with spikers. A spiker repeated *Luceria*. The name quieted the ward. Dozens of ravers and wall-bouncers became still and content as they reprised Luceria's name in a child's singsong fashion.

TV says Luceria is a RypStar. Myric is sure that she is more than a RypStar.

Myric has an abrupt and absorbing unprofessional need to hear Luceria.

He desires to receive her voice.

Yet he is not chosen.

To listen.

6

On the south bound metro. In the tube between Brighton and Coney.

> *"The sweet song that*
> *quiet your nightmares*
> *is Luceria. She is*
> *the Dark Light. She is*
> *Every Night. She is*
> *Blind Sight. She is*
> *True White.*
> *She is Love is."*

The thin alabaster-skinned young man croons with a lovely roar and a honeyed cadence. The song seems to emanate more from Denie's pasty statuesque body than from his mouth. He produces a beat by slapping his palms against his chest, stomach and legs. He flows through the train like cold smoke. Passengers bop their heads and tap their feet. Women dance as Denie continues to sing and slap his body.

> *"Her Love Light song is*
> *The Class of Death*
> *which cries for the lost you,*

yet only a smile will discover
  You in the embrace of
  Midnight Ivory.
Now everyone sing along!" Denie commands.

Everyone sings as the night train races below the bright city. The crowd knows the song by rote. They sing with smiles and stomp the floor of the subway car with joyous revelry.

Denie hops off the train when the doors open at Pershing Avenue. He prances down the waiting platform, singing the love of Luceria. He crosses over at the fairway just as the northbound train arrives. He dances through the open doors of the train car. Denie sings of Luceria's love.

  "She of Glass Heart
  That I make for you,
  I give to you,
  Luceria.
  She of Such perfect Dark
  Luceria.
  Forever Night and
  Love White. Luceria is Love."

7

Against his better judgment, Myric decides to visit TV. TV lives on The Ground. The Ground is constantly hot, muggy and bathed in stale artificial lights. The sun touches the natural ground of New York City with generous infrequency due to the tall and wide buildings fragmenting and cancelling the warmth and light of the brilliant orb. The reek and rot of The Ground permeates the skin. Life on The Ground is not recommended. RESPIRATOR REQUIRED read signs on Ground Levels One (natural), through Ground Level Five. Myric wears a plain black respirator that claims to filter out ninety-eight percent of all known toxins for up to one thousand hours. He has had this mask for weeks and is aware he should replace it. The Ground is a dangerous place. Armed Ground citizens are ready to take whatever comes their way. Myric exposes his chrome bodysuit. The bodysuit makes him impervious to all blades and most small arms fire.

Myric carries his pumper in his right hand, with his finger on the trigger. A bright red light indicates the pumper is ready to fire, alerting anyone feeling frisky.

"Are you in a relationship right now?" The short, pudgy gypsy asks Myric. She wears no respirator. Her teeth are flawless. Her eyes are bright red. She is unarmed.

"No?" she continues, "I can help you find your soul mate."

Myric looks at the old woman with annoyed curiosity. His station in life is visible: the gold badge (#72245674-SZ) on his belt. The gypsy does not display her license nor a bond number. What kind of idiot would prop a cop without proper city ID? He could arrest her and slap her into central lockup for a hundred hours. Yet, what was the point?

"Apathy. Too bad," says the crimson-eyed old lady.

Myric looks at the woman. She winks with a confident smile. Has she read his mind, or is it part of her pitch? Her illustrious eyes freeze his thoughts for a moment. He knows her eyes are not implants. Gypsies are renowned for their health. Their health is their edge in control of Ground Territory. He approaches the gifted red-eyed gypsy. Myric pulls out paper money that is folded and secured in a tiny pocket of his vest. He gives her twenty dollars.

"Who is Luceria?" Myric asks.

"A First Class Demon," is the gypsy's stoic answer.

Myric stares down at her. Her red eyes stand behind her words.

"How and why does she turn women into glass?" he asks.

"Such is the fragile nature of beauty. Luceria is an all-consuming Desire. A First Class demon."

"She was created. A learning program to study the language of the net," replies Myric with defensive reflex. He reaches for his cigarettes then notes his respirator. He bites back the urge to smoke.

"Luceria is indeed language.

Silence. Myric's attention is drawn to the flashing blue lights of a pot bellied fire truck as it zooms overhead, silent, through the structural maze of the City.

"How can I stop her?" Myric asks.

"Ignore her beauty and deny your desire." The gypsy's smile is like a howling laugh in the dark. It unnerves Myric.

He walks away. His intention unchanged and uninfluenced by the gypsy.

He is going to let Luceria into his heart.

*

The shiny metal door disappears into the wall on the left. Myric enters TV's home. The door zips shut. He pulls off his respirator and takes a deep breath of stale air. Gutted and ugly electronic parts clutter the narrow hallway. Myric approaches TV, avoiding unshielded trap rods, hot wires and a milieu of unfamiliar sharp-edged tech.

"What did the gypsy say?" TV asks. "I see everything but sometimes sound is static."

"She said that Luceria is language as well as a demon of desire. She also said I could beat her if I ignored Luceria's beauty." Myric glances at TV. TV looks anemic, and smells not unlike burnt hair. Myric looks away as he lights a cigarette. He exhales pale smoke with nervous disgust.

TV hands a rigid red lace spike to Myric.

"Again, I advise against spiking. First time could be last time." TV stares at Myric. TV's eyes were akin to a shaken snow globe, obscured by tiny flakes in constant motion.

"I have to understand her. Perhaps then I will understand the glass corpses." Myric holds up the red spike. Its weightlessness surprises him.

TV slides the Trigger to Myric. Myric picks up the finger-long joint.

"Two hits are all you'll need."

Myric lights the Trigger. Inhales deeply – chokes and coughs and spits. "Fuckin' taste like blood!" he states and spits again.

"Check. Hit again. No overload. Zip retreat. No promise of clean return. No traps for plain humans." TV states without looking at Myric.

Plain humans. Myric has neither default nor enhancement implants. This puts him at a disadvantage in so many ways. He refuses science for reasons he feels more than he understands. Myric hits the trigger. Coughs and spits. Tosses the trigger aside.

"You say you can find Luceria anytime you want. How?" Myric asks.

"Because I've tasted her song. I'm a disciple of her voice, but I'm too doped up to fall for her love song. That is the one that fucks up people."

"Right. So what do I do?"

"What the gypsy said. Ignore her beauty. Don't fall in love."

"Okay – pump her up." Myric tells TV.

TV dials in Luceria.

Myric snaps off the tip of the spike. He opens his mouth and spikes the inside of his cheek. He jerks and drops to a knee. He pulls the spike from his mouth. It falls from his loose fingers. He rights himself ... for a moment ... then he crashes to the floor.

Sitting on TV's floor, Myric watches the world on TV's monitors. Rain and snow assaults the Earth. Seas rage under a black sky. Chinese children play baseball. Lovers clutch and struggle in a tiny room. A nude man sits alone on the fine blond sand of an unknown beach.

Then Myric feels her subtle song.

Nothing to hear. Everything to feel.

Yes! Myric ejaculates! Rolling painful pleasure. He is everlasting, blinding and soaring because Luceria's song is a forever aria of celestial ecstasy. His stomach muscles flex and spasm. His hips pump the air. His cock is hot and inflamed and sperm empties from it. The pain surpasses pleasure and Myric wants more.

Don't fall in love with her.

Her song. Luceria. Such perfect Dark.

♥u

Such perfect Dark.

8

He is sensitive to light so the doctors keep the lighting muted.

He is sensitive to touch so surgeons have desensitized his mind with drugs.

He jerks and moans – another orgasm is always just a breath away! The dope they give him keeps him incapable of stepping over that threshold. Heavy petting without the pop.

He can think and remember yet these activities are a struggle. He has to fight the ever-present song and sensation of Luceria. She dominates his life and he has to remind himself that he is not happy about it.

"So this is the officer that was working on the glass corpses cases?" a voice inquires.

"Yes. I understand he was a very good detective," answers a nasal voice.

Myric uses the voices as an anchor and drifts out of the dope-induced fog. He looks deep into a familiar face and the new face that stands next to his bed. The new face has glasses and a large nose.

Dr. York, the man with the old face, makes the introduction.

"Detective Myric, this is Dr. Elvis Black. He can help."

"I propose an implant at the base of your spine that will shunt the sensations that plague you. Downside, no sex for you ever again." Elvis says with a dry smile. "Credit a good Trigger for your survival."

"Trigger?" The slim Dr. York questions the stout Dr. Elvis.

"Yes. A complex drug taken before spiking. It works best with traps but Detective Myric is plain." Elvis blots his meaty forehead with a white silk handkerchief.

"What possessed you to spike?" Elvis asks.

Myric thinks about the word then forces it out of his mouth.

"Luceria."

Elvis nods.

"What did he say?" Dr. York asks Dr. Elvis.

"Luceria." Dr. Elvis says. "She's a shared delusion amongst spikers. An urban myth if you will. The story goes that Luceria was created on the net to learn language and one day produced a universal tongue. A speech or song that drives one mad."

"I've heard that as well," offers Dr. York. "An organic song. A tune our minds are not able to process."

Dr. Elvis shakes his head, "Such debate about that phenomenon". He studies Myric for a moment longer. Then Elvis drifts away from Myric's bed and toward the door. Dr. York follows.

"Someone told me Luceria is a fractal aria," Dr. Elvis continued, "which makes no sense to me."

Myric watches the doctors leave the room.

Luceria does exist.

To ignore her beauty is to deny your desire.

Luceria Song is in his heart and on his lips.

Luceria Song is all and forever.

It is not a process. It is not trouble.

It is.

All.

Listen.

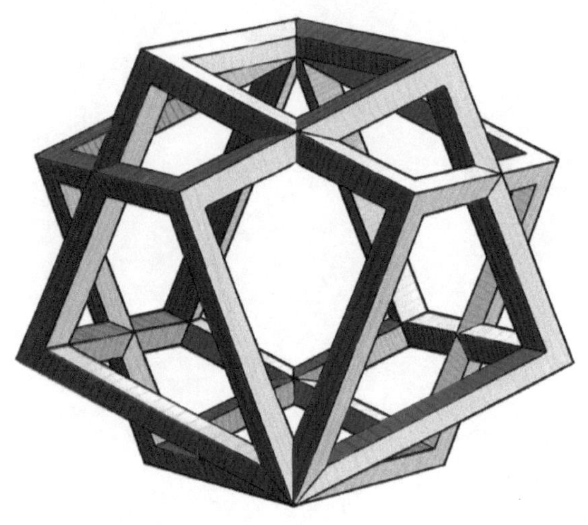

Homo Sapiens Inferior

by

Andy McKell

Andy was abducted by science-fiction in his teens. Exposed to American pulp magazines, he was hooked at First Contact. Subsequent exposure boosted the addiction until he was mainlining Asimov, Bradbury, Clarke and the whole author alphabet through to Zelazny, those long-gone heroes of mid-20th century science fiction. Then he discovered Tolkein and his fantastic ilk. A library of thousands of real paper books is preserved in Andy's home, assembled during his student years, then his servitude in the airline and computing industries in London and Luxembourg.

His consumption was only quelled by the appearance of the McKell offspring – three lovely and talented daughters – and the setting-up of his own web design company. Time became the real 'final frontier': time is so inelastic under normal conditions. But as the girls began to fly the nest, he sold the company and retired early. At last, there was time. It was the right time.

Time to power-up the muse and the pc and tap out the tales that have simmered long in his subconscious. Strangely, a few editors seem to like his works. And a few readers, too.

He hopes you continue to enjoy reading his imaginings.

I tried to be human. I tried really hard…

Just a kid, trying to be human.

Dad was talking to his friend as I passed the open study door. "Purity Laws? I'm not worried, Usebi. It's another west coast scare; it'll never spread across the whole continent. They see climate change, global economic collapse and now Ebola is returning. They're afraid; who wouldn't be? But it'll pass. We need to get our economy going again and get some aid in there."

"John, you are short-sighted. Crisis always leads to scapegoats. You don't hear the Ministers whisper together in the capital. Perhaps you should make plans."

"Plans for what? I'm not leaving my homeland. And where would I go? Europe? America? They're in ruins. No, we're much safer here in Africa." Then he noticed me lurking in the hallway, threw me a smile and gently closed the door, cutting-off my snooping.

I wasn't really interested. My mind was on girls–not just 'girls'; it was 'THE GIRL'.

Suzi. She was called Suzi. Usebi's daughter. And she was beautiful. Her eyes the deepest, thoughtful brown; her skin like chocolate silk; her smile like the sun breaking through storm-clouds, its glow spreading bright promise. Best of all, she liked me, too. We had known each other since forever, playing together before we could walk properly, just neighbours' kids–my dad an industrialist, hers a government minister. We were lucky, we were privileged, we were happy.

I didn't know I was carrying an ancient evil.

Yes, I looked different from most people: my hair was blond, my eyes blue. Suzi called me her vanilla ice cream, because of the hair.

I loved the way she smiled.

Then we changed, grew older. I burned inside in a way I didn't understand. Suzi seemed different, too. It was exciting, it was new, it was delicious and it was scary. Things were happening to our bodies and we ignored everything that was happening around us.

One day, she whispered in my ear, "I love you, too."

I heard things were changing in the cities, but we were far

from those. We ignored them. When it did come into our lives, it began with small things.

One servant was replaced, then another. Our parents set armed guards on our tails. They followed us everywhere outside the house. My frustration churned my insides. Just when we needed to be together, we were held apart by constant supervision.

Usebi began to travel into the capital with armed guards in a new, bulky limo. He gave Dad a lift every day. Usebi's personal guards dressed really smart, not like ours. His guys wore dark suits and ties, with weapons hidden in their jackets. Soon after, two more vehicles joined their commute. It had become a convoy of camouflaged vehicles with troops carrying automatic rifles.

About that time, I overheard Usebi pleading with Dad. "I beg you to think again. The tribal warlords are winning across the west. They've slaughtered politicians, teachers, doctors, and they're enforcing those damned Purity Laws."

"So-called 'science-based' racialism, heh? We saw that in Europe, Asia, America... But not here. We've moved on."

"Don't you watch our TV news? They were disapproving, but no longer. Some broadcasts smack of approval. Listen, these Laws appeal to desperate populations. We are heading for a tipping-point, I tell you. I urge you to make plans, my friend. Make plans..."

That same day, Suzi and I were down at the lake, swimming, keeping what her Mom called 'a chaste separation'. Somehow the guards' scrutiny felt different that day. As I towelled Suzi's back, I heard a deep-voiced muttering.

"I wouldn't let a thal touch MY daughter."

Suzi's guard didn't try to disguise his message by using tribal language. It was for my ears, although I spoke his language as well as he spoke mine. I didn't know what a 'thal' was, I just knew it sounded nasty. But all was well: I was with Suzi.

She asked her dad what 'thal' meant. She said he got angry and there was shouting in the yard and the guard was fired.

My own guard grew moody. I stopped going to school.

One evening, I found Dad explaining to Mom about the

factory and the redundancies. "What else can I do? The world is no longer consuming what we make. Not consuming anything much, anymore. Back to the Stone Age, out there. No internet, even. Nothing." Mom looked concerned. Dad gave her a big, comforting hug. "Don't worry, love. We're well away from the danger, here."

He hugged her again a week later when the mob smashed the factory windows and fired the trucks. She was crying. "None of your workers dare cross that picket line. They could have worked, produced something to sell, earned wages to feed their families. Why are they doing this? And why blame us? Thals, indeed!"

I heard Dad tell Usebi that some of the rioters were our own employees. It made no sense to me. I thought Mom was right. And I still didn't understand the slur. People call other people names all the time. I didn't realise there was a deeper, darker side to this one.

Another of our servants left, sobbing out her apologies. Mom and Dad said they understood, and it was not her fault. Dad gave her a thick envelope and wished her luck.

The power cuts started.

Usebi came over to say he couldn't give Dad a lift any more. The government was paying for Ministers' security only. His gaze wandered around a lot, from Dad's tie to his shoes, to something behind Dad: but not a lot on his face. Dad said he understood and, as a taxpayer, agreed with it.

Usebi grasped Dad's arm, at last looking him in the eyes, and spoke with urgency. "For God's sake, man. Things are changing. Think of your family. Make plans!" Then he left, walking away with slow footsteps, not looking back.

Dad tried to calm Mom, who was crying again. "Look, he came over personally. Didn't send a flunky or use the phone. He's a good man, a good friend. It will all turn out all right." He patted her arm in a way that had become familiar. I had the strangest feeling it was now to comfort himself more than her.

He no longer added, "We're well away from danger, here."

I saw Suzi's dad only once more.

*

When the soldiers came, Dad tried to show calm, but I could tell he was afraid.

The driver and a guard stayed with the jeep, smoking and talking quietly. A small, pompous man wearing a doctor's white jacket and carrying a medical bag strode up the stairs, a pleasant smile fixed to his face. He seemed harmless, as did the soldiers flanking him, their rifles held casually at their sides.

"Oh, Mister, why ask for phone calls? No need for talking to anyone. We are just taking some blood. We're taking everyone's blood. A little drop is all we need, because we already know what we shall find, don't we?" He actually winked at Dad, who relaxed a little.

Later, Dad said someone–Suzi's dad, business friends, someone, anyone–had intervened to make this go away. He trusted that wink.

It was a mistake. He had misread it. Yes, it did mean the test was a formality and the results a foregone conclusion, like he told Mom. But not in the way Dad had hoped.

The results arrived a couple of days later.

Two percent.

Mom, Dad, me–we were all 'two percenters', HSI-2.

Homo sapiens inferior.

Class 2.

Dad explained it to me with a choke in his voice. "Everyone whose ancestors moved out of Africa six hundred centuries ago has a little Neanderthal DNA in them."

Neanderthal? This made no sense to me. Neanderthals were all dead long ago, weren't they?

"Yes, but they left us a little gift, one that keeps on giving. When our ancestors left Africa, they met Neanderthals. There was interbreeding. Their offspring spread across the whole planet. So everyone has a little Neanderthal DNA in them, just one or two percent–everyone except those whose ancestors stayed in Africa and never met Neanderthals. The stay-at-home Africans are 'pure' Homo sapiens sapiens. You, me, your mother are not. Not a hundred percent pure. Two percent of our DNA is Neanderthal.

"Call it ancient revenge. After all, we did wipe them out." His chuckle was forced, his smile was fake. He saw my expression and turned away to hide his face. Later, I found an empty whisky bottle in the lounge.

So according to the Purity Laws, I was not totally human; I was a little bit Neanderthal. Like most people on Earth, I was Homo sapiens inferior.

In my case, Class 2.

I showed my new ID card to Suzi. She was puzzled, then smiled her big, wide smile. "This is just silly. You are still YOU. How can you be other because of a piece of paper?" She shook her head, dismissing the information. "I got a new ID card, too. Let's see what I am." She pulled it from her shirt pocket, that magical smile spreading across her face. It was still a game to her.

Mine was grey cardboard, its corners already starting to shred. My photo was roughly stapled on. Hers was a laminated photo card.

I wondered why mine looked so cheap, so temporary.

She giggled as she held hers under my nose. It was upside down.

"Clown!" We both laughed in the bright sunshine, as I took her card and turned it around so I could read the words. I remember the moment so clearly, frozen in my inferior brain. There would not be much more laughter.

HSS. Homo sapiens superior.

Suzi was pure human.

*

I heard Mom crying again. She'd heard about disappearances, camps, deportations, property seizures... I peeped around the doorway. Dad held her close. "That's in other countries, not here. People here have more sense." He could not hide how empty he knew those words to be.

"But what about the Jensens and the Ashokas and the other foreign neighbours? And your friends at the Chamber? They're all moving away, going somewhere safe."

"They are not foreigners; we are not foreigners. We were born here. This is our homeland. These are our people." He paused for a long time, then spoke quietly. "And where would we go?"

Later, I found him in his study, at the open safe, sorting through papers, selecting things to pack into his briefcase.

I tiptoed away.

Next day, Suzi met me at the lakeside. Our guards sat huddled in the shade of a nearby tree, smoking and gossiping, their rifles resting across their knees.

She was full of smiles. "I talked with Dad, told him to fix it. He said there was a vote about it in Parliament. He said that years ago, scientists took DNA samples from all over the world and those thal string things were only in the people not in sub-Saharan Africa! That's where we are. So everything's all right!" Her voice carried a triumphant note.

I wanted more. "What about the vote? The Purity Law?"

"Oh, he said he was very busy and we'd talk later." She thought for a while. "But you are African. Why are you HSI-2? I don't understand."

Neither did I, really. I understood the rules, but not why it was so bad to be me.

Another question came to me. "What about those taken to other countries? The Caribbean, America…?"

"They test everyone who wants to travel here. People with a non-African ancestor are forbidden to come. They have corrupted DNA, you see, so they are Inferiors, just like you–" She froze at my stare. "I didn't mean… I meant… Oh, I am so sorry. Let me hug–"

I felt a kick in my heart. I put up my hands in front of my chest, as if defending myself, pushing her back without touching. It was too late. The word had been spoken; it could never be taken back. She was beginning to use their vocabulary. Somehow, I knew it was just the first step towards a deeper change.

I scrambled backwards up the slope. I ran from her and the word, outrunning my guard, who strolled casually in my distant wake. I raced across the fields to the house, ran upstairs, slammed doors, ignored stunned servants. I shut myself in my room and threw myself on the bed. I lay in mental agony, testing the sense of loss I felt, my thoughts touching and drawing back from the imagined future like a tongue exploring a broken tooth.

I was losing her.

*

I overheard the staff talking about the rumours and the special 'Purity Action Force' being recruited. Cook yelled that they were stupid, slapping her hand hard onto the kitchen counter.

"It isn't true! My sons are in the army. My boys would never do such terrible things." Her voice rose to a screech. "Get out! Get out!" She chased them from her kitchen, scattering them like frightened hens. I heard the hack-hack-hack of cleaver blows, butchering some beast for our dinner. "People don't do these terrible things!" She said it over and over, as if to convince herself, to make it go away, or to make true something she feared was not.

That evening, the meal seemed extra-specially good and plentiful, as if...

*

Dad was wrong. Cook was wrong. Ordinary troops, ordinary people, might not do bad things, but the government had found people who would. After all, there was no other work since the factories closed.

The soldiers arrived in an open truck, drawing up outside the house in a swirl of dust and shouting. There was no warning. Their uniforms were new, with bright Purity Action Force flashes on their shoulders. We had ten minutes to pack.

Ten minutes. Two bags each.

They guarded the doors, as if we would try to run. Where could we run to? The sergeant flopped heavily into an antique chair, cocked one leg over the arm and lit a cigarette. The servants and guards didn't respond to our calls; perhaps they knew in advance, perhaps they were just scared and hiding.

The phones didn't work. The sergeant smiled smugly as Dad tried to contact Usebi, or the Ministry, or anyone...

"Oh, see how fast time passes. And how you waste it." He watched us gathering what we could in the time we had, flicking his ash onto the carpet and humming tunelessly, making a show of glancing at his watch.

Family photos, jewelry, legal documents, business records, clothes... all jumbled into bulging suitcases too full to close properly. Mom flapped about, asking if we should bring food or water. The soldiers looked at each other and laughed. One shrugged, as if to say, "Who cares?", without summoning up the effort to put it into words.

The sergeant called his men in before the time was up. "Your transport awaits, thals. Kiss your pretty house and land and factory goodbye. And keep a tight hold on those bags!" He kicked the nearest case. His laughter was contagious among his men. Something in his manner suggested we'd identified our most valuable and portable possessions for him.

Ashamed, mocked, robbed, we struggled outside with our cases. We threw them onto the back of the truck and struggled up to join them. Mom cried; Dad tried to reassure her, but he had nothing to offer except a hug and more empty promises. The soldiers followed, casual, careless, watching us like the helpless creatures we had become.

We bumped along the roadway into town, towards the camps, the station, the docks, the airport? No-one would tell us, no-one would answer our questions.

We sat, dejected, suitcases at our feet.

Something ahead caught Dad's eye. He gestured. A rising dust cloud ahead marked the approach of vehicles. Several vehicles. A convoy? Perhaps Usebi's convoy?

The distance between us grew smaller; the approach felt painfully slow.

Nearer and nearer.

Dad stood and waved both hands above his head like a madman. A soldier gestured with his rifle, cocked it.

Dad sat, white-faced.

We could see the approaching vehicles. Yes, it was Usebi's convoy. He was a government Minister. Surely he would stop this craziness?

The vehicles drew ever closer, their dust-trails looming larger, rising into that big, empty sky.

Mom was sobbing against Dad's chest. His gaze was fixed upon the approaching convoy.

The oncoming vehicles did not slow. The convoy guards

who had so recently protected Dad ignored us.

I saw shapes, human shapes, behind the smoked glass of the government limo, sitting in the rear seat. Suzi and her dad?

I raised my head, squinting through the sun and the dust. I could see nothing clearly inside the big, heavy car.

I hoped, prayed, that it would slow down, would stop; that he would emerge and make things right and I would hold Suzi in my arms and everything would be all right again.

The convoy didn't stop. It passed us by. It hid its disgrace behind the dust cloud.

I had to drag my gaze away, too hurt even for tears.

*

It plays out in my mind like a movie...

The beautiful girl in the long, black car watches the oncoming vehicle. She is thinking about meeting her boy. But then she sees that boy, bleak-faced, huddled among the cases in the back of the truck. She stares, disbelieving. She calls out to her father, tugs at his sleeve, points at the truck and its cargo.

He does not respond. He gazes unmoving out of the other window, away from the truck, perhaps to avoid seeing, perhaps to hide his shame, perhaps through fear.

She presses her face against the security glass, bangs on the window, breaks into sobs.

Tears run down her face. Drained, she whispers, "Goodbye, my ice-cream boy."

The clouds of African dust fill the distance between them.

And he is gone.

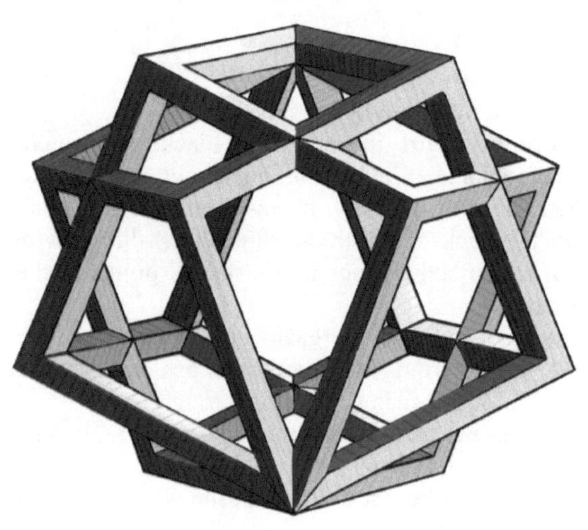

Face the Music

by

Siobhan McVeigh

Siobhan is a writer, copy writer, digital producer and film maker who sometimes helps out at Hoxton Street Monster Supplies. She has worked all over the place including San Francisco, Singapore, Sydney and at the European Space Agency. She writes about robots, comets and broken weather, and her work was performed by White Rabbit at *'Are You Sitting Comfortably'*. She is currently writing her first novel, ably abetted by her cat assistant/assassin.

Jess put down her mug of tea mid sip and stared at the receptionist.

"Built for hardship, that generation. They broke the mould when that lot went," the receptionist said. It could have been her dear old aunt talking. She had modelled some of the emotional range of the receptionist on her aunt Beatrice Antonia Fotheringale-Wight, but the similarity still surprised her. Not least because she had installed an algorithm based on how cats stalk their prey to improve response times on the switchboard and was in the middle of testing this very functionality. Aunty Bea had been by turns intrepid, wily, and stubborn but always very kind. The receptionist was a chip off the old block in many ways, reminding her so much of Bea that Jess smiled, then blinked back tears, as the familiar misery that old Fotheringale-Wight was dead and buried lurched through her.

"She's not gone," Jess said, sniffing. "You're so like her it makes things better in some ways and worse in others. I sometimes wake up and think she's still alive, that I'll come into the kitchen and she'll be there, you know."

The receptionist nodded and made a sympathetic "Hmmmm," as Jess had programmed it to, then paused, sensing how Jess was feeling, before passing her a tissue. The receptionist continued, "The first year is the hardest. And in the meantime, we will keep the business going. Remember our motto! We make more of you so you make more of you! Think about all the hard work you've put in over the years. Everyone knows that Sembler & Assemblage can handle anything! You have to fight to keep it going. It's what she would have wanted."

Jess yawned. More than anything, she wanted to sleep. The funeral last week had taken the last tiny bit of strength she had left. She still felt like she was spinning between work, her aunt's bedside on the ward and hunting across the city for whatever medication Bea needed that the hospital had run out of. Sembler & Assemblage, the place she had started from scratch and loved more than any other, the best robotic biohack joint in Shoreditch no less, seemed strange and irrelevant. She glanced at the headlines scrolling across the screen in the reception area. 'Arise, Sir Alistair'. Wait!

What? Jess turned up the volume.

"In other news, Alistair Handy, Health Minister and CEO of Dalebury Bank, has been knighted in recognition of his services to the nation in reducing the deficit," the newsreader said.

Jess whistled. Old Alistair Hands-In-The-Till Handy had pulled it off again. Rewarded for playing the sides off against the middle, in a desperate game where the real losers were people like her aunt, stoical to the end, her last minutes measured out by the rainwater dripping through a hole in the hospital roof into a bucket next to her bed. Jess wished she could change things.

*

Alistair Handy knew he was going to change things. Of that there was no question. The only thing he didn't know was how much time he had. All the way to Silicon Roundabout, Alistair gripped his wallet so hard his thumb and fingers whitened. The traffic held him in an embrace tighter than a trader holding stock in a bull market. He flicked through messages on his glasses, blinking to delete and winking to reply, as he muttered his instructions - a deal here, a small amount of pressure there, a reminder of past indiscretions for this man, a promise of lunch for that one. And each and every one of them now under investigation. At least his knighthood showed everyone that he still had the right friends. His chauffeur edged through the traffic and Alistair released the tension in his fingers, forcing himself to relax. Breathing deeply, he focused on the texture of the leather beneath his finger tips, stroking it gently. The finest calfskin, expertly treated and crafted into something that held his favourite thing. Money. Except his fingers kept returning to one point, where the leather had scuffed on something. As soon as he thought he had smoothed it over, he noticed the snag again, and try as he might he could not get rid of it. After what felt like an eternity they pulled up outside an imposing curved glass building overlooking Old Street and Alistair strode through the automatic doors.

"Sembler & Assemblage, how may I help you?"

Alistair looked at the receptionist. Her black skin glowed with an amazing lustre, each pore radiating beauty, and her makeup was so flawless that she seemed more like a doll than flesh and blood. He stood up taller, sucking in his slight paunch. He smiled and said, "I hope you can."

He hadn't made an appointment, but then as CEO of Dalebury Bank he didn't need to. He asked for the service that was not advertised. The one that everyone thought was impossible. He had barely sat down in the gothic wing-back chair in reception when a stocky middle-aged woman burst out of the lift and rushed over to him.

"Hi, I'm Jess," she said, thrusting out her hand and shaking his firmly. Her nails were short and the cuticles chewed raw. "I'll take you to the studio." She ushered him into the inner sanctum of the main studio, a secret room on the roof surrounded by bamboo with pink and blue leaves ("an early test subject," Jess was quick to explain as she saw Alistair looking at it). Alistair noticed that Jess was babbling with nerves, her pale skin blushing.

"Shall we get started then?" Jess said, finally.

"I'm waiting for you to get your boss, J. Ackland," Alistair said, frowning.

"I'm J.Ackland. You're talking to the Chief Technology Officer and CEO of Sembler & Assemblage. At your service."

Alistair refused to be disconcerted, though he blinked twice to alert his glass to order his security staff to pick up the researcher who'd given him the contact details and drop them from a lethal height. The name they had given him was correct, but still. He told J. Ackland that he needed their most deluxe, exclusive, discreet and complete service. The total resemblance model. The thing they called the Sembler.

*

"So Alistair, as long as you're happy, sign our NDA and contract, transfer the funds and we're good to go. Discretion is our middle name." Jess sounded bright and cheery, though inside she wondered what her Aunty Bea would have made of it all. She could imagine her snorting "Honestly Jess! Discretion is my big hairy behind!" Jess cursed herself for sounding like a complete idiot, an eager to please total idiot. What was happening to her? The old Jess would have made Alistair beg for her help. She didn't know if this was how her life was going to be. Was this what the receptionist meant when she said the first year was the worst? She watched Alistair scrawl his signature with his Mont Blanc pen and wondered how much of herself she had buried alongside her aunty. She wished that she'd asked him to leave when she still could.

*

As the weeks sped by, Alistair thought about what he would do once his Sembler was in place, duplicating him in his old life so he had more time. More time in the sun. More time on his yacht. More time with his family. More time with his mistress. More markets to explore. With Mars and the Antarctic opening up, he needed to be free to make the most of them.   After months of deadlines, scandals, and government inquiries, Alistair was finding his big city bank platinum directorship tiresome. It wasn't the investigators, he knew all of them well. It was the protestors. They were beginning to find all the virtual hidey-holes where he stashed his cash.

The hacktivists started to follow Alistair everywhere in real life too. His security team cleared his route and the police were of course cooperating, but his helicopter was his only sanctuary. At least the protestors couldn't cycle or walk or rollerblade around it waving placards at him like they did as he sat in his gridlocked Mercedes. He knew what they were shouting even though he couldn't hear it through the soundproofing. He only felt safe when he was in the air. Alistair blessed the mayor for using his special emergency powers to put nanokwik helipads wherever Alistair needed them. What was wrong with these people? All he did was what anybody would do, if they got the chance. And everyone was making money, it was all good, the sums added up if you wanted them to. Those idiots saying they were the

99% were lucky to have the trickle down from his geyser of genius. And he was not going to take the blame.

*

Back at Sembler & Assemblage, the product team worked day and night until Jess insisted they go home. She stayed on at the studio, nibbling on cold pizza and cursing as she ran the code again for what felt like the billionth time. The distribution pattern tags she'd set up to flag outliers were lighting up red. Alistair's profile was proving challenging to copy, and time was short. She stared hard at the interface space in front of her and yawned, flexing her fingers in their gloves to activate them and began again. She wanted to go above and beyond the brief. She always did. She pinched her fingers together and dragged more emotional components from the deck in front of her. Just so.

With only thirty-four minutes to go before the presentation, Jess put aside her gloves, yawned, and gulped two more koffeekaps. The studio had a state of the art shower which had an almost magical capacity to wake her up, so she crawled off to it. She was going to need her wits about her to get through the meeting with Alistair. She was still squeezing water out of her dreads when the 'whoompf whoompf' of a helicopter overhead announced Alistair's imminent arrival. She resented the helipad he had cut down the bamboos to install. She resented Alistair's insistence on doing everything face to face. But most of all she resented the fact that Alistair was so sociopathic that matching his personality required overriding the first fundamental principal of robotics, namely that a robot may not allow a human being to come to harm. Gritting her teeth, she went to greet him, but he cut her short and asked to see the Sembler. She hesitated.

"We've run into a small issue that we're sorting out, but the rest is done."

"Small issue? What kind of issue?"

"The hand keeps spinning round. Not ideal. Then there's the emotional stuff."

"Stuff? Stuff! This was all meant to go live last week!

I've got places to be and this guy - your Sembler machine - has to stay here. Do you have any idea what I will do to you if this goes wrong?"

Jess started to sweat. "Y-y-you could see it as a feature. We haven't got the tone of voice quite matching. Bit kind, bit friendly. Not you at all really. But it might be useful."

Alistair shook his head, wondering again if had he made the right decision to place his future in the, as he now discovered, possibly rotating hands of these geeks. All the smart money swore by them, but they were five days behind schedule. And the protestors were getting closer to him every hour, hacking the accounts that he paid the investigators not to investigate. Was it really too much to ask for this one, so very important, thing in his life to go right? Alistair stared at Jess and cleared his throat.

"OK, Jess. This is how it's going to be. You are going to fix this. I'm going to leave as planned. And this Sembler machine stays here at my office to face the music. And you are going to make this work or I will destroy you. Do you understand?"

Jess stared at Alistair, twisting the corner of her ironic retro Guns n' Roses t-shirt as a small tic flickered beneath her right eye. "Y-y-yes. Not a problem. Of course. Totally understand. You're right, of course. I do apologise. Please accept my... We'll do it right away."

*

Jess worked late into the night, debugging and testing, trying not to think about her words. 'We'll do it right away'. Why didn't she tell him to back off? She was his only hope, after all. She had let herself be bullied and she hated that. Her aunt would have told her to buck up and stand up to him. Jess would have stood up to him before. After all she had stood up to lots of little people who thought they were in charge of the universe. As founder and CTO it was part of her job description. She tightened a minute screw with her micro-pliers and stepped back. The Sembler's hands started to play Chopin nocturnes seamlessly, which was strange because Alistair didn't know how to play the piano, but at least they no longer turned three hundred and sixty degrees. She had stopped the Sembler sounding kind, but a new intermittent fault with some of the behaviour caused an altruism glitch. Jess debugged again, cursing.

The receptionist glided up behind her, extending an elegantly manicured hand. "Allow me." The tip of the red nail on her middle finger flipped up, and a tiny diamond coaxial cable whipped out and burrowed into the crease behind the Sembler's left ear lobe. Jess looked at the cable absent-mindedly, thinking that she hadn't used that extension, before registering the words she'd heard. She tore off her goggles.

"What are you doing?!"

"Helping," the receptionist said.

"I had it all under control!"

"That's why I'm here to help."

Never argue with a robot, Jess reminded herself. Especially the receptionist, who was the real power behind Sembler & Assemblage since Jess hardly knew herself through her grief. Even before all that, the lines of command had been a little blurred at times. The receptionist was the prototype for the emotional regulation engine that Jess was fine-tuning. Not only prone to sounding exactly like Aunty Bea, the receptionist knew Jess better than Jess knew herself. She had been with Jess right from the start, and her wickerwork chassis bore witness to the humble beginnings of Sembler & Assemblage, when Jess had raided skips to get materials, repurposing a broken patio chair to form the platform for the torso. As it was hidden behind a desk, Jess had never got round to upgrading it, though she had added new wheels so the receptionist could get up to the lift and into the studio to work all night after reception closed. Jess had augmented the receptionist's processors so that she could recharge at the same time as answering the phones on her day shift, keeping her online 24/7.

"What is it that you're trying to do?" the receptionist asked Jess.

"I'm trying to make this Sembler an exact copy of Alistair, CEO of Dalebury Bank... except..."

"Well?"

"It hasn't quite worked. He's going to kill me… really kill me."

The receptionist tweaked the cable, closing her eyes briefly so she could see the data, then asked, "How do you know that? It might work better than you can even imagine. You've done a good job. You're too good at snatching defeat from the jaws of victory. You might have done the thing you really wanted to."

Jess wasn't convinced, but after thirty-eight caffeine-fuelled hours she was past caring. She started to package up her work and cached it on the hub.

"OK. You're the boss."

The receptionist winked at her, rewound the cable with a high-pitched whine, then flipped back the middle nail before inspecting her manicure, taking one last look round the studio, and gliding back to the reception desk to dock and charge.

*

The Sembler Alistair, flanked by security guards, walked through the revolving doors of the headquarters of Dalebury Bank as, seventy flights up, the real Alistair stepped from the helipad into his helicopter. Alistair headed for the sweet freedom of a very remote, discrete and exclusive spa that asked no questions and said nothing when duplicates of the rich and powerful turned up at their marble-clad doors. He settled in to his new routine with a sigh of pure contentment. Meanwhile the Sembler was industrious. Identical in so many ways. First to arrive and last to leave. Always making money and moving it around, while the noose of traces and backdoors tightened round its neck.

*

Alistair drained the dregs of yet another Vesper Martini and watched the sun set as his little toe was massaged into an even more pleasing and relaxed state. His face was swaddled with steaming hot towels then shaved with a cut throat razor by a barber who came to his poolside lounger. He wondered how long it would be before the Sembler Alistair was caught. Strung up even. It really did look like things back in London were falling apart. Even water cannons could barely control the wave upon wave of demonstrators. But Alistair was safe, his money nested and cocooned so many times over that only he knew how to access it. The hackers were going to catch the Sembler, and only the Sembler. Any minute now, he thought as he ordered another drink.

"I'm ever so sorry Sir, but your credit has expired."

Alistair shook his head in disbelief.

"No, no, no. Try this." He offered another card. And another. And another. Each one was declined. Even his shell accounts.

Alistair hauled himself up to a terminal and checked his investments. They were all gone. Every single one. Heart hammering, Alistair flipped open his phone and checked the office cam. His Sembler was sitting there at Alistair's city desk, waving his arms and blinking his way through Alistair's custom-built interfaces, for all the world exactly like Alistair himself. The Sembler looked up and seemed to stare straight at Alistair through the cam, as if he could see him.

Alistair hugged his robe tighter round him, waving his useless pass key in front of the changing room attendant as he pleaded with her to open his locker. She refused, but eventually relented enough to give Alistair a pair of white fluffy towelling slippers embroidered with the spa's crest in burgundy red silk. Alistair shuffled past the sauna, grabbing an extra towel on his way, wondering how this could be happening to him. Where had he gone wrong? Even as the staff escorted him off the premises, depositing him unceremoniously on the road outside, Alistair was plotting his revenge.

He wasn't going to take this lying down. And he didn't need to. High frequency trading wasn't the only market Alistair had been involved in over the years. He walked miles to the nearest highway, then waited for a truck from a particular haulage company and ran into the road in front of it to make it stop. He shouted a few key names of the driver's bosses to persuade him to let him on board, then spent a tense twenty minutes using the cab radio to establish contact with the people-trafficking network one of his hidden subsidiaries still part-owned. A deal so murky that it was sealed in blood not bytes, leaving no digital trace. He'd always known it would come in handy. After an uncomfortable twenty-four hours in the base of the truck, he sauntered from the lorry deck as the ferry left Calais, dressed in a motley assortment of the driver's spare clothes, all of which were a little too small for him, and still sporting the spa slippers, no longer so fluffy. He found a very drunk man passed out on the ferry with size 10 feet, and carefully prised off his trainers, before hiding away on the truck again. He finally reached London and staggered out on the hard shoulder of the A12 outside Hackney Wick, the pins and needles in his leg almost making him fall over.

Alistair set off down the canal, footsore and weary, but determined to get to his Sembler and make him pay. He saw an unlocked bicycle propped up against a canal boat. From the laughter and greetings coming from inside the boat, he thought the bike's owner was probably on board. Seizing his moment he hopped on and pedalled off down the towpath, towards the city, as fast as he could.

Two hours later, covered in bike oil from where he'd twice had to stop to fix the chain when it fell off, Alistair stood outside the headquarters of the bank. He was surrounded by a group of call centre workers from a Dalebury insurance subsidiary who had marched from Cheltenham. Dressed in clothes that were too small for him, and trainers that were too large, smeared in oil and dripping with sweat, looking, appropriately enough, like he'd been hiding in a truck for days, Alistair was unrecognisable. Something for which he was grateful as everyone shared stories of how their lives had been ruined by the austerity measures of Alistair Handy and the disastrous double dealings of Dalebury Bank. Nobody realised that the Sembler was doing business as unusual. No news of Alistair's closed accounts had leaked out.

They reached the main entrance as the crowd broke apart. It had been hiding from Alistair's view a punk kid with a solar-powered angle grinder, who had cut two barriers into sections.   The crowd grabbed them and used them as battering rams to run at the revolving glass doors and wedge them open. They stormed up the stairs, throwing doors open along the way. They discovered the investigators smoking cigars, drinking champagne, and playing poker with the traders on the Forex exchange. Alistair wanted one thing and one thing only, to get his hands on the Sembler and push him off the atrium roof. And it seemed he was not alone in that desire, although of course everyone else thought the Sembler was Sir Alistair Handy himself.

As they surged up to the fiftieth floor, a strange hush fell over the crowd. The sound of a Chopin Nocturne (Op. 9, No. 2 in E-flat major) drifted down from the Director's office in the executive suite, relayed by the internal speaker system.   The screens on all the walls around them went blank, then started to show the results of the hackers' traces, tracking the trades coming from Alistair's Sembler. All the money was draining from the Dalebury accounts, transferring to adventure play grounds, schools, housing trusts, hospitals and youth schemes.

Alistair pushed his way through the crowd, climbing higher and higher, the Nocturne ringing in his ears, and was still ten flights of stairs away from his old office when everyone around him started to shout and cheer, whoop, whistle and applaud. He tried to edge closer to the Sembler, desperate for revenge, but was held back by everyone else. "Nah mate, you gotta listen to the music. Look at the screens! See what he's done! The man's a genius." Alistair slumped against the wall, tears streaming down his face. For the first time in his life, he was at a loss.

*

Over at Sembler & Assemblage, Jess sat with the receptionist, glued to the live reports coming in from Dalebury Bank, shaking her head in disbelief.

"The glitch... the altruism glitch. You said I'd fixed it..." Jess said. She looked again at the data feeds streaming live from the Sembler. The hospital Aunty Bea had died in was getting a new roof. The pharmacy contracts were all being renegotiated. Everything was changing. The Sembler was changing it. She had changed it. The receptionist winked at her.

"Didn't need fixing. It was a feature, not a bug."

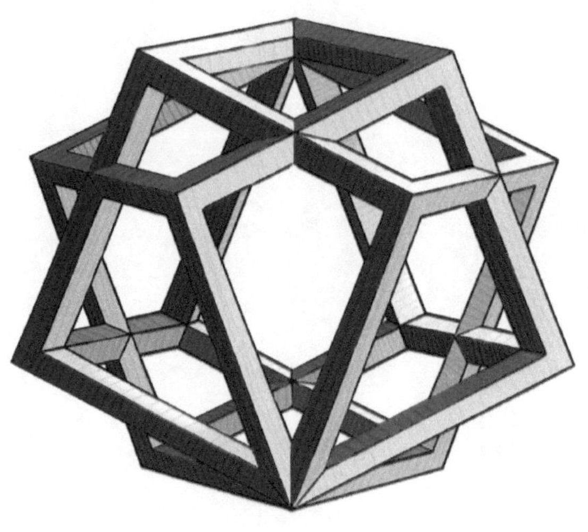

Degeneration

by

Robin Moran

Born in Yorkshire, Robin once again happily resides in Leeds after growing up in the insanity of London. Horror is her comfort zone, having read twisted tales and bone chilling stories since she was young so it's no surprise it has warped her writing mind. By day she's a primary school teacher and attempts to be relatively normal. By night she writes and puts characters through hell to see them squirm. Her first published story was in *[Re]Awakenings* (Elsewhen Press, 2011).

The pub was surprisingly crowded considering the recent worldwide fear. Even with the news report on the large screen television, people continued to down their pints, sip their wines or tuck into their food. Sophie included. Her table was covered in empty crisp and pork scratchings packets. Five empty glasses that had once been filled with frothy beer were now stacked and pushed aside to make room for five new pints. The third... no... fourth round?

Sophie was slumped in her seat, munching on the greasy onion rings she had ordered. She hadn't been paying much attention to her friends or anything else, too busy trying to get some food inside herself. Before coming out she had felt her temperature rising, despite it being the middle of winter. Normally she felt the cold, needing to turn her heating on as soon as September arrived. But it was now mid-January and she had had to turn down the heating in her flat because she had been so warm. When she had felt her forehead, it was slippery with sweat.

But she needed this night out. It was finally the weekend and she could make herself feel better after a couple of drinks. Maybe more.

Someone near the bar had requested that the television's volume to be turned up. Now she could hear the news report and she lifted her head to watch, ignoring the loud banter and giggling around her table.

The reporter spoke to Robert James, some loony who had taken his English Literature degree way too seriously. He had spent the last two years trying to convince and desperately warn people that there was a new threat to humanity. Forget global warming, nuclear threat or the annual ancient apocalypse: there was something happening in the world that was going to be the true end of humans and it was apparently all to do with a fear that sparked in the Victorian era.

Sophie sat expressionless, staring up at the television with a glazed look in her eyes as this James guy spoke.

"Their stories of the supernatural, science and horror represented a threat that they believed would continue to strengthen in years to come. Some saw science as a menace in Victorian society. It was an unknown mystery that was, all of a sudden, opening up doors to possibilities and opportunities. People were making discoveries and experimenting, which some naturally found horrific and frightening. Writers of the late nineteenth century took a good look at civilisation and fictionalised what it was fearing: science and decadence. These were the driving forces for this rapidly changing society."

Sophie recognised a familiar scent of cigarettes and hairspray. Her nose quivered as she sniffed and looked to see Eloise sitting back down next to her. Her friend snorted and nodded at the television.

"In other words, this modern day generation act like wild beast folk and we need to go back to being conservative and boring." She took her glass and gulped down the rest of her beer. "Bollocks to that. People are way too obsessed with how everyone lives."

"Look at that!" Sophie pointed to the screen where Robert James had once been. Replacing him were clips of police cornering a young man, taken from somebody's camera phone. The quality was slightly hazy and voices were muffled but Sophie could still make out what was happening. A young man had been trapped in a corner of an alley.

Or what used to be a young man.

Sophie felt her top lip curl up at the sight of him… it? The man was crouching next to some wheelie bins, a stance that was petrified and defensive. As the camera zoomed in, Sophie could see his fingers were flexed and that was the first sign of abnormality that told her this wasn't just some idiot criminal being chased down by the police.

His nails were long, curved and pointed. Sharp, needle-like tips that looked ready to slit open somebody's throat. He only had four fingers on each hand, swollen at the tips and held up to show the palms which looked lumpy and padded.

Like paws, Sophie thought. Are they actually…?

"Bloody hell. That ain't right," Eloise said, her nose wrinkling up.

As the camera zoomed in further, most of the man's face was covered in grey fur and Sophie could see the glaring yellow-green hue of his eyes and the pupils that had turned into black slits. When the man pulled his lips up he revealed thin, delicate fangs. His jaw opened wide and a short hiss followed before he started to yowl. A yowl that reminded Sophie of her cat at home, who would make that exact sound if he saw another feline in his territory. Low and sounding like a long 'noooooooooo'.

Hearing that sound coming from a human sent chills down Sophie's spine.

"Has he gone through surgery to look like that?" Eloise wondered aloud.

"I dunno," Sophie mumbled. She took another sip of her beer, making her head continue to tingle and buzz. She sat back in her chair, drooping as her mind turned fuzzy and she struggled to make her thoughts clear.

Robert James came back on to the television.

"You cannot deny this. There are cases around the world. These are not surgically enhanced people. There is no Doctor Moreau-style plastic surgery trend. People are actually turning into animals."

The sight of that man-cat-thing had turned her skin cold. Something was definitely not right, but the words that poured out of Robert James sounded utterly ridiculous. Sophie found herself laughing. Whether she actually found it hysterical or was responding nervously, she wasn't sure. But it had to be nonsense. People couldn't turn into animals.

She giggled again and, when her friends turned to her, she pointed at the television.

"People are turning into animals," she said, then chuckled.

Maddie was the only one in their group who wasn't laughing with her. She glanced up at the television report and bit her lower lip.

"Don't you think it's weird?" she asked. "There are so many cases of people turning violent and feral."

"Yeah. It's London," Eloise said, smirking.

"No. This is all over. Do you remember those mermaid carcasses they found on a beach in Norway last month?"

Their only male friend, Jay, sighed and set his drink down. "Maddie, seriously? It was all a hoax."

"Or what if people had actually turned into human-fish hybrid things?" she asked them.

A silence dropped around their table. Awkward glances

shared between Sophie and Eloise before Jay was the first to break by snorting into his drink. He reached over to pat Maddie on the head. Three, slow pats before she batted his hand away with a snarl. Sophie nearly spat out her mouthful of beer all over the table. Maddie had actually bared her teeth and growled at Jay.

"Did you just snarl at him?" she asked, cackling loudly with laughter.

"She's one of them!" Eloise shrieked, standing up and pointing at her friend.

Maddie scowled but shrank further into her seat as people turned to stare at the commotion. "Sod off," she muttered.

"You haven't been sprouting a tail lately?" Sophie asked with a grin on her face.

Her friend huffed through her nose. "You're all bell-ends."

"I always saw you as an ickle Yorkshire terrier. All yappy and trying to be fierce but you're really just amusing and cute," Jay said.

"And, again, you're a bell-end. If you all don't want to believe me then fine. Don't. But it's happening right under our noses and we're all too stupid or blind to see it. People are changing into these beast folk because we act like it. It's devolution."

Maddie gestured to the glasses on the table. "This is one of the keys to the change starting."

Jay gawped at Sophie and Eloise. "Uh-oh. And this is my fourth drink." He snorted, lifting three fingers up and took another swig of his beer. Beside him, Maddie shook her head and sighed.

"The decadent life is the key to the devolution of the human race," she said. "As we give in to animalistic instincts of alcohol, drugs, sex and violence, we start the degeneration in ourselves."

"You sound like that Robert James wanker," Sophie said.

Maddie rolled her eyes, her nostrils flared, and Sophie noticed she had begun to drum her fingers against the table. Sophie imagined steam pouring out of her friend's ears in a cartoon-style rage that she was so close to falling into. Sophie bit her lip to stop herself giggling at the image. Maddie was seconds away from flipping out and she didn't want to be the final straw in her growing fury.

Maddie clicked her tongue and grabbed her bag.

"I've seen it," she said. "My neighbour. I was coming back from work and he ran past me on the stairs. You should have seen him, it wasn't normal! He had all these fangs and there was blood on his face. And he had these ridged looking scales." She shuddered. "That and the greenish skin, he looked like a crocodile. When I got to my floor his door was open and his girlfriend had been eaten. He'd done that. Can you explain that?"

"Freak had surgery. And he's also a psychotic cannibal," Jay said.

"Is everyone having surgery these days? You really think this is just a sick trend? He looked completely human that morning."

Again, silence had fallen around their table as Maddie stared at every one of them for more answers, more sarcastic comebacks or jokes. Sophie glanced at Eloise and Jay who sat back, lips pressed tightly shut.

After a few seconds, he stood up. "I need a fag," he muttered and headed straight for the exit.

"I need the bathroom," Sophie said, standing. She swayed, almost tripping over her own feet. Her hands gripped the back of her chair as she tried to balance herself but the room had started to spin now that she was on her feet. Her body felt light, head buzzing and there was now a loud ringing in her ears.

She stumbled through the crowds, trying to walk carefully around people. Yet she still found herself leaning left and right as she staggered, hearing a cry of protest and swearing. What she thought was graceful dodging was actually violent pushing. She created a path through the groups, using her body to crash into strangers and shove them aside, not realising what she was doing until she saw the scowling face of an angry man leering down at her.

"Drunk bitch," he snarled.

Sophie flipped her middle finger, ignoring the shocked gasps she got in response. A bit of a dramatic reaction considering the language she could have chosen to use. If they had been horrified by a finger, those words would have sent them into a coma.

"Don't be so fucking old-fashioned," she slurred as she trudged away.

She used both her hands to push the bathroom door open, tumbling forward and falling into a girl who was walking out at the same time.

"The fuck?" the girl growled, knocking Sophie in the shoulder as she passed. Swaying, Sophie frowned. She was convinced that girl had snarled when she stumbled into her. A real, rumbling snarl.

And she was sure she had seen a glacial colour to the girl's eyes. The bright colour of blue ice. It was an eye colour she had never seen on anyone before, only ever in a husky.

An animal.

Don't start, she thought to herself, chuckling as she made her way to the sink. Maddie was welcome to be the paranoid one. The friend who believed in conspiracies and theories of the doomed future of humanity. That wasn't Sophie and she scoffed to herself, shaking her head over Maddie's idiotic belief in these rumours. Rumours that only belonged in the pages of a Gothic novel. Completely fictional. Nothing like The Island of Doctor Moreau or The Strange Case of Dr Jekyll and Mr Hyde could ever happen in real life.

She touched her arms and neck with cold water, sighing at the temporary cool down it gave her. She cupped her hands, letting the water fill up in her palms before she splashed it against her neck. Her skin felt hot to the touch. She was burning up again, feeling sweat gather quickly on her forehead and on the back of her neck.

Yeah. I've caught a bug, she thought.

She sighed as she tapped the water against her neck, gazing at her reflection to check the state of her make-up. Mascara gloop and her eyeliner had gathered in the corners of her eyes and had become messy, black sludge. She peered closer at her reflection, using a finger to gently wipe away the gunk of her make-up. Her nose was almost touching the mirror as she prodded at the corner of her eyes.

A glimmer of amber flickered in her iris.

She jumped back, blinking furiously. Her reflection looked stunned, eyes widened and lips parted to gawp at herself.

"No," she muttered, peering closer again.

No. Nothing. Nothing was wrong. Her eyes looked back at her, brown and almond shape. Completely normal. It must have been the light.

She laughed. Giggling over her brief panic but that laughter faded. She had noticed something else now.

Her long, black hair had been hiding most of her neck but she could see the start of her collarbone after she had flipped her hair back over her shoulders. The skin looked raised.

And green?

Sophie held her head up, tilting to the left so she could catch the light to see her neck better. With her free hand, she stretched the skin, pulling and tugging to examine the strange discolouration and texture she had developed suddenly. Her finger brushed against the lumpy skin and the heat of the pub no longer bothered her. Her heart felt like it was ready to leap out of her mouth. Or burst out of her chest since it was beating that frantically. Her body felt dipped in ice.

The lump was smooth to touch.

And it wasn't a lump.

She bit her lip, trying to fight against the whimpering and sobs she needed to make. She wanted to close her eyes and turn away but her body, her eyes, were fixed on the reflection in front of her. All she could do was shake and stare at those things. Those horrible, green things that were appearing, even as she watched. The skin shifted, turning green at first before rising up, forming a pattern she had seen on her aunt's python. When she lifted her left hand, she knew what the customers had been gasping at. The patterns were forming at a rapid pace across the back of her hand and neck, the green quickly becoming more and more luminous.

Scales.

She was developing scales.

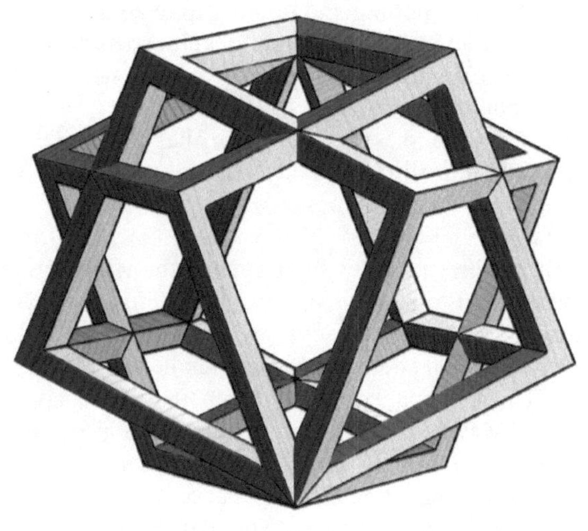

The Writer Did It!

by

Ira Nayman

In his past lives, Ira Nayman was, among other things: a cave painter whose art was not appreciated in his lifetime; several nameless peasants who died before their 20th birthday during the Dark Ages; a toenail fungus specialist in the court of Louis XIV; and Alan Turing's scullery maid.

In his current incarnation, Ira is the creator of *Les Pages aux Folles*, a Web site of political and social satire that is over 10 years old (that's positively Paleolithic in Internet years!). Five collections of Alternate Reality News Service (ARNS) stories which originally appeared on the Web site have been self-published in print. Ira has produced the pilot for a radio series based on stories from the first two ARNS books; "*The Weight of Information, Episode One*" can be heard on YouTube.

Ira has also written a series of stories that take place in a universe where matter at all levels of organization has become conscious. They feature Antonio Van der Whall, object psychologist.

Ira's Web Goddess tells him he should make more of the fact that he won the 2010 Jonathan Swift Satire Writing Contest. So, **Ira won the 2010 Jonathan Swift Satire Writing Contest**. In another life (but still within this incarnation) Ira has a Masters degree in Media Studies from The New School for Social Research which was conducted entirely online. He also has a PhD in Communications from McGill University. Ira taught New Media part-time at Ryerson University for five years.

Whoever created the Karmic wheel has a lot to answer for...

"Wuhl holy jumpin' cats, then!" Missy Mulholland, The Shootin' Sweetheart of Sandler's Gulch, exclaimed, "No offense meant." Missy looked at the six foot tall orange and grey tabby in the gold brocade bathrobe sitting at the desk to her left; it waved a paw and purred genially, as if to say, "None taken." Relieved, Missy continued: "If ah was of a mind ta kill someone, I'd do it the proper way: shootin' 'em in the back with mah sixshooters! Kin you see me killin' anybody by stuffin' a big ol' carp down their throat? 'Tain't mah style!"

I had to admit, Missy made a good point. And to be honest, I was hoping that she wasn't the murderer. She was small, with rough features and tangled blonde hair – my Bubbe would have asked me what I was thinking, falling for a shiksa from out west, but these were different times. Better times. Times when strong women were –

"I would imagine that changing one's *modus operandi* would be a way of diverting suspicion away from oneself," intoned Rich Uncle Moneybags, who sat on her other side. He was so short he was the only person in the room who was completely at ease sitting in the small desk/chair combinations that were available to everybody; in fact, there were times when I could have sworn the thick stogie he was constantly puffing away on was bigger then he was! The man seemed made up entirely of circles, but he looked smart in a tuxedo, top hat and monocle. Smart if you discount the fact that Rich Uncle Moneybags' white moustache looked like he had mugged a mop, I mean.

Missy was offended. "You take that back about my modest oper...brandy, mister, or we'll be exchangin' more'n words!" Her frilled arms slowly inched towards her gunbelt.

The Samurai standing behind her (Samurai don't sit. It's a thing with them – don't ask) grunted and spoke sixteenth century Japanese. Fortunately, I had done some work in the part of Anytown where...those people lived, and I had picked up enough Subtitlese to be able to follow what he was saying. The gist was that a true warrior does not disguise his actions in order to evade detection. A true warrior is proud of the work he does. Every second sentence out of Feng Chi's mouth had something to do with true warriors. My shrink,

Melinda Gottlieb, would have said that he was compensating for something. I don't generally argue with people in shiny black body armour who carry swords that are almost as big as I am, though, so I saved the thought for my next session.

I raised a hand to stop the discussion. "Oy, why do you people want to give me such *tsuris*? Nobody is going to be killed, here," I commanded. "I asked you to come tonight because you're all suspects in the murder of Desmond Concannen, gentleman inventor." I could physically describe the dead man, but I hadn't heard of him before his estate had asked me to investigate his murder, and when you've seen one urn full of ashes… To be honest, I had been on the case for several days and, although I had many suspects, I had run out of leads; a good friend of mine, Hercule Marple, had suggested I gather the suspects together in one room and shake them up to see what came loose. Did I have a better idea? Naah. So, I went with that. "Nobody murders anybody when you've gathered all the suspects in one room! It just don't work that way!"

"Well, thank goodness for that," said Jules Flippe-Flappy, the beanpole of a man with a long face and oversized ears, who sat on the far left of the group of suspects facing me. Ain't no easy way to say this, so I'll just come out with it, already: Flippe-Flappy was black. And white. He had no colour at all. "Because…Death. Death. Death./Nobody wants to smell your stinking breath/On the backs of their necks./Especially when they're having –"

Oh, yeah. And he frequently broke into song for no apparent reason. He was good, I'll give him that: you could practically hear the orchestra playing behind him. Still. I held up a hand – I must have been a children's crossing guard in another life – and he immediately stopped.

Mister Giggles, the alien cat thing, purred and looked languidly at Missy. We all understood this to mean, "Well, you do have a strong motive for killing Mister Concannen. After all, he knocked up your sister and then abandoned her." Everybody in the room got the sense that Mister Giggles couldn't see why such an action would be a bad thing and thought Missy was overreacting.

"I ain't the only one," Missy sneered. "That dang

gentleman inventor done invented hisself a gizmo that made it possible to travel to distant planets. Seems ta me your planet was one of the ones we done made it to, Mister Giggles. Only, we killed alla you cat people – yer the only one whut done survived. I imagine that's a right powerful motive to kill a man."

Mister Giggles waved a paw in her direction and made a low growling noise in the back of his throat, causing the table to gently vibrate. "Did that happen over four hours ago? Honestly, I can't be bothered to purrsue anything that happened more than four hours ago!"

Feng Chi grunted. Twice. Then, he pounded his open hand with his fist for emphasis. Then, he grunted again. He either said, "The true warrior does not allow the destruction of his civilization to go unavenged!" or "The duck charger screams out to be sacrificed at Stonehenge!" Gimme a break, here: my Subtitlese is a bit rusty, and he spoke fast. Real fast. If I had to guess, though, I would say it was the first one.

The cat creature licked one of its paws and slicked back the fur on the top of its head. Then, it languidly purred: "I wouldn't be so quick with accusations, if I were you. Or, have you forgotten the Electric Samurai?" I don't mean Mister Giggles spoke in English with a purring voice. I mean: he purred and we understood what he meant. I don't know, it must have something to do with pheromones or something.

The Samurai brought his fist down on a nearby chair/table so hard that it splintered into a thousand pieces. It was the third since he had entered the room. I was going to have to pay for that, but what are you gonna do? Argue with a Samurai? I like my *kishkes* on the inside of my body, thank you very much!

But, uhh, perhaps I should explain. Ordinarily, these things are held in the apartment of the detective, all very civilized-like. But my apartment? Oy! Don't ask! A shoebox has more room and a sewer has a better view! If I had tried to get everybody into my apartment, only the Samurai would have fit – the rest of us would have had to meet in the hall! So, I asked my *Rebbe*, and he said we could use a room in Beth Tchochkes Synagogue. It was a standard Hebrew classroom, with rows of chair/tables facing a desk at the front. The brick walls were painted white and adorned with old notices of High Holidays, children's art and posters that attempted to make you feel guilty for not sending all of your material wealth to Israel. I haven't exactly been a pillar of faith since the Big Man and I had a falling out over the Gutman debacle of seventy-three. Whatever that was – I'm a little fuzzy on the details. One too many blows to the head with a blunt instrument, probably. Still, whenever I got an eyeful of one of those posters, even I couldn't help but involuntarily reach for my wallet.

Anyway, I was sitting behind the teacher's desk because I'm the *schlemiel* who called this zoo together – no offense to decent, hard-working caged animals anywhere. I got a lotta respect for what they do. Who am I? The name's Schwartz. Shlomo Schwartz. I'm the Kosher Detective. When something don't smell...you know...right, you call me. Except on Shabbas. Don't get me wrong: I got nothing against working on Saturday; as I mentioned, I wasn't exactly Abraham or...or...or somebody else who was prominent in the faith – you see what I mean about not being a believer? However – okay, Moses. There you go. I wasn't exactly Abraham or Moses. I got his name from a movie, but it still counts. Anyway. As Maimonides – that would be Myrtle Maimonides, my landlady – used to say, "You ask somebody to work on the Sabbath and it's like doing it yourself. You gonna finish that potato *kugel*, or what? You don't, I'm only gonna throw it out!"

I'm not really sure what that has to do with anything, but it was damn good potato *kugel*. It would have been a shame to have to throw it out.

So. Yeah. The Samurai. Feng Chi. Concannen had developed an android, The Electric Samurai, that was intended to replace battlefield soldiers. Feng Chi got wind of it (a Ninja friend had told him, because what are Ninja friends for, right?) and challenged it to a duel. It stared at him blankly because what does an android know about warrior honour? When Feng Chi came at it with his sword, it defended itself, because that android sure did know about fighting. They fought for seventeen hours, with much thrusting, parrying and exquisite wire work. In the end, Feng

Chi fell to the ground, exhausted, expecting the Electric Samurai to cut off his head. So violent, these warriors! Anyway, when he looked up, the Electric Samurai had sheathed its weapons and started walking away. Feng Chi did not even have the energy to grunt his disgust at the machine's back. Ever since (about three weeks), the man had walked the world in search of redemption for what he saw as his failure as a warrior.

Feng Chi grunted in Subtitlese: "There is no honour for the warrior to kill an untrained man, unless so ordered by the penguin." That last word may have been "emperor." There are no guarantees in this life.

Flippe-Flappy started laughing. Everybody in the room looked at him. "Honour?" he asked. We could all tell it was a mere prelude. Sure enough: "Honour/Gives the Samurai a boner." It was a tune with a nice melody, but the lyrics? Oy! "Honour is to the Samurai/What fast cars and faster women are to a certain –"

"You're a fine one to talk," Rich Uncle Moneybags cut him off. "Sing. Communicate in whatever fashion suits you. Are you not a member of the Pointdexter Brigade?"

Flippe-Flappy, who had put his clasped hands to his chest in anticipation of throwing them open, stopped in mid-note and left his hands where they were. "How...?" he squeaked. Tunefully, but still.

The Pointdexter Brigade, I should probably mention, was a group of professional song and dance men (I am not being sexist when I say this – they were all men, for reasons which will immediately become apparent), who spent their weekends dancing naked in the forest except for white conical hats that were constantly falling off their heads (what'd I tell ya?). They were rumoured to spend some of that time in rituals involving baked beans, although whether they ate them, snorted them for their hallucinogenic properties or filled their shotguns with them and used the tasty side dish to hunt pine cones was a matter of some dispute. Pfeh! This was supposed to be some kind of protest against the accelerating rate of technological advancement in society, but, you ask me, it was just *meshuggah*. Brainiacs at Anytown U., my Alma Mater (loosely defined – I passed through it once on my way to the Anytown School of the Streets) had written papers on the negative correlation between men dancing naked in the forest except for white conical hats that were constantly falling off their heads and a slowing rate of technological change. Still, hope springs eternal. When you're *meshuggah*.

"La la la la la," Flippe-Flappy trilled. Contorting his face, he made noises halfway between a cow mooing and the engine of a Ford woody station wagon turning over. Missy gave me a "What in tarnation is that fool doin'?" look. I just shrugged. I could have explained that he seemed to be warming up, but I was afraid that if I interrupted him, he would just start the whole process all over again.

It was the right call. A couple of seconds later, Flippe-Flappy crooned: "If you believe I killed Concannen, your head must be made of cement/The Pointdexter Brigade has always been non-violent!"

Mister Giggles purred, causing Flippe-Flappy's face to turn tomato. You know: red. Then, Flippe-Flappy angrily sang: "Nobody knows where Joe Funicular got that tank, son/But his actions were not officially sanctioned!"

The motives were flying faster than bitter recriminations for past wrongs at a Passover *seder*. Still, I had a feeling that somebody was missing... Snapping my fingers, I pointed at the person sitting at the desk on the far left of the group in front of me. "Rich Uncle Moneybags, we have yet to hear your motive for wanting Desmond Concannen dead."

"My motive?" Rich Uncle Moneybags looked shocked that I would even consider the possibility that he had done anything so distasteful as committing murder. "I am so wealthy, I have people who look after the people who brush my teeth in the morning! Do I sound like the sort of person who would cold-bloodedly –" A tinny version of a song that somebody would later tell me was AC/DC's "Money Talks" started playing. Rich Uncle Moneybags pulled an object out of his coat pocket and looked at it. "If I may have your indulgence for a brief period of time," he told everybody, holding up a stubby finger, "my response is urgently required."

The object was a small metallic square with a screen on the

front. On the screen were a variety of colourful images. Rich Uncle Moneybags put the object to his ear and talked to it. Pfeh! They tell me it's a telephone, but I don't believe them. A telephone has a circular dial and a receiver the size of a banana that you talk into and listen to. And it comes in two colours: black and deeper black. What Rich Uncle Moneybags had? A cheap parlour trick, you ask me.

"I see," Rich Uncle Moneybags said. "Stay the course." Then, he pressed a button on the screen of his device and pocketed it anew. When he saw the looks others were giving him, he said, "Don't hate me just because I'm wealthy."

The Samurai grunted twice and made a gesture of punching himself in the face. My impression was that this was his way of saying, "I hate you because you are a weak pudding of a man."

Mister Giggles made a low growling noise in his throat: "I hate you because you smell of burnt cedar chips and overcooked mutton."

"I don't done hate you on account of you have lots o' money," Missy said. "Shoot, my uncle Septimus done made millions lots o' times, and he still told the funniest jokes in alla the southwestern Pecos! Naw, I done hate ya cause of where ya put yer hands when you and me was walkin' into this here room!"

All eyes turned expectantly towards me. "What? Now it's my turn? I'm the detective, here. I have to be dispassionate – I can't afford to hate anybody." The eyes weren't buying it – they could be relentless, those eyes! – so I finally had to add: "Alright! *Shoin*! I…like you less than other people because you think having fancy schmancy machines makes you better than those of us who don't!"

Rich Uncle Moneybags sighed. "I walked right into that one, didn't I?"

Half the people in the room mumbled agreement. Eventually, all of their eyes turned expectantly towards me – did I mention the whole relentlessness thing? Problem was, I had lost the thread in the tattered tapestry of the case. I knew we hadn't gotten to the confession yet – I should be so lucky! Maybe the shredding of the alibis? Hercule Marple had told me that that's usually what came after the discovery of the motives, but I wasn't sure if we were there quite yet.

Excuse me if I wanted to get this right. *Rebbe* Kellerman says I got a need to save the world. Let me tell you, pal, I seen the world, and it's beyond my help. That wasn't it. I was very much aware that this could be the biggest case of my career, even bigger than the Pizzicotti triple homicide! I...I couldn't remember any of the details of that case...or, for that matter, any of its generalities – anything about it at all, really. I could infer that murder and somebody named Pizzicotti were involved – although whether it was three killings or three Pizzicottis was unclear. Still, inferring is not knowing; I resolved to reread the case files when I got back to the office.

"Are we going to be here much longer?" Rich Uncle Moneybags groused. "Time is money, and I'm getting poorer just listening to all of your nonsense."

Mister Giggles, representing the feelings in the room, hissed at him. No need for translation there. Then, I snapped my fingers and pointed at him. "We still haven't dealt with your motive for killing Concannen."

"What possible motive could I have had?" Rich Uncle Moneybags puffed on his stogie. "We had been business partners for years – Desmond had created a large number of lucrative technologies for me. Killing him would adversely affect my bottom line."

Feng Chi grunted at least a dozen times, punctuating his remarks with hand gestures that looked like rock-rock-scissors-paper-paper-paper-Spock? Rich Uncle Moneybags looked at me. I laced my fingers and flexed them, creating an audible crack. This was going to be tough.

"As I understand what the Samurai has said," I translated, "there have long been rumours that you had an interest in...other tortoises?"

Feng Chi grunted angrily.

"Sorry. Universes. You have an interest in other universes. You had given Concannen the task of creating a machine that would allow you to travel between universes. At first, he worked on the machine in the spirit of furthering the...spit take booby prize?"

Feng Chi grunted a correction.

"Right. The scientific enterprise. Knowledge for the sake of knowledge and all that. Only, as time went on and it looked like Concannen was about to make a breakthrough, he started to become suspicious of the fact that you would never give him a straight answer when he asked why you wanted this device. That's always when the trouble begins, isn't it? When scientists question the motives of their benefactors?"

Feng Chi, offended, grunted.

"Yes. Right. That was my editorial two cents worth – don't blame Feng Chi for that last comment. Anyway, Concannen stopped working on the machine, so, in a fit of rage, you pulled down a carp that you had mounted on the wall and killed him. What do you say about that?"

Mister Giggles grinned Cheshirely and purred, "Yes, indeed. What do you say to that?"

Rich Uncle Moneybags didn't seem to be put out by the accusation, but his round features were so simply drawn he could have been feeling anything. I wondered if he had made his fortune playing poker. He took a long, contemplative drag on his cigar, then blew thoughtful smoke rings into the air. "If Desmond had been killed by a stuffed carp," Rich Uncle Moneybags finally responded, "There would have been traces of formaldehyde or some other taxidermic chemical agent in his system. However, according to the coroner's report, there were no such traces. Desmond was killed by a freshwater carp."

"Aww, that's just so much shootin' into tha breeze!" Missy scoffed. "Yaw could afford a whole boatload o' fresh carp if ya was of a mind ta kill somebody with 'em!"

"You can't argue with forensic science, little lady!"

"Who?" I asked.

"What?" Rich Uncle Moneybags asked.

I was confused, but my experience is that is the first step to solving a case, so I tried my best not to show it. "Look," I said. "In his long monologue back there, Feng Chi pointed out, in his gruff, barely articulate way, that you could easily have obtained a freshwater carp if you had wanted to kill Concannen. Are you calling the Samurai a lady?"

Feng Chi growled at the cartoon of a wealthy capitalist.

Rich Uncle Moneybags blinked, which consisted of a

straight line appearing and then disappearing in the middle of his eyes. Before he could respond, however, a song came from one of his pockets. I would later find that it was ABC's 'How to be a Millionaire'. Holding up a pudgy finger, he said, "Your indulgence." He listened to the phone for a few seconds, then said, "No. Under the circumstances, best to hold off on further action in this matter. Right. Be in touch soon." Then, he pressed a button and the 'phone' disappeared back into his coat pocket.

"Now, about –" I started.

"Of course," Rich Uncle Moneybags had regained his composure. "Anybody could have bought a carp – that's hardly evidence that I killed Desmond."

The Samurai. The cat. The obscenely wealthy person – I ticked them off one at a time on the fingers of my mind. Okay, all the suspects' motives were now accounted for. If Marple had been correct, it was time for the alibis. "I need to know where you all were at 7:32 Tuesday night."

Mister Giggles purred. "I was at home. Cleaning my fur." I guess I must have looked at him funny, because he added a low growl: "My tongue is not much bigger than your common housecat, but I have the body of a fully grown man. It takes a long time, okay?"

"Jumbo?" I nodded at the Samurai.

Feng Chi grunted a couple of times and stomped his feet. He wasn't sure what "Jumbo" meant, but he was pretty sure he didn't want to be called it. The stomping meant, "I was at home. Meditating."

"You got any witnesses?"

Feng Chi grunted, breaking another table for emphasis. "Meditation is a solitary activity!"

I turned my attention to the older man. "What about you, Moneybags?"

"That's Rich Uncle Moneybags to you, shamus!" he sneered.

"No, I wasn't saying your name, I was trying to use a pejorative nickname to – never mind. What's your alibi?"

"You know, I am under no obligation to respond to your interrogatives. In fact, I may just…"

He suddenly stopped talking, his mouth becoming a large,

surprised circle. I turned to the door of the room to see what had tied his tongue. It wasn't the cat, obviously – I would have seen that. No, something was shimmering in front of the doorway; I could barely make out the letters of the Hebrew alphabet above it. Two people shimmered into existence: a man who looked like a Crackerjack box with limbs and a, you should pardon the expression, coloured woman with hair that would have flattered a rat's nest. They introduced themselves as Crash Chumley and Noomi Rapier, Transdimensional Authority investigators. Their identification cards were very impressive, if you like that sort of thing.

The Samurai grunted and slammed his hammy fist into the brick wall. Crash looked at me expectantly. I shrugged. "Either he needs to go to the bathroom really bad, or he wants to know what a Transdimensional Authority is. Translation is such an inexact science…"

Chumley looked at Rapier, who deferred to him with a shrug of her shoulders. "The Transdimensional Authority monitors and polices travel between dimensions," he explained. "If you're outside of your home universe, doing something you shouldn't be doing, we find you, stop you and take you back to where you belong."

"He's been practicing that for weeks," Rapier confided in a low voice.

Mister Giggles purred, which we all took to mean, "But, we are all from this dimension."

"Aah, yes, well, that's a little…complicated…" Chumley started.

"Whoa! Whoa! Whoa!" I interrupted. "This is my case, boychick. You don't get to start making with the explanations until after I have caught my murderer!"

"And you are…?"

"The name's Schwartz. Shlomo Schwartz. I'm –"

Rapier clapped her hands together in delight. "You're the Kosher Detective!"

"You've heard of me?" I couldn't keep the pleasure out of my voice.

"I have all your books!"

"All my…but, I don't…" I didn't.

"Nice hat!"

"This isn't a hat, lady," I defensively told her, "it's a fedora. I always wear a fedora, even in the shower. Plays hell with shampooing my hair. And I have to get a new one every three weeks. But it helps me stay in character." Like I said, I'm not religious, but some habits die hard.

Chumley gave Rapier, who was grinning madly, a questioning look. "What?" she replied. "Before I was a science fiction geek, I was a mystery geek."

Chumley gave her a look that asked a different, but related question. "Oh, somebody says that to him in every story he's in," Rapier explained. "It gives him a chance to talk about his love of fedoras. It's kind of a running –"

The Samurai gave a long grunt and pulled imaginary hair out of his bald head. I didn't have to translate.

"Right. You live in a universe designated by the Transdimensional Authority as Earth Prime 5-1-3-0-2-4 dash theta," Chumley explained. "Your universe exists in a symbiotic relationship with Earth Prime 6-5-4-7-8-4 dash eta."

"Symbiotic universes exist where two universes are conceptually intertwined, where actions in one affect the other, and sometimes vice versa," Rapier explained Chumley's explanation. "The one that most people are familiar with is the relationship between one universe and the universe that hosts its pantheon of gods. Sometimes, the gods come to the first universe to start wars or impregnate fair maidens or engage in other hijinks. At the same time, if people in the first universe stop believing in the gods, their hijinks powers start to wane, to the point where it could threaten their very existence. The two universes are intertwined. Uhh, symbiotically."

As Rapier began a pause to catch her breath, Chumley took back control of the explanation: "Your two universes have a unique relationship. All of the people who live in this universe are characters in fictional stories that were written in the other universe, but never read or otherwise shown to an audience."

"But…but…but," I sputtered, "lady here said that she had all of my novels. The novels where I was the main character.

How –"

"Except for *Murder Most Presbyterian*," Rapier corrected. "In that one, you only appear at the end and solve the mystery before you return to your vacation in the Catskills."

"Just my point. If – how many novels did you say I was in?"

"Thirteen novels and at least twice as many short stories."

"Harrumph. If I – were they were popular? My novels?"

"I don't think now is the best time to indulge your ego in–"

"No, no, well, I mean, yes, but I am building to a point, here."

"Oh. Well, yes, in their day, they were very popular."

"Yes, well, there you go. How could I have been in a story which nobody had ever read if I was the hero of a popular series of stories?"

"As best we can figure," Chumley explained afresh, "Hanna Moscovitz, the author of the Shlomo Schwartz mysteries, must have written one before she died that was never published. Her fans have traded rumours of a lost manuscript on Internet message boards for decades since her death – your existence here would lend credence to those rumours."

I snapped my fingers and pointed at Chumley. "That's why I can't remember the details of my most famous cases! They could have been mentioned in the missing manuscript, but if they were read in this other universe you mentioned, they couldn't be referenced in this one!"

"Exac –"

"Poppyrot!" Rich Uncle Moneybags blurted. "Utter tosh and bosh and that. Even if what you say is true – and my inclination would be to call bullponies on it – none of us have anything to do with that other universe. This is a murder investigation that is strictly limited to this reality!"

"Ah," Chumley said.

"Well," Rapier added.

"There is this writer on Earth Prime 6-5-4-7-8-4 dash eta named Etienne Carlyle," Chumley expositioned. "He writes mostly fourteenth century gothic science fiction murder mysteries – a niche taste, to be sure, but his fans are very loyal. A couple of weeks ago, Earth Prime 6-5-4-7-8-4 dash eta time, somebody used a very naughty – very illegal – device to control his brain from this universe. What did they force him to do?"

Chumley looked around the room in anticipation, but nobody felt the need to prompt him, so, a little disappointed, he continued: "They forced him to write short stories whose main characters were people who lived in this universe and post them on Smashwords. When his fans started reading them, those people would disappear from this universe as if they had never existed. Now, you're probably asking yourself: why would somebody do that?"

Chumley paused again, but more briefly, as if he didn't expect anybody to try to answer his question this time. Nobody did, so he continued: "Because somebody close to the Desmond Concannen case had found out that this person had killed the gentleman inventor and was blackmailing him. Whoever the killer is didn't know who the blackmailer was, but he had a group of suspects, and was eliminating them one by one. So, the ultimate question is: who would do such a thing?"

Chumley paused several seconds before he added: "No, seriously. That wasn't a rhetorical question. Carlyle didn't know who was controlling him from this end. Any help any of you could give in solving this would be greatly appreciated."

We looked at each other for a while, but nobody knew what to say. Eventually, Chumley, looking around the Hebrew school room, turned to Rapier and asided: "Well, this sure takes me back."

"I didn't know you were Jewish," she responded.

"I'm not. My parents wanted me to have a well-rounded education, so they sent me to a different religious school every semester throughout high school. Ask me about the term I spent at the Church of the Flying Spaghetti Monster some time."

You know how, sometimes, when one part of your mind is distracted, another part of your mind actually comes up with the solution to a problem? You know, when you're listening to *The Wonderbread Mystery Theatre Three Quarters of an Hour* on the radio and you suddenly come up with a proof for

Fermat's last theorem? Well, I may be no genius, but even I know that when you put two and two together, you get a family of twos.

I snapped my fingers. "Say, Chum…ley. Was one of the people whose existence was erased from this world a girl?"

Chumley consulted a notepad that had suddenly appeared in his hand. "Yes. Her name was Missy Mulholland. Her shorthand description was 'The Shootin' Sweetheart of Sandler's Gulch.'"

I pointed at Rich Uncle Moneybags. "You knew that a girl had disappeared from here. You tried to cover it up in the confusion, but you knew, even though there was no trace of her existence in this reality. The only way you could have known that was if you had masterminded the whole *megillah*!"

Rich Uncle Moneybags took a long puff on the cigar that always seemed to be in his mouth but never seemed to shorten. "Son, I've got more lawyers than you've got hairs on your head. So, I would think twice before accusing me of illegal behaviour if I were –"

Mister Giggles purred contentedly. "Okay. You got me. I'm the blackmailer. I was prowling around R.U.M. and Koch Industries labs in South Outer Anytown. I had heard the rumours about Desmond Concannen building a machine that could transport you to another universe, and I thought, *Purrfect! He could help me get to a reality where my homeworld still existed!* Don't ask me how I got in the building – the feline guild would never forgive me for giving away such a basic trade secret. Let's just take it as given. As I approached the door to Concannen's lab, I could hear two voices shouting: the inventor and the rich purrson. I could also smell the unmistakeable odour of carp. I had no idea that it was going to be used as a murder weapon – honestly! I just assumed that it was dinnertime. I'm always ready for dinner. When I heard choking noises coming from the lab, well, I panicked and ran. The kind of man who is capable of choking another man to death with a carp is capable of anything!"

"Well," Chumley started, but now that I knew what was going on, I wasn't about to cede the case to him.

"Well, Rich Uncle Moneybags, what do you have to say to

that?" I asked.

"I'm not saying word one until there is a phalanx of lawyers between us," Rich Uncle Moneybags sneered.

"Still," Chumley started. I gave him such a look! A small smile threatened to break out on his lips, and he gestured towards the suspect.

"Still," I said, "we know enough to have a pretty good idea of what you were up to. Concannen refused to continue working on the interdimensional flying machine –"

"We call them Dimensional Portal^{TM}s," Rapier whispered to me.

"Right. Concannen refused to continue working on your Dimensional Portal, so you –"

"^{TM}. Dimensional Portal^{TM}. It's very important to our lawyers."

I supressed the urge to roll my eyes. "Right. So, Concannen refused to work on your Dimensional Portal^{TM}, so, in a fit of rage, you force fed him a carp."

"Pah! Some detective you are!" Rich Uncle Moneybags snorted. "Desmond had already finished the Dimensional Portal^{TM}!"

"Of course. I suspected that that might be the case. You must have killed him because he was no longer useful to you."

"Noooooo, I killed him because the idiot insisted upon registering a flight plan with the Transdimensional Authority! How was **that** going to help keep my secret plan secret?"

"Of course. That would have been my second choice."

Chumley cleared his throat. "The, ahh, interview is going very well, Mister Schwartz. I was wondering if you would allow me to interject one small question of my own."

A compliment he paid me? A real nugget of praise? Of course, I would allow him to ask a question after the big lug paid me a compliment. I gestured towards the billionaire.

"Thank you. Rich Uncle Moneybags, if the Dimensional Portal^{TM} had been completed, why didn't you use it immediately to return to Earth Prime 6-5-4-7-8-4 dash eta?"

"I thought I made it clear that I'm not answering your questions!" Rich Uncle Moneybags snarled.

"If you will allow me..." I suggested.

Chumley looked like he was repressing a desire to scratch his head. "Be my guest..."

"So, the Dimensional Portal ^{TM} was finished, but you didn't use it. Obviously, it was out of gas –"

"It runs on hydrogen, the most abundant element in the universe."

"Or, Concannen hadn't given you the keys –"

"You start it by pressing a big green button."

"You crashed it into a dingo that had randomly appeared in the lab the first time you tried to –"

"No! No! No! No! No! Gaaaah! I'm not from this world, okay? I lived most of my life in the other universe – one day, I woke up to discover that my mind had been switched into...this!" Rich Uncle Moneybags poked himself in the belly. "Going back in this body wouldn't do me any good – nobody would believe it was really me! I had to find out where my original body was and figure out how to get my consciousness back into it!"

Chumley and Rapier exchanged a look. Hoo boy, the look they exchanged! "Okay, what?"

"We know somebody who controlled people's minds across dimensions – this might be an extension of her work," Chumley stated.

"But, she's been in a maximum security prison since we caught her a few months ago," Rapier added.

"So, what're you going to do?" I asked.

"Mmm," Chumley mmmed. "I think I can convince the Transdimensional Authority's Poet Laureate to spend some time on Earth Prime 6-5-4-7-8-4 dash eta –"

"Leonard is always complaining that he doesn't ever seem to get a vacation," Rapier approvingly agreed.

"Exactly. While he's there, we can hopefully prevail upon him to write stories featuring the characters – sorry, **people** who were erased from this world and immediately transfer them to Earth Prime –"

"That's where our headquarters are."

"As long as nobody on Earth Prime 6-5-4-7-8-4 dash eta reads his stories, everybody should reappear as they were."

"Well, probably not **exactly** as they were. For one thing, they may speak in verse for a little while. Still –"

"Hold on!" Rich Uncle Moneybags put in. "If you're planning on bringing everybody back from oblivion, there can be no murder charges for what happened to them. Habeus corpus, my friends. Habeus bloody corpus!"

Chumley favoured him with a warm smile. "Attempted murder, then."

"I'm not sure that conceptual homicide is against the law. Once my lawyers get through with you –"

"We have you dead to rights for communicating across universes without a permit," Chumley's smile vanished as quickly as it had appeared. "We take that sort of thing very seriously at the Transdimensional Authority."

Chumley motioned to Rich Uncle Moneybags to turn around so he could put handcuffs on him. At first, I thought it must be some kind of joke – Rich Uncle Moneybags' wrists were so thin, the manacles would fall right off. Then, the other shoe dropped – right on my *furshlugginer kop*.

"What are you doing with my suspect?" I asked.

"I'm taking him to Earth Prime to serve time for his crimes against the multiverse."

"You can't do that! He killed a man with a carp – nothing you do is going to change that!"

"Have you ever read the Treaty of Gehenna-Wentworth?"

"Umm…not that I'm aware of."

"Consider yourself lucky. It's been on *People Magazine – Multiverse Edition*'s list of ten most boring documents for years. Last year, it tied for number three with a book of Vogon poetry. Still, I'm sorry but it gives the Transdimensional Authority jurisdiction in this case."

Rapier laid a hand on my arm. "If it's any consolation," she enthusiastically told me, "that was the most brilliant use of the Clouseau Technique for interrogating a suspect that I have ever witnessed! Congratulations!"

I had no idea what she was talking about, but, yeah, it was some consolation.

*

A couple of days later, I was sitting in my office, nursing an ice cold skim milk (what I know from ulcers? – oy! – don't ask!) and looking at the front door where "rehcrA dna ztrawhcS" was written when I snapped my fingers. Of course! rehcrA must have been my partner on a case in a book that was popular in the other universe. I would never know why he was no longer around, but I was satisfied that a minor personal mystery had been solved.

A thin figure wearing a big flowery hat and sixguns appeared behind the frosted glass. Could it be the woman who disappeared from my investigation of the Concannen case? Before she could even knock, I shouted, "Come in!"

A woman with hair of straw and a strong chin walked into my office. "Mister Schwartz?" Missy Mulholland asked.

"That's what they call me," I shot back.

"A Transdimensional Authority investigator told me I oughta done catch ya later. Her name was…Naomi? Said ya did a kind thing for me?"

It was love at first sight. Again, probably. I beamed at her and waved a hand towards the chair on the other side of my desk. "Sit. Sit. I'll tell you all about it. Can I offer you some skim milk?"

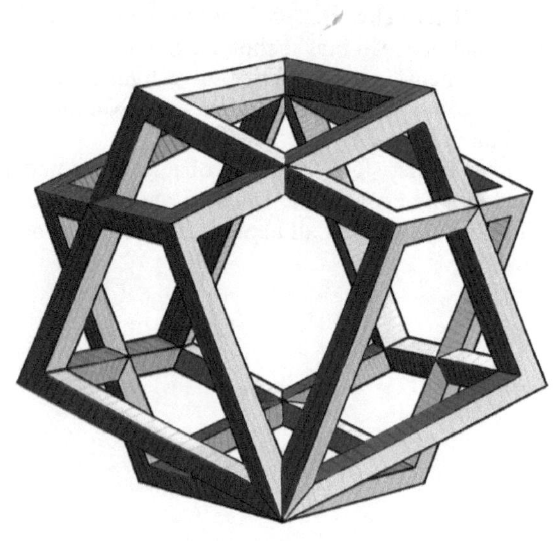

The Girl in Black

by

Christopher G. Nuttall

Christopher G. Nuttall has been planning sci-fi books since he learnt to read. Born and raised in Edinburgh, Chris created an alternate history website and eventually graduated to writing full-sized novels. Studying history independently allowed him to develop worlds that hung together and provided a base for storytelling. After graduating from university, Chris started writing full-time. As an indie author he has self-published a number of novels, but has also had eight titles published by Elsewhen Press, including the best-selling *Bookworm* series.

His *Royal Sorceress* series about Lady Gwendolyn Crichton is set in an alternative 1830s, some sixty years after British scientists discovered the scientific basis of magic (which enabled them to win the American War of independence). The series began with *The Royal Sorceress*, followed by *The Great Game* and then *Necropolis*. The next installment in the series, *The Sons of Liberty*, will be published by Elsewhen Press in 2016. Chris is currently living in Edinburgh with his wife, muse, and critic Aisha and their one-year old son Eric.

The Girl in Black takes place before the end of *The Great Game* (1831), just prior to Olivia's kidnap.

My Lord Mycroft.

Doctor Norwell, as you are no doubt aware, has requested that a full account of the affair of the Saint of Grimsby be written for the Royal Archives. As my work for the country is considered a state secret, I am forwarding the account to you beforehand so you may edit it to preserve the secrets of our great nation. I look forward to your comments on the matter.

It was my task, as the threat of war with France loomed over the country once again, to monitor the actions of the country's few remaining Papists. While some believe the threat of a Catholic Restoration to have died with the Young Pretender, the prospect of a threat presented by Catholics within our country cannot be discounted. France, as all are aware, dominates Rome and the Pope himself is a French mouthpiece. Accordingly, as a Charmer of the second rank, I move between the various Papist households, making contact with a number of His Majesty's agents. It was from one of them that I first heard rumours of a saint.

Father Peter, at least on the surface, is one of the few Catholic priests allowed to move freely within Britain. His freedom comes at a price, as he is well aware; it is his duty to watch and record those who take Mass openly, those who take it secretly and those who would take it, if they dared. It galls me to depend on such people – the secrets of the Confession are open to us, if we merely pay the Father what he demands – but he is reliable. I met up with him in an isolated house and we fell to talking. My Charm, of course, permitted me to extract more from him than he might have preferred.

"There is a rumour of a young girl who works miracles," he said, after we had discussed the loyalties of the most prominent Catholics in the country. "They say she speaks with the voice of God."

I did not, of course, believe such blasphemy, but rumours can spread quickly if they are not nipped in the bud. Accordingly, after drawing all of the details I could from him, I rode to the home of Sally Harcourt, an elderly woman who has remained firmly Catholic through several wars and innumerable persecutions of Papists. I must confess that I found her rather remarkable. She is and remains the type of woman who is the core of Britain's greatness, but her stubbornness condemns her to the fires of hell. We took tea together and, using my Charm, I urged her to tell me what she'd seen.

It was difficult work. Mistress Harcourt is a stubborn old lady and, while she never quite realised what I was doing, she knew *something* was wrong. I will spare you a complete recital of everything she said and merely summarise. She had been attending a service with a number of other local Catholics when a fisherman brought in his young daughter. The girl went into a trance, levitated up into the air and spoke truth. It chilled me to the bone, I must admit, when it became clear that the girl had pointed an accusing finger at John Rotherham and accused him of being in the pay of London. You will be aware, of course, that Rotherham is indeed one of our agents.

And then things became truly terrifying. The girl called down the wrath of God and Rotherham burst into flame. She fainted at the same moment; her father, with many prayers of thanks to his Lord, helped her to leave the chamber. Mistress Harcourt left shortly afterwards, deeply shocked. I would venture to say that this 'proof' of her religion was enough to harden her soul against my Charm.

Mistress Harcourt, of course, agreed with the prevailing opinion that the young girl was a saint, although there are no recorded incidents of *any* saint (male or female) incinerating a grown man. I suspected there was another explanation. The girl was a magician, either capable of using multiple talents, like Master Thomas, or covertly assisted by another magician in the congregation. A Talker or a Sensitive would, perhaps, have been able to pull John Rotherham out of the crowd and identify him as a spy. Rotherham could hardly be expected not to be thinking of his report to London when he saw the girl levitate herself into the air.

This was clearly more dangerous than I had supposed. I bade farewell to Mistress Harcourt, using a limited amount of Charm to ensure she forgot the specifics of my visit, and headed at once to Grimsby. Brave as I am, I dared not walk into the lair of at least one magician without intensive support from the Royal Sorcerers Corps. I reached the city as night was starting to fall, asked a Talker who worked at the Sorcerers Hall to send a message to London, and waited for the response. When it came, I was ordered to take a room in the local inn and wait for Lady Gwen.

I must confess that I did not find the thought reassuring. Master Thomas had been a firm hand, guiding the policies of the Royal Sorcerers Corps; I found it hard to believe that a sheltered young girl could possibly take his place, even if she was a Master Magician. But I knew better than to protest, particularly with war threatening the country. I left my details at the railway station, found a room and settled down to wait. In all honesty, I did not expect to be summoned until the following morning. I was wrong.

The landlord knocked loudly on the door seven hours after I had put my book aside and gone to bed. I glanced at my watch – five in the morning – grabbed for my jacket and opened the door. The landlord informed me that I had a visitor, waiting downstairs for me. Mindful of the propriety of being alone with an unmarried girl, I slipped the landlord a small tip and asked him if we could use one of the side rooms for a private chat. He was surprised, but willing.

I must admit that I was not one of Lady Gwen's supporters when she assumed the role of Royal Sorceress. A young and largely untested magician – and a girl, at that – could not, in my opinion, fill Master Thomas's shoes. And yet, knowing that she enjoyed the support of some of the most powerful men in the land, I decided to give her a chance as I walked down the stairs and into the meeting room. If nothing else, she *was* a Master Magician.

She surprised me. I had expected a young woman in a fashionable dress, not someone wearing male clothing. Indeed, had I not known her sex, I would have honestly mistaken her for a slightly effeminate man. She lacked stubble, of course, and an Adam's Apple, but without knowing to look for such details I would have missed them. There was little feminine in her movements, none of the reluctance to be forward of aristocratic womanhood or the blunt plainspoken attitude of a commoner woman. Her clothing disguised her figure perfectly.

"Mr. Davidson," she said. Her voice was low, but firm. "The Sergeant told me a great deal about you."

I confess the thought worried me. Sergeant Hamilton, the Master-At-Arms of Cavendish Hall, was never one of my biggest supporters. We Charmers are rarely popular when we do not use our powers to *make* people like us. Indeed, everyone who has anything to do with us worries constantly that we might be affecting their thoughts. But I swallowed my fears and waited for her next words.

"He said you were a good man," she added. "And quite observant."

The Sergeant, of course, was observant himself. He had seen dozens of young magicians pass through the doors of Cavendish Hall. Many of them would have been more useful, certainly more open, than a second-rank Charmer. I couldn't help wondering if I was being flattered, before I decided that it was unlikely. Lady Gwen didn't strike me as the sort of person to pour out unjustified praise.

"Thank you," I said. "You came quickly."

"Lord Mycroft wants the whole affair investigated as soon as possible," she said. "When can we leave?"

I glanced at my watch. "We can go now, if the landlord will pack me something to eat," I said, "or we can go after breakfast."

"We'll go after breakfast," Lady Gwen said. "That will give you plenty of time to brief me."

The landlord was kind enough to supply a breakfast of porridge, eggs and bread, which we ate in the sideroom while I told her everything I knew. Lady Gwen agreed with my assessment, remarking that she'd developed her powers when she was very young. I had the impression that something bad had happened at the time, accounting for her near-complete exclusion from the London social scene, but she refused to be drawn on the topic. There was no way I could draw more out of her, not without using Charm. And she would almost certainly notice if I tried.

"We will probably not be particularly welcome when we arrive," I said. "Do you want to go as an official investigator?"

"I have authority to investigate any and all cases of suspected magic," Lady Gwen answered, bluntly. "I'll go as myself."

"Yes, My Lady," I said. My cover as a travelling salesman was likely to be blown, if word spread, but it couldn't be helped. "What will you do if the child is a magician?"

"I'll take her away," Lady Gwen said, shortly. "It will be better for her to be raised by her fellow magicians."

"And we cannot leave her in Papist hands," I added.

Lady Gwen nodded. The Pope had made the mistake, back when Cavendish first proved the existence of magic, of proclaiming it the work of the devil. France and Spain promptly started killing every magician foolish enough to reveal his powers, while Britain, on the other hand, sought to use them. Even now, after the French reversed their policy, their magical corps is far inferior to ours. To the best of our knowledge, they have never found a Master Magician.

We finished our breakfast, collected an official carriage and driver from the local magicians and drove off to Salk's End, where the girl and her father were supposed to live. It was a tiny fishing village, barely eking out a living; the villagers, according to the taxmen, were fond of smuggling goods from France into Britain and vice versa. Even so, I was struck by the poverty as we drove into the village and down towards the girl's house. Grimsby, Hull and the other major towns had sucked the prosperity from the village. I was surprised that so many people actually *remained*.

But perhaps I shouldn't have been. Too many of them were Catholics and it was hard for them to get a job elsewhere.

We parked the carriage outside a rundown hovel, ordered the driver to wait and headed down the path. The stink of rotting fish hung in the air as we approached; I could see a small boat resting on the beach as we walked around the house looking for the door. I am a confident swimmer, yet I would not have cared to go out onto the waters on that boat. Even a skilled sailor would have problems handling it if the weather turned rough. I found myself looking eastwards, towards the open waters, and wondering if an invasion fleet was lurking just over the horizon. It all seemed so safe and tranquil, but the threat of war was very near.

Lady Gwen rapped on the door with her cane and waited. I was on the verge of proposing that we kick the door down when there was a rattling sound from inside and the door opened, revealing a grim-faced man in grimy clothes. He was, perhaps, one of the ugliest men I'd ever seen. I found out, later, that his name was George Barton and he claimed to be related to the Nun of Kent, although this was never actually proven (and seems unlikely.)

"Yes?"

"I am here to investigate reports of your daughter possessing magic," Lady Gwen said, in her most officious voice. She sounded very much like a man at that moment. "Please will you take me to her?"

"My daughter is a saint," Barton insisted. He looked very much as if he had no intention of budging. "You will *not* call her a filthy magician."

"I'm here to establish that she isn't a magician," Lady Gwen said, lacing her voice with subtle Charm. It was nowhere near as skilled as my own work, but I had to admit that she definitely had more skill with Charm than had Master Thomas. "Please will you take me to her?"

The beauty and danger of charm is that it allows the victim to come up with their own justifications for their behaviour. George Barton wanted – needed – to believe his daughter a saint, so he convinced himself that we would prove she had no magic and, therefore, that her powers came from God. He turned, beckoned us to follow him and led the way into his house – his hovel. The outside was bad enough, but the inside was worse. I would sooner have grown up in a tenement in Glasgow than that tiny hovel. The floor was filthy, the walls were mouldy and I really didn't want to know how they washed. I sincerely hoped that they swam in the sea. The stench alone was enough to turn my stomach.

Barton tapped on a door and opened it, revealing a young girl kneeling on the stone floor. I was struck at once by just how ... *strange* she looked, although I could not put my finger on why. She was around nine years old, with long blonde-brown hair and a dark dress that reminded me of a nun's outfit. A copy of the bible – the latest version authorised by Rome – lay on her lap, open to the Book of Exodus. And there was something utterly expressionless in her eyes, so much so that I couldn't help wondering if she was drugged.

Lady Gwen knelt down on the floor. "Hello," she said. "What's your name?"

"Her name is Cecelia," Barton said. "She rarely talks to strangers."

"Wait outside," Lady Gwen said. "Both of you."

I did as I was told and, while waiting, bounced questions off Barton. It was a frustrating experience; Barton appeared completely convinced that his daughter was a saint, but seemed to be totally unable to recall any specific details. His only comment on the death of John Rotherham was to say that God had punished him for his crimes. He was a little more forthcoming on the subject of his late wife, who had died giving birth to his daughter. She had, apparently, been a zealot. Her name was completely unfamiliar to me. I discovered, later, that she'd been kicked out of her own family for excessive zeal, back when they'd been doing their best to make peace with the king.

"She was a holy woman," Barton told me. "She made me what I am."

I kept my thoughts to myself as I glanced around the hovel. It was no place to bring up a child. Barton himself slept on a mattress that needed to be replaced, although it was unlikely he could afford anything better. I couldn't help feeling sorry for the girl and prayed, silently, that she would turn out to be a magician. We couldn't justify taking her from her father and handing her over to another family if she wasn't.

But when Lady Gwen emerged, she looked downcast.

"I couldn't find any traces of magic," she said, as she closed the door behind her. "She was very reluctant to talk."

"She's a saint," Barton announced. "She has no truck with the devil."

Lady Gwen nodded, gave him a guinea – I'd venture that it was more money than he'd seen in his life – and headed for the door. I followed her, breathing a long sigh of relief as soon as I could smell the salt air again. The hovel had stunk so badly that my clothes would need to be cleaned thoroughly – or simply discarded once we returned to Grimsby. Lady Gwen said nothing, but I was sure she was as uncomfortable as myself.

"That was a very strange girl," Lady Gwen said. "She certainly isn't *normal*."

I looked at her. "How so?"

"A girl of that age should be bright and inquisitive," Lady Gwen said. "Or, if her parents are strict, very submissive and obedient. But *she* wasn't responsive at all. There was no sign she was even *there* while I was talking to her."

You will know, of course, that while I am unmarried, I do have two younger sisters. They had been quite embarrassing when I'd been a lad – their sense of humour was definitely mischievous – and they drove their governess wild, but they had definitely been very active and determined to cause trouble. I still smile whenever I think about the time they'd play hide and seek with their tutor, rather than getting down to work. And, by their standard, Cecelia was *very* odd.

"Perhaps she's touched in the head," I said.

"Perhaps she is," Lady Gwen said. "I can't read thoughts directly, but I can normally sense emotions. There was almost nothing in her mind at all."

I considered it. I'd been taught, years ago, that a strong mind could block out a mind-reading Talker, if he had sufficient skill. "Did she block you?"

"If she did, it's a very odd block," Lady Gwen said. "I sensed nothing, as if she wasn't there at all. She would have needed magic to do that, but I didn't sense a *hint* of magic surrounding her."

I frowned and forgot myself. "Are you sure?"

"Yes," Lady Gwen said. She didn't sound angry at my tone. "I can usually recognise another magician, even if the specific talent isn't recognisable. But I didn't feel anything from her."

"Me neither," I admitted. I normally feel a little uneasy when near an undeveloped magician, but Cecelia hadn't triggered that feeling in me. "And yet, we know that magic is involved somewhere, don't we?"

"Yeah," Lady Gwen said. "If Cecelia isn't the magician, there must be another one or two hanging around nearby. I think we'll be attending the next Mass."

We drove back to Grimsby, where Lady Gwen sent a preliminary report to London and I consulted with Father Peter to learn the time and place of the next Mass. Barton, it seemed, was fond of attending a Catholic Church some distance from his village, even though it meant getting up very early in the morning and walking several miles. Father Peter reported that several of the local Catholics were already talking about requesting a papal commission to investigate Cecelia and confirm her claims to sainthood, even though appealing *anything* to Rome is in flat contradiction of the Edict of Tolerance. Something was definitely odd. Most of our remaining Catholics know to keep their heads down, but now they were doing something that would definitely incur London's wrath.

"If the French are involved, they may be looking for an excuse to start the war," Lady Gwen speculated, afterwards. She'd taken lodgings at the inn, rather than the Sorcerers Hall. I had a feeling she was enjoying the freedom that a male guise brought her. "Their own people are not keen on the idea of yet another ruinous war."

I nodded in agreement. The French have fought us in seven successive wars and lost badly every time. Effective hegemony over Western Europe – and a union of crowns with Spain – does not make up for losing control over North America or for the simple fact that George IV rules an empire greater than Alexander's. One has to admire their persistence – they have come up with hundreds of plans to invade our native soil – but their rationality is something else. Every war they have fought with us has cost their peasants dearly.

"They use religious faith to keep the peasants in line," I said. It was true enough. The Pope in Rome wouldn't dare say anything to contradict France while the French held a dagger to his throat. Their network of priests served as secret agents, keeping an eye on the population; those who dared confess to anything less than complete loyalty were rarely seen again. "If they can convince their population that the next war is for the freedom of Catholics in Britain, they might be able to avoid trouble."

"Perhaps," Lady Gwen said. I could tell that she was

troubled. "But all that will happen is that a great many Catholics will wind up dead."

Privately, I disagreed. The military threat from Catholic or Jacobite families might be long over – they had been unable or unwilling to rise when the Young Pretender crossed the border – but those that remained stubbornly practicing their faith were hardened by decades of legal oppression. Even a relative handful of them might be able to cause trouble, if the French crossed the waters; the mere act of destroying a railway line would make it difficult for us to move reinforcements around the country. It would be better, perhaps, to offer the English Catholics the chance to move to Catholic Ireland or even to emigrate to France. But they wouldn't be welcome in either place.

Going to Mass is never easy. The authorities, for reasons that date all the way back to Martin Luther and Henry VIII, are very nervous about the Mass. So is the mob. The mere suspicion that someone might be hosting a Mass is enough to provoke violence on the streets of London, where fear and hatred of Papists runs strong. Even in the days of the Edict of Toleration, Masses are only permitted in certain churches and carried out by registered priests. Catholics like Barton have been known to travel for miles just to attend a Mass, which made it easier for me to slip into the congregation. I had been, in my persona as a wandering trader, to Mass several times; Lady Gwen, still in male guise, was introduced as my business partner.

The church was packed. Rumours, clearly, had been spreading far and wide. I saw a number of faces that I recognised, including several men who publicly claimed to have renounced the faith. I made careful note of their attendance for later attention – there was no reason to attend, unless they wished to take the Sacrament – and watched from the rear as the building hummed with conversation. Nothing secret would be discussed, of course; they knew they were being watched. But there was no sign of Cecelia by the time the service began. Father Peter handled it, despite his divided loyalties; I had to admit there was a certain majesty in the whole ceremony. But it comes with the price of obedience to Rome and that, as a pure-blooded Englishman, I can not tolerate.

It had nearly reached its end when Cecelia made her appearance, walking into the church accompanied by her father. It was hard for me to see her face from where I was sitting in the rear of the building, but there was something in the way she walked that sent chills running down my spine. Was it even the same girl? There was a confidence in her movements that I hadn't seen when I'd first laid eyes on her. She walked with the attitude of a crowned queen.

Lady Gwen leaned forward, watching Cecelia carefully. I wondered, briefly, what she was thinking. Women are often more observant than men. If I could see that something was different, that something was wrong, Lady Gwen could see it too. *Was* it the same girl? I wouldn't have thought Barton could deceive us, but I might have underestimated him. If he'd drugged another girl and passed her off as his own ...

No, I decided, when Cecelia reached the foot of the altar and turned to face us. It was the same girl. But she was active now, her face gleaming with holy purpose.

"Magic," Gwen whispered.

The spell snapped. Cecelia was, deliberately or otherwise, projecting an aura of pure Charm at the audience. *I* couldn't do that! I needed to speak to influence someone with my powers; the simplest way to cripple a Charmer had always been to simply tie and gag him. Cecelia, on the other hand, was pulling people into her spell. They believed in her sainthood because they *wanted* to believe in it, on some level. The most effective Charm is always when the target only needs a small amount of convincing to do something.

Cecelia rose into the air, just like a Mover. Lady Gwen sucked in her breath, harshly. Her senses were far more attuned than my own. If there were other magicians in the audience, she would have sensed their presence; their absence, in many ways, was even worse. Cecelia was using multiple powers ... and *that* made her a Master Magician.

"There is a false priest in this room," Cecelia said, as she span in the air. The sheer *power* in her voice was incredible. She combined the force of a first-rank Charmer with the subtle skill of a second-rank. I *knew* she was trying to steer my thoughts and yet it was hard, so very hard, to think clearly. "He serves the King of England instead of God."

She turned to look at Father Peter. "Confess your sins and receive absolution."

Father Peter looked as if someone had struck him across the face. I had always thought of him as a strong-minded individual, but he knelt at once and started to babble out a tearful confession. It struck me, suddenly, that he must have felt more than a little guilt over his dual role to have collapsed so easily. The Mass is, of course, a reaffirmation of a community as well as a holy rite. And *he* had given hundreds of such ceremonies in his time.

"Go forth and sin no more," Cecelia said, when he had finished.

The words held the power of true compulsion. Father Peter couldn't possibly disobey. I stared in horror as he stumbled from the church, tearing off his robes as he passed. He would be useless as a spy for the rest of his life. Cecelia turned, her gaze sweeping over the watching congregation. They were transfixed, unable to move, yet I could feel their fear beating on the air like a living thing. Cecelia was looking right into their very souls.

"You committed adultery," she said, looking at a fisherman. Her gaze switched to a middle-aged woman seated in the front rows. "You ate meat during Lent."

The fisherman caught fire. His screams and the stench of burning flesh shocked the crowd out of their paralysis, his neighbours stumbling to escape before they caught fire themselves. The church was suddenly alive as everyone tried to run, to flee her accusing gaze. Lady Gwen levitated herself up into the air as the pews emptied; I clambered up the wall and watched as the building emptied. Cecelia seemed unconcerned by her fleeing audience; she kept pointing at people, telling the world their sins and incinerating them.

"Stop," Lady Gwen said. "You're killing them."

Cecelia stabbed a finger at Lady Gwen. Flames exploded around her, but she was untouched; I saw, in the light, a translucent bubble surrounding her. I breathed a sigh of relief as Cecelia stared in horror, her face shocked to the bone. Had she really believed she was a saint? Or had she merely been unable to comprehend the true nature of her powers? There was, and remains, no way to know.

Lady Gwen landed on the ground in front of Cecelia. "You have to stop this," she said, very quietly. I clambered down from my perch as she spoke. "Whatever you think you're doing, you're not."

I hurried towards her ... and froze as Cecelia turned her gaze on me. Her power struck me like a physical blow, ripping through my mental block and burrowing into my mind. I was completely exposed before her. Lady Gwen stepped between us, blocking her stare; I fell backwards as the connection snapped. And Cecelia ... threw back her head and screamed in anger and fear. Seconds later, her power ripped through the building, tearing up the pews and throwing them at us. Lady Gwen raised a shield as the walls started to crumble: she shouted at me to run as her shield started to stagger under the weight of successive blows. I ran, feeling Cecelia's power beating against my mind, and almost stumbled over her father as soon as I was outside the church. Moments later, the building collapsed into rubble. Lady Gwen and Cecelia appeared in the centre of the debris, completely untouched.

"Oh, Jesus," Barton was wailing. "Oh ..."

I grabbed him. "Make her stop," I shouted. I didn't bother with subtle Charm; I shoved the order at him as hard as I could. "Make her *stop*!"

Her father gibbered – I wondered if his mind had snapped – and then he stumbled to his feet and walked towards Cecelia. She was floating in the air, wrapped in power; it was hard, so hard, to tear my eyes away from her. And yet, as her father approached, she turned to stare at him ... and then stopped. She simply fell out of the air. The power beating on the air vanished at the same moment ...

... And all that was left was Cecelia, lying on the ground.

Lady Gwen bent down next to her and touched the girl's forehead with her fingers, trying to sense the girl's mind. She must have seen something, in that final moment, because she rose and rounded on Barton. He tried to stumble backwards before realising that I was right behind him.

"You caused this," Lady Gwen accused. "What did you *do*

to her?"

Barton tried to avoid the question, but Lady Gwen hammered his mind with magic until his defences collapsed. He'd tried to bring his daughter up to be a good little girl, he said, yet she'd developed magic, which he'd believed to be a curse. Somehow, he'd come to believe that she was a saint instead, that she wasn't a magician on her own, but merely a conduit for God's power. I couldn't help wondering if she'd accidentally charmed him into believing she was a saint, perhaps when she'd started showing signs of magic. It is far from uncommon, even in Britain, for children with magic to be disowned or beaten by their parents. Barton would have believed in his daughter's sainthood because he *wanted* to believe in it.

And then others had come to believe in her too.

Lady Gwen killed him, there and then. It is perhaps the least of the horrors of that damned day that I felt nothing when I saw his body fall to the ground.

There remain only a few issues that need to be cleared up.

Lady Gwen believes that Cecelia, as an untrained magician, accidentally damaged her own mind. She locked away her powers outside of church, burying them so deeply that neither of us could sense their presence. Perhaps through madness, she boosted some of her powers to truly staggering levels. Her Charm and Talking skills were both superior, at least in raw power, to anything I have seen among adult magicians. As quite a few Talkers, at least, have ended up in Bedlams because they couldn't control their abilities, Cecelia may have had similar problems. The more powerful the ability, the harder it is to control.

Cecelia herself seems to have reverted to the silent mouse persona we observed when we first laid eyes upon her. There is no visible sign of magic; Lady Gwen reports that she was able to pull impressions and images from her mind just after her collapse. However, as it is quite likely she has a fractured personality, I strongly advise that she be kept under close observation for the remainder of her life, well away from vulnerable people.

Father Peter was caught some distance from the church, begging for alms. His mind appears to have been completely snapped by the experience, as he alternates between tearful confessions and attempting to do his duty as a priest. He has been moved to a Bedlam in Doncaster, where he will be held until recovery or death.

The survivors of the church have been shocked by the incident, according to our remaining agents. I believe that the situation deserves careful monitoring, but there are no grounds to believe that they pose any more of a threat than they already did. It would be advisable, however, to use the incident to further discredit the French. If the survivors – and those who hear about the incident at second-hand – come to believe that the French turned Cecelia into a monster, rather than a saint, it can only rebound to our benefit.

As of writing, there is no evidence to suggest the French were actually involved.

In conclusion, I must note that Lady Gwen lived up to the legacy left behind by Master Thomas. I was expecting either a fainting flower or an aggressive 'lady' of the Trouser Brigade. Instead, I got a calm and capable investigator who saved my life when Cecelia lost control. You can be assured that she will have my full support in future.

I trust this account meets with your approval.

Solomon Davidson, Charmer
Royal Sorcerers Corps

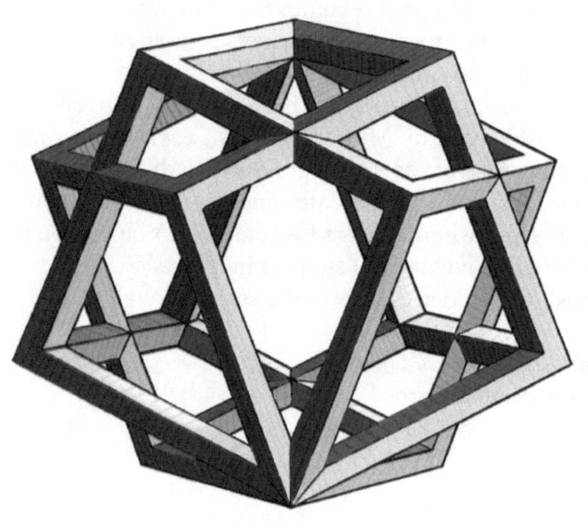

Hide and Hunt

by

Susan Oke

Susan Oke has been a storyteller all her life. The eldest of three sisters she would entertain with off-the-cuff bedtimes stories on a nightly basis. Actual writing of said stories had to wait until she was a proper grownup. When the last of her three daughters—can you see a pattern here?—went off to university, Susan discovered the true meaning of unfettered time and space. Well, she was still working fulltime, but you know what I mean.

And then writing happened. Short stories at first: in anthologies (Tree House Press, Kindofahurricane Press, and now Elsewhen Press), magazines (*Words with Jam*, *Silver Pen*, *Writers Tribe*), podcast (*Cast of Wonders*), and some flash fiction for *Sein und Werden*. But behind it all was the novel, of course. A novel that she started as part of her MA in Creative Writing, and that she is now busily putting the finishing touches to.

Susan hails originally from Yorkshire, but has spent the last thirteen years living in London, where she worked in the Higher Education sector. She is now a full-time writer, and is loving every minute of it.

I press my back against the wide bole of the tree and try not to breathe. But my body won't behave and gulps ragged lungfuls of air. I squeeze my eyes shut. Any moment now the Hunter will find me, and it will all be over.

Beyond the rasp of my breath, the forest is silent. I can't stand it any longer. My eyes snap open and I stare wildly around at the twisted trunks of ancient trees, each one harbouring its own collection of shadows. Stubborn tussocks of grass and patches of frozen mud pattern the uneven ground. Above, stark boughs net the sky, some threatening to bud, others still dusted with snow.

Father's voice echoes in my memory. *Useless. Weakling.* My shoulders hunch and I bite my lip. He's right. It's my fault I got separated from Tara. The Hunter got between us and I panicked. Now he can pick us off one at a time. I dig my nails deeper into the crumbling bark. I have to get back to Tara, somehow. The makeshift bond that exists between us is only good over short distances. I'm too far away to sense more than the rough direction I need to travel, like a faint magnetic pull. She's somewhere in the northwest quadrant, third maybe fourth circle.

I narrow my eyes and inspect every straggly bush for twitching branches, ears straining for the faintest rustle of leaves. The silence is unnerving. I take a deep breath—the air still has the after-bite of winter—and my chest spasms. I have to cover my mouth with both hands to stifle the cough. The shadows remain stubbornly empty. Perhaps I really am alone out here.

Only one way to be sure.

I step away from the tree and into a mottled patch of sunlight. Nothing happens. No telekinetic punch to send me sprawling to the ground, no smothering net of tykae energy to leave me bound and helpless. I jump back behind the bulk of the tree, sweating and cursing. The Hunter must have doubled back. I've got to warn Tara!

Sending a broadband telepathic call across half the forest is easy, but setting up a private link is a lot trickier, especially if you don't want anyone else to know you're doing it. Eyes closed, I picture a glowing strand of energy following that magnetic pull; I stretch it thin as gossamer and then give it a mirror sheen. That should be enough, I hope, to deflect any scans and keep our conversation secret. All I have to do now is maintain the focus. Not as easy as it sounds. Face screwed up in concentration I *reach* as far as I can… Tara grabs my questing link, strengthens it and makes it secure.

<Alden! What are you doing?>

I can feel how angry she is. She's bound to be, given the risk I'm taking. If the Hunter catches even a hint of our t-talk, he'll be able to pinpoint our location.

<Tara, the Hunter—>

<Shut it. You need to move. Now.>

Through our t-link I can feel her crouched by the granite shelf that marks the northwest edge of the fourth circle. <But—>

<Idiot, you can't hide at the Lightning Tree, it's one of the first places the Hunter will look.>

Oh, yeah.

The lightning tree has a huge gash in it from, you guessed it, a lightning strike. It's a great place to hide. Or would be, if the Hunter didn't know about it too. I flinch as the buzz of a tykae scan rakes the far side of the tree.

<Too late. He's here.>

My legs tremble with the need to run. Frantically, I strengthen my defensive shield; it will deflect the Hunter's scan, at least while my strength holds out, but it can't hide me from plain sight. And pretty soon the Hunter will be right on top of me. My chest feels tight and there's a scream building in my throat. I press my lips together to stop it getting out.

I'll have to make a break for it. I crouch, ready to run.

A telepathic scream reverberates across the forest. It's Tara. She's in trouble. I risk a glimpse around the bole of the tree and catch sight of the masked Hunter as he turns and lopes off westwards.

Tara's telepathic whisper tickles and is gone. <Run! Meet me in an hour. Third circle, south-east quadrant.>

I'm already running as the t-link breaks, terrified and grinning at the same time. Tara is drawing the Hunter away from my position. She's giving me a chance. I head east, dodging through the trees, senses straining for any hint of pursuit. A low hanging branch dumps old snow on my head as I scramble past; thorns hook and claw at clothes and exposed skin.

At first light, when the six Prey had scattered into the forest arena, I'd revelled in the sense of adventure. Tara had to tell me to stop bounding around. "It's like being out with a puppy," she'd said, scowling. Now the light feels treacherous, like it's pointing me out: Here he is. Come and get him.

I slow to catch my breath. Most of the snow has melted, though stubborn pockets lurk in shaded dells and amongst the thicker copses. If I'm going to survive this, I've got to be smart. I fight off a sinking feeling in my gut—my older brother, Zand, never tires of telling me how pathetic my tykae skills are. Focus on practicalities: my canteen is almost empty. I drain the last mouthful and come up with a plan.

It's hard work balancing speed and stealth, but I make good time cutting south through the forest. Relief makes my legs feel a bit wobbly when I finally spot the Lovers' tree, named for the way its trunk, split into two at the base, twines around itself. Its roots hump and snake into the stream, forming a perch for me to balance on as I refill my canteen. I drink greedily and then glance up through the branches; from this angle they seem to claw at each other as they struggle to catch the pale spring sun, making the whole look more like a fight to the death than an embrace.

This is as good a place as any to rest up. From here I can cut southwest towards the rendezvous point. I sit with my back to the trunk, feet braced on the thick roots and listen to the gurgle and chatter of the stream. A faint splash and pop sets my heart racing. It's just a stupid fish.

Master Tomak's dry rasp replays in my memory: A warrior's mind is clear. A warrior's mind is focussed. Only then can he effectively command the tykae energy that resides within him. Only then can he win!

Without thinking, I pull my lucky stone from my pocket and roll it in the palm of my hand. Its surface is perfectly smooth, except for a crease that forms a streak of purple across the bottom two thirds of its length. At every fifth turn I trace the crease with my thumb and then start the count again. My heart slows to a trot and then a steady walk. With a frown of concentration I set the stone turning slowly in the air, using a whisper of tykae to both support its weight and control its spin.

"Hey look, it's the noik." The low-voiced call comes from behind me.

I grab my stone from the air and scramble to my feet. Dyl is half-hidden by a spiky evergreen. He's a year older than me, tall and skinny with whipcord muscles.

"Where's Tara?" Dyl asks as he pushes his way out of the bushes. "Let me guess. She's sent you to hide out here, while she takes on the run for Home Rock by herself."

Home Rock is the final goal for all the Prey. It is a man-high fist of granite set into a clearing and surrounded by seven roughly concentric circles mapped out across the forest. Home Rock stands in the centre of the first circle and marks the finish point of the game.

"No. We're meeting up at—" I snap my mouth shut, feeling stupid. Of the three teams fighting for victory against the Hunter, only one can win. The less they know about our plans the better. I straighten up, trying to look casual. "So, where's your partner then?"

"Right behind you," Mika says. She gives a snort of contempt. "Don't know why you were selected to play. Anyone can see that you're useless." Mika is fifteen, just like Tara, with the same blue eyes and braided snow-white hair.

I've got a place because Father pushed for it. And what Father wants, he gets. Zand said I'd be lucky to survive the first hour, and Father's face had twisted into that half-frustrated, half-disgusted expression that's always hovering behind his eyes whenever he looks at me. I decided, there and then, that this time I was going to prove them wrong.

I back away from Mika, face flushed, not trusting my voice, but not able to keep quiet either.

"I'm old enough."

I turned thirteen two days ago, so yes, I am old enough, just. But that isn't what Mika means. She's talking about my off-template looks: blond hair instead of white, grey eyes instead of blue, more stocky than skinny. Like that makes any difference. I'm just as good as the rest of them—that's what I keep telling myself, anyway.

Mika closes the distance between us. "What? You think you can come anywhere near your sib's score? Zand must've laughed himself sick when you got a place."

Dyl moves to my right, bracketing me between them. "Must be hard having a wimp like you for a sib."

"You're on the run, aren't you?" Mika says. "I bet the Hunter has already taken Tara out and you're just looking for a place to hide, maybe earn a couple of survivor points."

"No, he hasn't! If anyone can beat the Hunter, it's Tara."

She already has two wins under her belt; one more and she'll be raised to the rank of Hunter herself. And anyway, I'd feel it if Tara was taken. From the look on their faces I've just told them exactly what they want to know.

"Poor little noik, did you get lost then? Or have you given up already?" Dyl is smiling that sickly smile of his, buckteeth jutting between pale lips. I flash my own perfect teeth back at him. A small victory.

We're pretty close to the seventh circle that marks the outer boundary of the game, if you step beyond that it's an automatic forfeit. Not that anyone would. Better to be dragged out broken and bleeding than be branded a coward.

"I'm not a noik." The words are out before I can stop them. Taunts like that have followed me all my life, but today the barbs sink deep. After all, here I am, the genetic throwback, running and hiding while Tara takes all the risks.

Mika shuts Dyl down before he can say the obvious. "That's enough."

She pulls up her vest and I watch, open-mouthed, as Mika unwinds a length of rope from around her waist. That's against the rules! Prey are supposed to use just their wits and natural talents to defeat the Hunter. That's the whole point.

"We need to make our move. See if Tara's opened up a gap for us to slip through."

Dyl pounces. And I go down hard, stone knocked from my hand. Mika wraps me in a vice-like telekinetic grip, while Dyl trusses me up good: hands behind my back, feet hobbled.

"You're wasting time," I gasp. I can taste blood. "I bet Nyki's team is already closing in on Home Rock."

"Nah, the Hunter took them out an hour ago. It's just us

and Tara now." Mika looks pleased with herself.

Dyl grins and draws back his foot for a kick, but I'm ready for him. He yelps as a loop of tykae catches his foot in mid-air. I tighten my grip and watch as he hops and curses, arms swinging wildly for balance. Mika laughs and grabs him around the waist before he lands flat on his face. She holds onto him until he stops fighting to reach me.

"No wonder Zand's so mean," Mika says, looking me straight in the eyes. "Having the likes of you as a sib would screw anyone up."

"Yeah," Dyl spits. "No one wants a noik in their bloodline."

I want to scream at them both. I want to take the memories of all the things that Zand has done and shove them into their heads. But instead I just lie there, trembling and blinking. It's my secret. I can't let anyone else see what my life is really like.

Mika clamps my ankles in a painful telekinetic grip and starts to drag me across the uneven ground. I grit my teeth, determined not to cry out. There's no point in struggling. I've got no chance against the two of them.

"Here's a good spot," she says. They dump me in a bank of snow. I shake my head and blink away ice crystals. "That should keep you busy until Tara comes looking."

"Feel free to call for help," Dyl says over his shoulder. They both laugh.

A surge of anger sets me struggling, but the rope just bites tighter. I stop when I start to slide downhill, my legs disappearing into a much deeper drift. I can feel the slope where the ground dips sharply beneath me. Instinct sets me pulling up tykae energy, ready to create a cocoon of warmth to snuggle in. I stop myself. That's what they want me to do. Use up all my strength fighting the cold, leaving Tara to face the Hunter alone.

A numbing ache spreads through shoulders and hips where they press against the cold ground. I use a sliver of tykae to try to lever myself into a sitting position, but instead end up chest deep in snow. There's a layer of solid ice under the drift and the combination of body heat and weight is enough to create a slide that, at any other time, would have been fun.

"Hey! You can't leave me here." Panic forces the words out. I slide a little deeper. Keep still. Calm down. I need my lucky stone. Where...? I remember the jolt as I hit the ground, Dyl busy punching while Mika consolidated her telekinetic hold, and the stone spinning away from me. I launch a low level scan, testing for its familiar resonance in the surrounding bushes.

Nothing.

My stomach clenches. Maybe Dyl or Mika picked it up. The thought of someone else touching my lucky stone kindles a furious determination. I close my eyes—trying to ignore the ache building in fingertips and toes, and the cold squelch of snow that's found its way up one trouser leg—and send delicate tendrils of tykae energy to investigate the binding securing my hands. It's a complex twisting pattern of knots that I haven't come across before. My heart sinks. It'll take too long. My priority has to be Tara. I've got to warn her about Mika and Dyl. It means admitting that I let myself be captured. But what's new there? It's what they're all expecting.

This time I'm too far away to sense her presence. I'll have to fish for her. Digging deep, I fashion a dart, needle sharp and just as bright, one end trailing a gossamer thread of energy linked directly to my well of tykae.

I focus on the dart, imbuing it with part of my awareness. With a pulse of energy I *reach* blindly: third circle, southeast quadrant. It's too far and I know it. Still, I've got to try. I push harder probing, probing... Come on, Tara. You have my telepathic signature. Please be looking out for me, just in case the runt you got saddled with has got himself into trouble.

The thread flickers. Collapses. With a gasp I let it go. It would have been too easy to find her on the first cast. I shift the angle, more south than east, and try again. I can feel myself unravelling, energy spooling into grey nothingness.

<Tara, please.>

It's a whisper, tightly wound around the thread that defines me. It hurts. Like I'm being scraped out by a rusty blade, bleeding what's left of my energy into the void of not-Tara. I can feel myself falling, and there's nothing I can do about it.

A shudder runs through me and I open my eyes. For long seconds nothing makes sense; the world is dim and grey and cold. I try to shift position. Suddenly I really need to pee.

Not now!

All I can see is dirty snow. My shoulders must've carved a hole as I slipped further down the slope, leaving me with space to breathe, but little else. No choice now. I've got to get out of here My thoughts are as sluggish as my body, and at first I can't get a grip on what tykae energy remains to me. It's hard, tracing the intricate tangle of knots that bind my wrists. Once I've got the whole thing pictured in my mind, I'll be able to figure out where to pull…

…the ache in my bladder spikes…

NO! I will not be found tied-up and soaked in pee. Father will never forgive me and Zand will crow about it forever. I blink away tears, telling myself it's anger and not panic that's blurring the world. Come on, this isn't so different from all those times Zand left me locked in the cellar. Over the years, I've learnt to ignore hunger and thirst, and yes, the need to pee. I call it my daydream strategy. I invoke it now, even though I know it will waste valuable time. But what choice do I have?

I'm seven years old. Zand grins as he hands me the Box. It doesn't feel too bad at first, just a warm buzzing in my fingers. The sensation gradually turns into a burning itch that worms its way into my hands and then, as tears begin to prick, winds crimson bands of pain around my wrists. I drop the Box, rubbing at my hands and trying hard not to cry.

Zand laughs. "I knew you couldn't do it." He sneers at my snuffling attempts to hide the pain. "You're such a baby." The taunt hurts. Master Tomak doesn't blame Zand when he drops the Box.

I can hear the Master's dry, patient voice whispering the lesson over and over. "Close your mind to the pain. Focus only on the task."

I pick the Box up, slot my fingers into the holes and trigger the test again. The mechanism inside the box is tricky; you have to find the switch to turn it off. Closing my eyes I stretch out my senses, feeling my way through the twists and turns of miniature cogs, gears and levers: looking for the right sequence of pull, push, twist and turn that will release the switch and stop the pain. I'm sweating; my fingers and hands feel like they're on fire. But Zand is watching, so I can't give up. I stifle a gasp as pain lances up my arms. Zand is saying something, but I can't hear him. Tangled in the intricacies of the Box my mind can't spare a second's attention for anything else.

Click.

A small cube rises from the centre of the Box; the subliminal hum cuts off, the pain stops. I open my eyes to find that I'm on my knees.

Zand pries the Box from my numb fingers and silently examines it, turning it over and over. He's frowning. I can feel the question at the front of his mind. How did you do that? But he doesn't ask. Instead he turns his back on me and walks out.

I come back to myself with a loud sniff. My wrists are on fire and there's an awful pricking in my fingertips. It takes me a moment to realise that my hands are free. I force numb fingers to deal with the less complicated knot that hobbles my feet and kick my way out of the snowdrift. Stumbling like a drunkard, I relieve myself against the nearest tree. Only then do I try and figure out what happened.

There's no way that Tara could have got back to me in time, even if she knew where I was. I examine the rope; it hasn't been cut. Maybe Nyki? But why would she help me? No—I shake my head, trying to clear it—the Hunter has already captured Nyki's team. It's hard to think straight.

Find Tara. Make the rendezvous.

I stumble through the forest, defensive weave wrapped tight. The sun is overhead. For a moment I'm glad of its almost-warmth. Then it hits me: I'm late. A twisted root catches my foot and suddenly I'm on my hands and knees on the ice-hard ground. I want to let go and just lie there. I want it to be over. But the game will go on until all the Prey have been captured, or someone gets past the Hunter and touches Home Rock. I remember the look on Father's face and push myself to my feet.

Third circle is a fat circular strip of land thick with broadleaved trees. As I step through the gap between two gnarled trunks an arm clamps around my chest, its strength augmented by a crushing band of tykae. A hand slaps across my mouth.

"It's me," Tara whispers, her voice hoarse. "Stop struggling."

I go limp and we both end up in a tangle of limbs on the forest floor.

She pushes me away, frowning. "You're soaked through. What happened to you?"

"Mika and Dyl," I say.

Tara snorts. "That bitch. Thinks she can sneak a win by taking out my partner? Well, she's in for a surprise."

Tara smiles and I smile back. I can't quite believe it. The exhaustion sloughs away, though I still feel dizzy when I get to my feet. I don't think she notices.

"No sign of the Hunter," Tara says. "Chances are he's busy bagging Mika and Dyl. Now's our chance."

I do my best to mimic the careful prowl of her movements as we cut straight across second circle and close in on Home Rock.

<I'm going to make the run.> Tara's about ten strides south of my position, hidden amongst the trees.

<Wait. We still don't know where the Hunter is.>

<C'mon Alden, we can win this!>

Her excitement is infectious. I can't help grinning.

<I'm closer. I'll do it.>

<I'm the fastest.> Exasperation stripes Tara's words. Her tone softens. *<Get ready to distract and defend.>*

Tara sprints like a deer flushed from cover. In five thundering heartbeats she covers more than half the distance to Home Rock. I want to yell with excitement. There's a flicker of movement to my right.

<Tara!> Too late. The force of the tykae strike lifts Tara into the air before sending her sprawling face down on the rough, pebble-strewn ground.

A sharp barking laugh cuts the sudden silence. The Hunter steps out of green shadow into the sunlight dappled edge of the clearing: a tall stringy adolescent, snow-white hair coming loose from the single braid down his back, face masked by the likeness of a ravening wolf.

"Come out. Come out. Wherever you are."

The sound of his voice is like a slap. I drop to my belly, heart hammering. It can't be Zand. It just can't. Instinct kicks in and I pour every last drop of tykae energy into my defensive shield. Over the years I've perfected the art of concealment, an act of simple survival growing up with an older brother like Zand. I feel his scan slipstream over my shield and skip beyond my position.

Right now, the best tactic is to abandon Tara, circle round and wait it out. I might get another opportunity when Mika's team makes their run. After all, only one member of a team has to touch Home Rock to win.

It's what Tara would do.

But I can't move. I watch, transfixed, as Tara struggles to rise. Blood darkens one side of her face; thick, slow motion drops spatter the ground as she raises her head and rolls onto her side. I yearn to *reach* out and touch her mind, but that's what Zand is waiting for. He can use an active link to backtrack my location. Tara starts to push herself up into a sitting position.

"Last chance," Zand says, too loud in the green-gold stillness.

Zand has that look on his face. The familiar paralysis takes hold and I bury my head in my arms. Hunters are not allowed to step inside the first circle, but Zand doesn't need to. Tara yelps as she's dragged across the clearing, her ankles bound in a savage telekinetic grip. It's against the rules to use excessive force to subdue the Prey, but Zand doesn't care about the rules. He just cares about winning.

My brother gives the treeline one last raking look, and then leans over to place his hand on Tara's scratched and bleeding leg. Skin-to-skin contact, that's all Zand needs to inflict his punishments. I know what comes next; my body trembles with remembered agony.

All choices flee when Tara begins to scream.

I cower under the bushes, trying to block out the sounds tearing the air. I can almost feel the needles of tykae energy piercing my body. Zand is laughing, the way he always does when he's got me trapped and thrashing at his feet.

The screams cut off. I peer through the bushes. Tara is

curled into a ball, her body shuddering. She draws a breath and lets out a wracking sob.

"What's it to be? You or the girl?" Zand shouts across the clearing.

I feel sick. Tara's hands scrabble weakly at the pebbles as she tries to crawl away. Her whimpered "please" tears something inside me. I step into the clearing.

"I knew it." Zand's face twists with disgust. He stabs a finger at me. "You should've run or stayed hidden. You might still have had a chance to get past me."

A mountain of anger and hurt lodges in my throat, damming the words that I've practiced night after night for this moment. Instead I weave my fury into the lattice of my defensive shield.

At least Tara is quiet now.

"I want to thank you," Zand says. "For leading me to Tara. I would never have found her without you."

Suddenly I'm cold all over. I glance across at Tara, furtive and guilty. She's curled in a ball, not moving.

"Tara's good. I'll give her that. It was a smart move, drawing me away from you. Almost worked too."

"You doubled back," I say flatly.

"Yeah," Zand smirks. "Found you pissing up a tree."

The last word is half-shouted as Zand thrusts out a hand. The energy strike sends me staggering backwards, but I keep my feet and my silence. Zand never stops until you beg, and sometimes not even then. I retreat, drawing Zand as far away from Tara as I can. He swipes at the branches blocking his path as he skirts the edge of the clearing, but I know he won't risk automatic disqualification by stepping into the first circle itself. That's the one rule he won't break.

Zand's grin is all teeth. He pulls something from his pocket and tosses it up into the air. I flinch away and then realise what it is. The stone—my stone—catches the light as it twists and falls. With a cry I *reach* for it. The instant of relief as my telekinetic fingers close around its smooth surface is blasted away by a roar of white agony. The ground leaps up to smack me in the face. I squint at a world reduced to a smear of blue-white edged with a creeping darkness.

I have to get up. I have to face him.

Gasping, one hand cradling my ribs, I struggle to rise. It's my brother's harsh laughter that finally gives me the strength to lock my knees and stand.

"You're not…" It's hard to get my breath; my chest hurts. "Not going to win. Not this time."

Zand just glares at me. I can feel his fury beating against my faltering shield. "You're done," he hisses between clenched teeth. "This time tomorrow you'll wake up in the dorms and I won't have to look at your noik face ever again."

So that was why Father pushed me into the game: one final test before consigning his faulty offspring to the dorms where all the unwanted end up. The betrayal threatens to swallow me whole. I clench my fist and feel the hard shape of the stone press into my palm.

"You won't get rid of me that easily," I spit back at him.

I know that Mika's team is still out there; if I can distract Zand for long enough they might have a chance. I don't want to win anymore. I just want Zand to lose. My brother raises both fists. I can't keep him out for much longer; pretty soon it'll be me screaming.

The click of scattered pebbles fills the clearing. I stare, eyes wide with surprise. Zand turns in time to see Tara slap her bloodied palm against Home Rock.

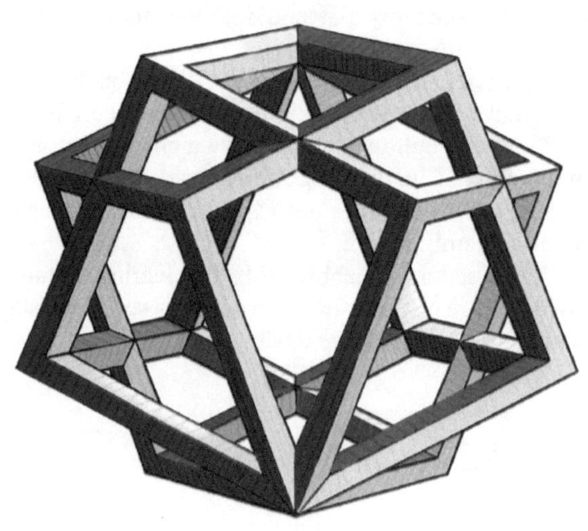

The Song of the Sky

by

Sanem Ozdural

Sanem Ozdural was born in Ankara, Turkey in the 70s, and spent her childhood from age seven onwards in England. Happy days at a quintessentially British boarding school in Surrey helped forge her character and tastes, not to mention lasting friendships. Making her way to the U.S. she studied economics at Princeton University. After graduating from Boston University School of Law, she moved to New Orleans where she practiced as a prosecutor and civil litigator, and spent seven wonderful years living in the French Quarter. In 2004 she migrated from New Orleans via Washington, D.C., reaching New York City in 2006, where she lived and practiced law until 2013. She is currently teaching business law at Koç University in Istanbul.

Sanem was an avid bridge player until the tenth round of revisions to her debut novel *LiGa*^{TM}, although she is now thoroughly enjoying an indefinite bridge sabbatical, and imagining all sorts of stories that feature absolutely no bridge or chess. In the second book in the *LiGa* series, *the **Dark** shall do what Light cannot*, Sanem took us to Pera, a place which lies beyond the Light Veil, on the other side of reality. There are light trees there that eat sunlight and bear fruit which, in turn, lights up and energises (literally) the community of Pera. There are light birds that glitter in the night because they have eaten the seed of the lightberry. She also introduced us to Shadow, the formidable soul of Pera Fundamental to the life of every person in Pera is the *Book of Shadow* – not so much a single book as a library of stories, poems and songs that inform the psychology, sociology and mythology of the Perans. *The Song of the Sky* tells how the light tree and the light birds came to be as they are today.

I want to know how things work! I want to understand why!

You must watch and listen to the voices of the world to know and to understand why. Close your eyes and ears and truly, deeply listen to the Song of the Sky...

THE SONG OF THE SKY

The Sky seems empty only to those who cannot fly...

We are many
We are One.
We are unseen under the Sun
But under the Dark One, we sparkle as if touched by the golden hand of the Sun.
In the deepest ocean where the Sun never ventures, and only the Dark One adventures... Our cousins glimmer and flicker like tiny morsels of the Golden One.
Under the stars we dance with a blue green fire in the darkest forests, and we glow in earthly corners under the black mantle of the Dark One.
Indeed we do. Under the Sky at night, each and every One.
And the Sun?
She is asleep in the River; she cannot see us, not one, not Anyone.
Unseen by the Sun
But not unseen by Everyone.
Have we borrowed the light of the Sun?
No indeed. Light is not the sole domain of the Golden One.
Light can indeed be worn by Anyone from the deepest ocean to the darkest forest
Anywhere, anywhen...

*

There is a pond in a forest. The surface of the pond is unbroken, disturbed only by concentric ripples caused by various insects, flying, hovering, dipping and diving but never quite breaking the surface skin of the pond. For those that fly and hover on the surface, the pond is the World.

There are trees in the forest that surround the pond. Each tree is a World, and the forest, too, is a World.

There are also two worlds that exist both within and without the world of the forest. These two worlds are defined, not by the physical domain of wood, trees, earth and water, but by light. While there are significant overlaps, the world of the forest by day is startlingly different from the world of the forest by night. For instance, fireflies do not dance in the world of the day. This is simply the way of things, and it will never change.

*

The bluest sky is reflected in the deepest ocean, and the moods of the ocean change with the motions of the Sky: from the wildest to the mildest.

The ocean is one world, and it consists of many worlds. There are also worlds in the ocean, like the forest, that are defined by light, or more particularly sunlight: its presence and absence. There are creatures of all sizes that exist within these two worlds. There are overlaps, to be sure, but the differences sparkle! Literally. Like fireflies dancing in the forests in the night, so do creatures in the sea sparkle and glitter like starlight. This is the way of things, and it will never change.

*

One day, a small bird swooped down from the Sky. She swooped in an arc across the Sun's bright golden eye.

By all accounts, it was a blue bird with a sharp black beak and ruffles of white in its tail feathers. These accounts, of which I speak, are to be found lapping gently upon the shore, for it is there, they said, that the small bird first found its place. It was cousin to the seagulls, said eyewitnesses that sparkled in waves at night. So many eyewitnesses are hard to discount.

The time of day is important, say our analysts, and who are

we to argue? As previously mentioned, the bird was arcing across the golden Sun, but what was not mentioned was that it was at the time when the Sun was but a few steps from her rest, sinking, red-gold, into the horizon. It was the between-time for the worlds of night and day.

The bird grew hungry, and indeed, this was the reason for its soaring approach in the first place, we are given to understand. Our eyewitnesses tell us that the bird was a swooper of some note, and the small fish that had caught its sharp eye hadn't the shadow of a chance. Now, this small fish was not part of the bird's regular diet, for it (the bird) belonged to the world of day, and the other (the fish) was a dark dweller. But the bird was hungry, as we have ascertained, and in that state, was not particular about its palate, and swallowed the fish in haste.

Our eyewitnesses once again recount that this fish was a sparkler like them. Due to the nature of light in water (it does not go as far as light on water), creatures that belong to the world of the Dark One do not necessarily appear at the same time as nighttime dwellers on land. Some, particularly those that inhabit the deeper reaches of the ocean, are forever locked in a world of utter darkness, broken only by such light as might be produced by them. The small fish that the bird espied was not a creature that dwelt in the nether portions of the sea, but nevertheless, its life revolved around a lightscale different to that of the bird that flew above the sea.

Is the timing so important? we asked. And we were assured by our analysts that this was the cause of all that came to be in the thereafter, and who, in the world, are we to argue with such authority?

But one fish? One single fish? we retorted, could hardly be the cause of all that followed. Not *all* that followed, some of it perhaps, we conceded.

It was not one fish, replied the analysts reasonably; it could not be one single solitary sparkler in the sea that caused an event of such magnitude. But it was the beginning. Not the beginning of the end, but the beginning of the beginning…

*

The forest is close to the sea in this place. These worlds –
that of the forest and of the sea – co-exist comfortably within
a short geographical distance. The forest was a convenient
distance for one blue bird of distant sea gull extraction, and it
grew accustomed to exploring this new space where it found
plenty to forage for in the pond.

We have already stated that the bird belonged to the world
of day but, with that one fish, had started to find its
alimentary niche in the between time when the Sun wanes,
but before the Dark One completely reigns. The bird was a
stickler for things that worked, and it had found that hunting
at twilight gave it a competitive advantage over its brethren.
Good for the bird! we applaud.

In any event, the little bird took its newfound advantage to
the world of the forest, and started to hunt and forage in the
twilight hour. Now, remember that these are two different
worlds that the little bird had started to inhabit, and when
doing so, even the most careful and assiduous traveller is apt
to make a mistake, a misstep, a miscalculation…

*

We will leave the narration of the next part of this tale to our
key eyewitness, our one and only Shadow:

*Now, the small bird flew around the pond, for water was
the place she best knew
And she flew…
Longer and longer she flew, looking for a morsel or two
All through the day the little blue bird flew…
And as the light grew dim, brothers, what did the bird do?
She could not see as well as before, for her eyes belonged
not to the world of the other, the one they call the Sun's
brother.
No, indeed, the little bird's eyesight was not accustomed to
the half light.
And as she flew, keeping her eyes trained on the surface of
the pond for a morsel or two…*

She caught sight of a flicker, a glimmer, a tiny flash of bluish light, similar to the sparkler she'd first caught in the water. With her eyesight none too keen, the little bird assumed it was the same thing and swooped low
Reaching for the bluish glow…

*

…The blue-white flicker danced a complicated step in the waning light. It was quite a sight, said our keen eyewitness. A tiny star-like mite dancing to an unheard strain in the Night. This dancing light turned out to be, not a fish as the myopic bird surmised, but a winged denizen of the night, out to snare himself a mate, and perhaps a bite. As our keen eyewitness would say: these are things that happen in the Night. It is the way of things, and it is right.

This tiny sparkling dancer has been called a firefly by those who do not inhabit the world of the forest. But in the forest they are known as star dancers. Names can be confusing, especially when they refer to the same thing.

In any event our blue bird turned out to be a philosopher in this instance, and when it had gulped down the unsuspecting mote, it might have blinked a few times on account of the unfamiliar flavor, but went ahead, undeterred, on her route.

And the little bird decided that since this sparkler in the night was easier by far to catch than the little fishies, she would do best to stick to the pond rather than the sea. Besides, the wind tended to be less wicked on account of the trees.

This went on day after day, and many moons waxed and waned as the residents of the forest watched the little bird's progress…

And all the while, the little bird lived amidst the flowering trees, all through summer's greenery and stayed on in the forest, as the air got colder.

*

In time, it is said, the blue bird found a mate, who had found his way from the beach in the same way as the first bird.

This, too, is the way of things: it only takes one to make a path.

My kin, this is the way of things. This is how it all begins.
Over time, the birds grew in number, now living under the shade of trees instead of flying across the sea.
And like the first blue bird, they foraged for winged creatures instead of sparklers of the sea...
And one day, one small bird, descendant of the original blue bird, picked up the fallen fruit of a tree...

*

As the little bird ate the fruit, the seed of the tree was transformed by its alimentary canal, report our researchers. Our analysts confirmed that this is a reasonable, and moreover *probable* explanation for the events that unfolded in the thereafter. Our analysts remind us that the blue bird and its descendants had grown accustomed to consuming the star dancers in the forest as part of their regular diet. To put it succinctly: they ate insects that glowed with an inner light. These birds ate light.

And so, when this unassuming descendant of the original blue bird ate the seed of a tree ... What tree was it, you ask? After careful research our analysts have placed it in the same family as one solid, stocky character with large, flat, dark green leaves and a soft sweet fruit with a velvety purplish brown skin – known by certain non-forest dwellers as a *fig*. Names *can* be confusing, as we established, and in the forest this tree is known as much for its girth and its shade as for its fruit. By those who shelter beneath the expansive welcome of its leaves or nibble upon its honey-sweet fruit, it is known as the sweet shelterer.

Can you guess what came to be? Of the seed of the tree that the bird that ate light swallowed?

*

luminescent

blue   white   bright light

blue white   sparkling glittering star-like

bejeweled diamond bright   in

darkest Night blackest sky

branches black and bright with star-like glittering flickering marble-like

sweet shelter   shelter bright in darkest Night   velvet black

under moonlight   sit under sky-dark leaves studded with starlight

Come, sit

Under me

I   am

Light   Tree

We are many
We are One
We provide shelter under the Sun
But when the day is done
We glitter like stars under the Dark One
And we are seen
By Everyone
Who can say
We are None?

That, at least, is the account of our eyewitnesses, including none other than our star and one and only Shadow who happened to inhabit the very pond next to which this remarkable (might we say *miraculous*?) event occurred, and we do have it on the best authority (our analysts) that this is the most *probable* explanation for the birth of the first Light Tree. THE FIRST LIGHT TREE!

Shadow also related that it, too, occasionally found shelter from the Sun under the dark, velvety leaves of the first Light Tree. Our Sun is a good sort in many ways, but there are times when she – quite unintentionally – is apt to get ahead of herself in the heat and brightness departments. She can get just a tad overzealous; a bit of a workaholic, say some of our analysts (we know they mean it in the best possible way), who does not always know when enough is enough… and that is exactly when large, dark, velvety leaves provide the most welcome relief. Until the Sun comes to her senses, of course, and either gives way to her brother, or at least pulls some cloudy curtains to cover up some of her blasting brightness! What a sizzler!

And the fruit of the Light Tree? The original Light Tree, that is… We wonder how different it might have tasted from the kind one gets nowadays, which has such a distinctive flavor, and of course, the aroma, well, can only be said to smell of light! Our researchers, as always, seek to enlighten us on this point, but it has proved elusive thus far. Our analysts, on the other hand, who have spent countless days poring over what data the researchers have been able to glean, suggest – they stress there is no certainty – that the fruit is likely to have been lighter in texture and translucent, illuminated like a beacon by the cold bluish light of the seed of the lightberry. As everyone knows, the flesh of the lightberry nowadays – a most distant incarnation of the original – is dense and dark, almost black, unwilling to let the light of the seed shine through, and the only time that the Light Tree is able to appear in full lightful splendor is during the awakening season when it flowers. Oh, the flower of the Light Tree! That transcendent translucence shining like liquid stars decked out in glorious hues of pink, purple and blue. What a sight to behold in the Night!

Yes, yes, I hear you say, we all know the beauty of the flower of the Light Tree, but do get on with the story.

And who better to recount the next chapter than our star, the inimitable, the one and only Shadow, our key eyewitness:

So the tree grew
And the birds flew
   until they grew tired and rested upon the bough of the
tree...
and flew
     until they became hungry and nibbled upon the berry of
   a tree
that ate light...
      and still they flew
Through the air the birds flew
Beating their wings, gently at times, gliding, fluttering at
times
   Upon the blue canvas of the sky
     They flew.
And the Sun shone
   all day long
Upon the blue canvas of the sky through which
   the birds flew
Did the birds fly at night too?
   Yes, so they did. They flew all along the black mantle that
the Dark One
     had flung across the sky
In darkness they flew...
Even when the dark was complete, my kin
When the sky was blacker than his dark eyes
Blacker even than the starling's wing...

How? You are right to ask. How could these birds, relatives (distant) of a certain blue bird with uncertain eyesight, manage to fly through the night sky without encountering some serious mishap?

They were aided by the Light Tree. Guided is a better word, perhaps. They were *guided* by the Light Tree, let us say. We saw how the light of a sparkling fish (inadvertently) guided the little blue bird to a new life in the forest, and then it was the bird who in turn helped guide the birth of the Light Tree, so the guidance appears to have come full circle as a steady diet of the berries of the Light Tree transformed those distant descendants of the original blue bird into something altogether different... I *could* tell you, but I would not do it

justice. For the end of our story let's listen to the Song of the
Light Tree:

Fly! Soar!
In the
swelling sky, fly
As high as you wish,
Bird
As long as you must,
Bird, fly...
There is nothing to stop you
Nothing can stop you,
Bird, fly!

So fly!
Are lit like stars, Bird
Your wings, Bird
High!
So you can fly!
Even in the night, Bird
There is light, Bird
Fly!
Higher, Bird
High!

This is the way of things. As it was then, so it is now...

(From The Book of Shadow)

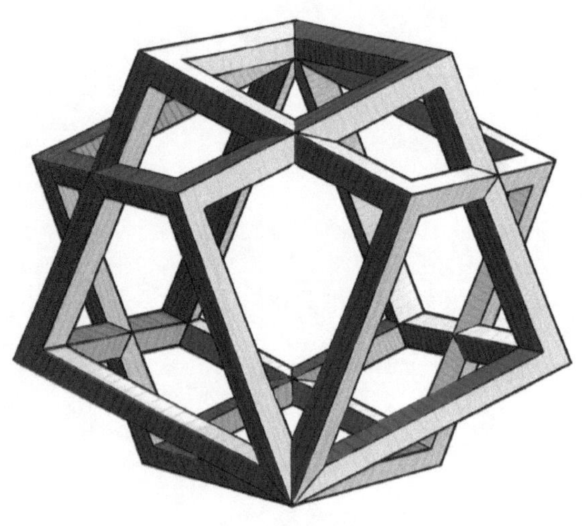

Forbidden Fruit
And so Eve tempts the devil

by

Tanya Reimer

Born and raised in Saskatchewan, Tanya enjoys using the tranquil prairies as a setting to her not-so-peaceful speculative fiction. She is married with two children which means among her accomplishments are the necessary magical abilities to find a lost tooth in a park of sand and whisper away monsters from under the bed. As director of a non-profit Francophone community center, Tanya offers programming and services in French for all ages to ensure the lasting imprint and growth of the Francophone community in which she was raised. What she enjoys the most about her job is teaching social media safety for teens and offering one-on-one technology classes for seniors.

Tanya was fifteen when she wrote her first column. She has a diploma in Journalism/Short Story Writing. Today, she actively submits to various newspapers, writes and publishes the local Francophone newsletter for her community, and maintains a blog at Life's Like That. In 2014 her debut novel *Ghosts on the Prairies, A Sacred Land Story* for adults, was published by Elsewhen Press, followed by *Petrified* a young adult Whispering novel, from Sunbury Press. In 2016, Elsewhen Press published *Can't Dream Without You*, a novel from the Dark Chronicles set in a post-apocalyptic Canadian landscape where Whisperers are trying to return to immortality.

I

I liked this town. I'd been here two days, but it was home. Not one rule was thrown at me, not one diabolic idea. I knew we should move on, but damn, it was hard. Maybe it was the wide-open spaces or the quiet streets. I always did like places where I could think.

A satisfying crunch echoed in the car when Eve bit into her apple.

Maybe it was her.

I parked and glanced out the window of our clunker. Sally was picking apples off her trees along the side of the motel, in shorts that were too short for the weather. She waved, and Eve leaned against me to wave back.

Sally ran the motel we were parked in front of. Eve took a shining to her, but then again, Eve loved everyone with a heavenly passion that amused me.

Taking Eve in my arms, I said, "Something homey about a town where everyone waves to ya, don't you think?" I was ready to bite into her apple with her, but a familiar zap sizzled in the backseat, grinding my nerves.

Still, I didn't miss a beat. Brushing the pendant around Eve's neck, I tapped into the power of Hell. The shiny apple locket was the smallest link-up I'd made, yet it was the most powerful as it transported the desires of those touching it, interweaving magic and technology in a way only I understood.

Responding to my need to protect her from the Hell I tried to escape, she fell asleep in my arms. I rested her gently against the seat before facing the devil in the backseat who had dropped in on our lovely moment.

He looked confused, but his memory gun was pointed at me so I couldn't use his sudden displacement within the worlds to my advantage.

"Xaphan, you're a hard devil to find," he said.

"Means I don't want to be found." I was activating the link-up kit hidden in my pocket as I spoke. "You going to take me back?" If these devils were finding me, it meant my brother had chosen sides. His betrayal wasn't a reality I was ready to face.

"You coming peacefully?"

"Depends."

He had his name embroidered in gold on his uniform, ranking him as Adam's soldier. Adam was the oldest devil in Hell. He ran Hell with more rules than I could break, but I was trying.

Rule number one was no apples, ever. I used it to my advantage, by connecting the link-up to the apple I took from Eve, then I tempted my guest with it. He grabbed it, curious.

"What is it you desire?" I asked.

Our eyes met as my disposable kit sizzled, vanishing him with it, leaving behind a fine grey powder as his desires dropped him in a new reality, apple and all.

Reaching around Eve, I opened the glovebox for a new disposable link-up kit. In my phone case, embedded in the plastic were two disks. I needed to make more tonight. I inserted one in the link-up. It was ready to transport, so I hid it in my pocket.

I was far from relaxed when I bit into another apple and returned it to Eve's hand. Then I brought Eve back with a passionate kiss I teased on her lips.

II

She smiled as I pulled away. Eve had a smile so powerful it could blow out my worst fears. My eyes lingered much too long on her lips, then they journeyed to the pendant snuggled against her bosom. I let the moment consume me, the taste of apples on my lips.

"The necklace is sexy on you, Eve." I touched it playfully. We were parked, but neither of us was eager to get out.

The locket warmed under my fingers, promising me all the powers of Hell to play with. Running my fingertip over it, I couldn't even feel the seam concealing the disk. Really, I was brilliant. More gifted now than I'd ever been. The rush tormented me, then my fingers slipped off and sneaked under the warmth of her red top. I was dizzy, suffering the fiendish power she held over me. I returned my fingers to the pendant so that I was in control again. The difference between power and loss of power was that easy with her under my fingertips.

She didn't need to know how hard it was for me to balance the two. Her ignorance kept us safe. Yet I wanted to let her in on my secret. I suppose this was my weakness. I always craved this connection to others.

"I love it, Xaphan, almost as much as I love you." Her long lashes moved slowly as she passed me her apple.

Love. I was beginning to understand. Her eyes devoured me while I broke rule number one with her, losing myself to the moment, enjoying the apple, one forbidden bite at a time.

Gosh. She was heavenly. No wonder I didn't want to return to Hell. "You like this town? We could buy a house here. You could make friends. We could have children and our own apple trees…"

"In no man's land?" she cut off my dreaming, but her voice held a bit of energy to it, so I didn't lose hope.

"I thought we were searching for your brother." She studied the crummy motel in front of us. "What would we do here?" She rubbed her thumb and finger lightly, a trait that promised rule-breaking fun.

Eyes closed, I let out a content groan. "I can't wait to find out."

"Isn't it important to find your brother? I thought we had to save him?"

Thing was, we weren't looking for my brother, we were moving around so he couldn't track us. I was cursed with the ability to create things, like the link-ups allowing inter-world travel, but he was gifted with the power to undo everything I did. It's how things balanced in the universe.

Still, thinking about my brother was hard. "He'd like apples." I glanced out the window, a deep regret drowning me. I fought back tears, missing him. When he showed, would I be able to send him off as easily as I had the other soldiers? I had my doubts. He would see my weakness, even if I didn't know it yet.

Eve took the apple from me. Her lips puckered so she could suck the juices from the core. I followed each swallow until she licked her lips, done. Turning to me, she said, "They don't have a dance club and I'd like to dance tonight."

My grin broadened like the devil I was. "We don't need a club when we can dance under the stars." I liked dancing with her. We didn't dance in Hell. Nope. We slaved. Endless work to keep us busy, because eternity was too long for a lonely starving devil. We worked our tails off day and night in hopes that we'd save the universe from collapsing on itself. Stupid, since I'd never seen evidence that the universe needed us to do this eternal labour. In fact, many worlds, like the one we enjoyed now, thought we were an evil myth. Appreciation like that made it even less worthwhile.

She rubbed my leg, waiting for me to open the door for her like the gentleman I pretended to be. I enjoyed the lingering smell of apples before I pulled the key from the ignition, a little amazed I could handle such a simple task when she had her hand on me like this.

"The city life has you spoiled," I teased. "This country life will do us good."

I was home.

Not even Paradise was this awesome, and I stayed there for twelve glorious years. A slave entranced by the beauty of those forbidden angels. Gosh. That was a good time. But nothing compared to this balancing game of power I enjoyed with Eve. Here, I was somewhat in control, yet always on the brink of losing it to her. It was a maddening rush of addictive pleasure.

Her thick brown curls were a wild, angelic mess. I studied her eyelashes. My favourite part of her. They were so long, that often, when she kissed me, they brushed against my skin, whisking away any form of control I thought I had.

I closed my eyes as her hand wandered to places females of Hell weren't allowed to explore without a permit.

Even if she left me tonight, I'd enjoyed every indulgence we'd shared.

We sat in the quiet car, in the motel parking lot, me a victim to her touch without another car in sight. Not a soul to save me. Not a bird to hear me hum peacefully inside. Nothing but us. Free and wild. Saintly and hellish.

I glanced over as she leaned forward. The pendant dangled toward freedom, stirring something in me that wanted to feel this way forever. "I'm tired of rules. When I'm with you, I feel *unlonely*." It wasn't the word I wanted. What was this feeling? How could I describe the warm happiness inside me? "I don't want to go back to that emptiness I was forced to endure. My brother figures rules are for our safety, but I've never felt as safe as I do right now. I'll carry this warmth you give me for eternity. Rules rob us of this freedom to make mistakes, to question everything." Again, freedom wasn't the right word. "There's just a certain *magic* in me that wants to create things when you're around me." I was getting closer.

Regardless, it was a good feeling, but I was a greedy devil and the more it warmed me, the more I sought to deepen it, to share it. I had no idea what *more* involved, yet I felt my creativity ignite when I whispered, "I hunger for more."

She pulled out another apple as if that might satisfy this craving. "I am not good for you." She didn't give me the apple. "You're easily entranced by my touch."

This was true, but I desired it anyway. "I can handle it," I promised her, like an out of control maniac. "You are my only good memory, and I want more."

"Surely you have one childhood memory that pleased you?"

Not of Hell.

"The best memory I have was when I discovered my talent. The joy I felt was replaced by longing when I was forced to move into a lab away from my brother to work under constant supervision and endless rules." I sat back with a heavy sigh.

Her hand settled on my thigh and shivers shot through me when she brought the apple between us.

I opened the door and leapt out before she got me to confess everything.

III

The motel had a musty smell. Eve bumped into me as I stopped in the doorway. Something was wrong. With a last breath of freedom, I flicked the light.

A somber glow enveloped the room.

My brother lounged on the bed with a link-up kit open on his lap. I missed him so much I forgot how damned I suddenly was.

"Eve, could you wait in the car? Seems my brother found

me and he looks in trouble.”

“Just a minute.” Vassago dropped the link-up kit that had brought him to me, discarding it on the bed. He came to us with three even strides. His movements were so smooth, they reminded me of dancing.

He stepped too close to Eve. I shoved him back. There was no way I'd let anyone from Hell near her. Not even my brother.

“She has a disk on her.” He snatched her purse and the bag of apples Sally had given us earlier.

Eve reached for them. “Hey!”

I guided her hand down. “I'll come get you in a minute. Okay?” She smelt like sweet apples and it was hard to pull away. “I'll get it back,” I promised her. “Don't worry. I know how to handle my brother.” I had no idea how this would play out, but her safety was my first concern. A woman like Eve would never survive Adam's rules. She belonged here, with me. I nudged her out the door before Vassago grabbed her necklace, too.

Vassago already had the purse unzipped and had dumped the contents of the bags on the bed. I watched him work, curious to learn what he sensed in her purse. Until I created more, there were only a few disks left. I controlled them and would never put one in her purse.

Proving me wrong, he pulled out a tiny disk from Eve's face powder kit.

I kept a straight face, but my insides freaked out. What was Eve hiding?

“I'm finally able to live the way I want,” I assured him.

“You think this is living? Breaking rules and mutilating your body?” He pointed to the serpent tattoo on my arm. “Eating the forbidden fruit.” He picked up an apple. The shine to it entranced him for a moment. He licked his lips and forced down a swallow.

“Hauling me in will do nothing for you, but if you bite that apple, you will feel the rush of breaking your first rule.” My promise came with a wicked smile.

He set the apple on the bed, tragically. “I am here to save you. I can't help this sense of duty I have. It's my gift, my curse.”

"Noble, but believe me, brother, I don't need saving. I can't suffer a life of eternal loneliness and neither should you. We deserve better. We'll live here. Free and wild. Sally said she was looking for a devil to warm her bed. She has three apple trees. Three. Eve could introduce you. We could dance…"

He took a deep breath. "We belong in Hell with the rest of the devils. We have everything we need there."

"We're missing a few delicious things." I pointed to the mess of apples on the bed.

Still, he persisted, "I trust that Adam's rules keep us safe."

"From what? Happiness?"

He shrugged. "It's not my duty to understand his rules."

I leaned closer to him. "I make my own rules. I decide what's safe for me."

"Xaphan." He sighed. "Link-up travel is not for you to enjoy. None of this was created for you."

"Why not? It's my power to craft these things, yet you imply they should hold no worth to me? What type of impossible rule is that? Why can't I take pride in things I slaved for? Why can't I experience the pleasures of other worlds? Why can't I come here and teach what I know?"

"It's another devil's destiny to use these link-ups. One who can handle the pressures of these worlds. Look at you." His scowl deepened. "I'm worried about you. Besides, you create these things so I can contain them. As higher life-forms, it's our duty to stay ahead of those less gifted. You create problems, I solve them. Someone else shares this knowledge with the other worlds, adapting it to their technology and magic."

Higher life-forms? We were at the bottom of the naughty list. I rolled my eyes as Eve had taught me to do, then I picked up her things, returning them to her purse.

He snapped a picture of Eve and me from my hands before I could toss it in her purse. It was a silly black and white photobooth picture with four candid shots.

"What are you doing in this image?" he asked, eyeing it, reminding me of how he'd studied the formula to the Measles Virus I'd made in Medicine Studies. He'd made short work of that virus. Annoying, yet impressive.

"It's called laughing. You're almost a thousand years old,

don't you think it's time you experience profound joy? I can't go back. My happy is with Eve."

"I don't trust her." He studied the picture from different angles, trying to find fault in it. Or maybe he was wondering how many more rules I'd broken.

"We were raised to fear females, but those teachings were wrong, Vassago. These gals have much to offer us: companionship, fun..." I didn't know how to describe the feeling bursting in me. "It motivates me to be so powerful, I foolishly let her have it."

His intense stare of the pictures deepened. "You met her here?"

"After I left Paradise."

"Paradise?" He glanced at me. "You survived?"

Ah Paradise. I melted into the memory, picking an apple off the bed and crunching into it. "It's a world all of Hell should visit. Not one rule anywhere, just wild pleasure. Don't ask how I escaped. It's a blur of forbidden fruit and lust, yet I somehow fit a disk in my link-up. Eve found me under an apple tree."

"How many worlds have you visited?" He came in closer to smell the apple, sweet juices sprayed him as I bit into it again.

"Six so far. I've planted permanent link-ups in each. They keep in contact with disposable kits I make. Link travel is now possible anywhere within those six worlds, by anyone. All I need is to insert a disk." Of course, I controlled the disks.

I handed him the disposable link-up kit from my pocket.

"They burn up?" A bead of sweat formed on his forehead, but he wasn't looking at the kit. His mouth watered for my apple. "This means you can escape any world, even Hell." Even distracted, he saw the brilliance in my creation. "That breaks rules 5157 and 6492 of World Travelling Law."

Rules. I was sick of them. "Wanna break rule number one of the Sacred Law?" I tempted him with an apple. "Sally has sweet apples."

"I missed you," he admitted, taking it from me. "Nothing the others do is a challenge like this. You push me to be smarter, to think outside the laws." His eyes remained on the forbidden fruit. "To try new things."

"I'm free, Vassago. I planned to visit other worlds, but this one requires more study. I think for myself and live with this incredible complete feeling that warms me inside. I belong here."

"The devils of this world—"

"People."

"What?"

"They're called people within this world."

"Oh." By our definitions, devils were saviours, angels were tempters, and people were free-thinkers. He frowned, something so unlike him it was amusing.

"If they are free-thinkers, they have the right to know that devils like you come here to mate their females."

"The females do not belong to them."

"Then they are controlled by them?"

"They are considered equals." I'd had a hard time with that concept, so I gave him a moment to absorb the possibilities. "It means they demand loyalty and respect, but they also return it. The way your eyes wandered Eve will get you slapped by her, and a punch from me will follow."

His brows went up, excited at the idea.

"When my children ask who their mother is, I plan to share amusing stories about her." I smirked. "About her laugh, her smile, her silly ideas. Not show them a pamphlet on how females need to be contained in cages for breeding I am only allowed every thousand years." I tightened my fist, determined to find a way to free the females of Hell.

He sat on the bed with the apple and pictures, staring at both. Thinking.

I sat beside him, easing the picture from his grip. "I can be in control if I choose to be, or I can give her control, trusting her to bring me pleasure and intense joy."

"The female out there is the mate you want to tell your sons about? A person not even from our world?"

"Not a doubt."

"Adam says their hands seduce, touching we can't refuse. We must wait until we are older and wiser to mate. These forbidden fruits have you drugged. Tempting you."

"The only rush they give me is because I know I am

breaking his most sacred rule. We can refuse the touching but a smart devil chooses not to. It's crucial for me to know the mother of my children. To sleep with her, to hold her, to protect her. It's incredible to feel her..." I wanted to say *power*, but that word would scare him. *Love?* He wouldn't understand. "*Gifts.*"

"She will never be your equal. We have freedom in Hell if we follow Adam's laws." He pulled out his memory gun. It drew directly from the magic of Hell. One blast and I'd forget all this.

My teeth pierce the skin of my apple. A drop of juice tried to escape and I licked it with a content groan.

"The secret about a freedom-thinker," he continued with less enthusiasm, "is that she will require the truth before she makes a decision."

That was worse than forgetting. I couldn't tell Eve the truth.

"She will not wish to have children with a devil. She will never trust you once she finds out you have the power to make her do your will."

"She can counter that, controlling me with her touch," I pointed out, as if that made our relationship less dangerous.

"I challenge you to use this disk or tell her the truth." He handed me the disk he'd found in her powder.

So this was his solution.

I fondled the disk with one hand while I snacked, thinking. It was old, made to escape Paradise. Who had made it? Unless Vassago planted it? I couldn't ask him without raising doubts about her. Devils had zero tolerance for out of control females.

I cracked the disk. "I present this challenge instead: I will tell her the truth, you will bite into that apple."

He nodded, accepting the challenge. "Then we will see the truth. You know how much Adam underestimates you?" Vassago chuckled. "He asked me to show his soldiers how to link-up. He thinks that if we put your mate's life in the balance, it'll force you to return with me. I didn't of course. I know you'll have prepared for this, and it would cost him good soldiers. Even my memory gun will not change your core beliefs. You must see the truth for yourself. I'll challenge you until you do."

I panicked. "Soldiers have already been by. If you didn't send them, who did?"

We stared at each other. This was a development we had not anticipated. Another devil had copied our gifts? Impossible. Still, he wouldn't lie to me, nor I to him. We were destined to challenge each other, not destroy.

I handed him the last disk from my phone case.

"Where does this one lead? It's so different, I didn't even sense it."

"This is why I have no fear of Adam's soldiers. It's fueled on desires, taking you where your heart lies. I will always return to Eve. If you plan to use it, I recommend a little stopover in Paradise. Not a hungry devil there, promise."

He held the disk. "What's it like? The connection to a mate?"

"Find out for yourself." I yanked my desire disk from him and put it in his link-up kit.

"Your female out there, could she show me this connection?"

"It annoys me that you think of her this way. Get your own girlfriend. I don't share when it comes to her. That's my rule."

His voice was barely audible. "Friend? Ah, but that's the trick, my brother. If you give her the choice, she might choose another. Don't you see? By giving yourself this freedom, you've created a trap where you might get burned. Adam is right, it's better to contain them and never feel loss."

Thrill surged through me, shooting me to my feet. I needed to do something creative. "She can pick anyone, yet she's waiting for me. I know this, because if her desires change, she'll be whisked to them by the link-up I placed around her neck."

"And when she doesn't choose you?"

I couldn't imagine that day. "I'll find another to connect with. If that doesn't work, I'll link-up to Paradise and visit those angels. But in this moment, my desires are with Eve." Again, *desires* wasn't the word I wanted to use.

While he thought about what I'd done, I examined his kit. It was a copy of my first attempt; every wire, every gear, every thread of demonic magic weaving through it. Now my last disk was nestled in it, ready to show me his desires.

"Since you went on the run, Adam hooked me up with a tracking device. If I stray, my dreams correct me. It's mighty annoying." He rubbed his forehead. "He sees everything I do."

"Enslavement." I tossed the apple core and dug through my pack for a magnet and fine needle. "Put your head flat against the wall."

He did, but he grabbed his kit and gun first, as if I might use them on him while he had his back to me. Much to my amusement, he was still clutching the apple.

I ran the magnet over the back of his neck until I felt the pull of the tracking device. "Don't move, this will pinch." I slipped the needle through his skin and into the device. "It's deactivated. Freedom is that simple to achieve. Your dreams will be your own, my gift to you." While I had him pinned, I activated the kit he held.

It was old and took a moment to power-up.

"You know," he said, looking at the desire disk that warmed while I trapped him to the wall. "If you desire her, I just have to contain her in Hell and you'll follow."

I dropped the needle and dived for the door while Vassago vanished, apple and all.

Eve waited outside, leaning against the hood of the car, her arms crossed, a fury around her that was rousing.

The relief at seeing her still in this world was deep. We would have to run. I handed her the purse and brushed the locket, ready to erase her memory, but guilt swept over me and I couldn't do it. This was no longer my desire. I wanted her to know the truth. No more lies.

"So you introduced your brother to Sally," she snapped. "Here I am waiting, and you sneaked out the back."

I peeked around the corner of the motel. Sure enough, Vassago was petting Sally's St Bernard, chatting with her, enjoying his apple one bite at a time. He glanced at me, lifting his bitten apple, enforcing my challenge from earlier.

"I have a secret to tell you," I confessed, watching him with Sally. "You might leave me once you know, but it needs to be said." My gut was in knots. "My brother and I are from another world known as Hell. A place that enslaves and calls it evolution." I waited for her to vanish. When she didn't, I continued, "My weakness is your touch, but I use the pendant to connect with the power of Hell and fight it. This connection comes at a price: you are linked to this power. Your desires will be granted."

"So if I no longer wish to be with you, I can leave?" She looked thrilled by this news.

"Yes."

Vassago was solving Sally's apple-reaching problems by lifting her on his shoulders. That broke a few rules.

Eve brushed a hand along my jaw, bringing my attention back to her. "I come from Paradise, a world that requires us to please everyone. Our evolution is at a standstill, too, because you can't please everyone without destroying yourself."

"How did you get here from Paradise?" I glanced at her purse. "The disk you hid... How?" Had I forgotten to deactivate a disk from their end? I might have. I could barely remember my escape. *A hand guided mine to insert the disk.* Was it possible I brought Eve here? Or had she brought me? Was her desire so strong, I was trapped to her? Had I lost the freewill I so desperately craved?

"How much do you understand about the locket?" I asked.

Her fingers lightly traced my tattoo, snaking up my arm. "When I touch it, I feel the connection to those who wish to find you and I will them here."

She'd been calling Adam's soldiers to us? "Why?" I asked, dumbfounded.

"I don't mean to, but this joy I feel, I wish I could bring it to others. Long ago, before your existence, before Paradise and Hell even existed. I lived here with a devil named Adam. He was cold and cruel, ruling the land with an iron heart. I tried to bring joy by sharing our wealth, but he caught me offering an apple to another devil." She dropped her head.

I brought her chin up with a finger, so our eyes met, understanding how Adam's rules protected us from the pain of betrayal. My world would have been so different had he enjoyed the way her ideas balanced his.

"I vowed to never be controlled by another this way. This

locket will allow me this freedom." Eve batted her long eyelashes. "But what if I hurt you?"

"Hurt?" I now knew why Adam's safe world bothered me so much. "I am the devil of creation. I don't fear my deeper emotions, Eve, I need to experience them. You are my *inspiration*." Yes, that was the word forever eluding me. "You inspire me to be more, to want more, to push my creativity, exploring it at impossible levels. Because of you, my brother and I will change the worlds. You are my muse."

Power erupted in me, dying to be unleashed. I saw countless possibilities, ideas I had to tempt... but first, I savoured the fruit on her lips, tasting the magic.

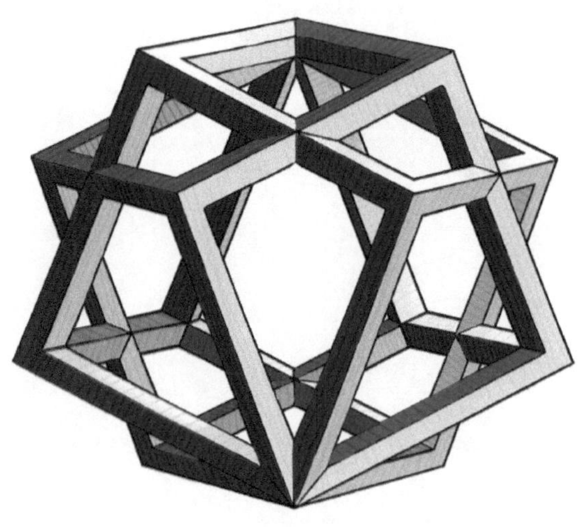

Precipitation

by

Chloe Skye

Born and raised in the idyllic green countryside outside London, Chloe has spent most of her life dreaming about high-tech dystopias where the only green is neon.

Having spent a few years working on other people's fiction, she finally got around to writing things herself; cyberpunk and space opera, since the only thing she loves more than the neon cityscape is the depths of space.

Currently, she's trying to blend the two.

The sky was slowly clearing, a muddy blue showing through the clouds for the first time in what felt like weeks. Rain had been pelting November hard, and every surface was slick with water, a patina of oil adding its own sheen to every puddle below the fifteenth storey.

Ryan sat astride the low wall of her balcony, absent-mindedly kicking her bare foot through the liquid that had collected in the fabric shielding the balcony below. The splashing noise barely intruded into her consciousness as she stared at everything and nothing in particular.

The morning's light added its own tint to the wet surfaces of the city, and Ryan could see rainbows in the splattering droplets.

All in all, it was a beautiful day for ugly deeds.

Ryan watched as a clearance car snaked along the upcity pavements five storeys above her and sloughed water off them, into the air and down onto the lowcity roads below. Sunlight sparkled through the falling droplets, giving them their own gilt shine. It looked, for all the world, like upcity was pissing on lowcity.

"Even the architecture does it these days," Ryan muttered to herself in a low voice, before lifting herself up and over the balcony wall and back into her apartment. 'Apartment' was generous, but it was home and it was hers; not even on loan, as she owned it outright.

Stripping her nightclothes, she dropped them in the vague vicinity of the laundry basket and stepped into her bathroom, hugging the chill tiles of the shower, angling the head away whilst she carefully twisted the dials to the exact point between where it stopped being hot enough to brew coffee, and hadn't become 'ball-clenchingly cold', as Syke had always described it. As close to comfortable as the damn thing came, but she'd not change it for the world; the intricate game of balance had become part of her morning routine.

Besides, she'd found there was no better way to wake herself up than the sudden shock of too-hot or too-cold water.

Half an hour later, clean, only slightly too cold, and smelling faintly of the cheapest shampoo she could find that actually worked, Ryan stepped out of the bathroom, towelling her short hair. She froze momentarily, all her muscles tensed, as she heard a Police flickercar buzz past the building, siren blaring. The blues and their siren faded away fast enough, however, and she forced herself to relax.

'You gotta calm down, they never saw us.'

Kayala's voice echoed in her head, and she shook it to dislodge the sound. Kay had been right, she knew, but Kay had disappeared off the radar less than a week after the run and none of the team had heard from her. She'd struck out on her own and left November, for sure, and there was no point holding onto runmates who were out of your life. Wisdom of a life on the streets.

Or, Ryan thought, *a life off the streets* – runs at ground level almost always turned out to be a bad idea.

She shook her head again ruefully and, dropping the damp towel in the same general area as her nightclothes, flopped onto her bed. She reached out to the table beside it for her link and slipped it around her wrist, fitting it snugly. She tapped the link's small screen, and in turn it tapped into her wired neurosystems. Its display fizzled into her line of sight as it superimposed its translucent writing into the corners of her vision:

9:37am
28 degrees, 18 adjusted

3 messages
  1 – Johnathan Sykes
  2 – Unknown contacts

Ryan double-tapped the point on her knuckle that activated the link's gesture control, and her fingers flashed through the motions as she rolled over onto her back and stared up at the ceiling, watching the gold light gradually slip from it as the sunlight moved across the room.

Since she was neither interested in Viagra, nor in helping a lunar regolith prince move money around, she deleted both of the spam messages, and opened the one from Johnathan;

'Syke' as he preferred.

It was overlong and rambling, just like the man himself.

She scanned it quickly, and then again in more detail. None of the watchwords or alarm phrases.

Relaxing back into the bed, Ryan thumbed her knuckle again, turning off the link.

Syke wanted to meet up at the market in Henderson Plaza for breakfast.

In all, it was almost surprising in how normal a request it was. Ryan smiled to herself as she formed the thought.

Things don't always have to be quite so interesting I guess.

With just over an hour before he wanted to meet, she rolled off the bed and dragged herself to her feet, running a hand through her hair to test its dampness. The filament towel had done a good job, so she just roughed her hand through the short curls and left them to do their own thing.

Glancing again at the temperature displayed by her link's UI, she dressed, pulling on her favourite jacket and sequestering her ID, cash and a knife through the hidden inside pockets. No need to take a gun to lunch, but one could never be *too* careful.

Running a quick checklist to be sure she had everything she needed, she ran an inventory of her kitchen to see if anything was running low. Or, more to the point, running so far past low that she should probably buy more. She was doing well though – nothing so low she could be bothered to carry it back for herself, at least. Certainly not from Henderson.

Nodding in final readiness, she palmed the control for her door locks and stepped out into the wide landing outside her apartment. The building's managers actually spent some of the rent on upkeep, so it was unusually clean and neat, and nearly all the lights worked nearly all the time. It was, really, quite upmarket for this area of the city. Though not without its hazards.

She dodged backwards as her door quietly swung closed,and pressed herself to it as a running gunfight blistered past her. The four children were using empty bottles and sticks as weapons and engaging in all-out-war down the corridors and through-ways of the building.

"Hey! Watch where you're shooting!"

"Sorry Mrs Waters!"

"Mrs?" she shouted at their retreating backs, incredulous.

Low chuckling followed its owner up the corridor as one of the mothers paused beside her.

"Aren't I too young for kids to be calling me 'Mrs'?"

"Well, you're past ten, dear."

Ryan made a sulky harumphing sound and glared at the disappearing children before turning back to her companion.

"Anyway, this old biddy is going over to Henderson for early lunch, do you or the other families want anything from the market?"

The older woman smiled gratefully.

"If there's any of those fresh-grown pears like last week's batch, I'd appreciate it. Most else we can get downstairs."

Ryan nodded. "Sure thing then, I'll keep an eye out."

"Thanks Rye."

She smiled her deeply lined smile again, and un-hurriedly made her way after the disappeared warfare, whilst Ryan turned and made her own way to the staircases at the other end of the hall.

She dodged and danced around a delivery man clambering up to the 20s, as well as the kids from her floor when they came sprinting down past her, the sticks now apparently become swords. Managing to avoid being run through, she reached the ground floor, and crossed the small courtyard to the main atrium. The hydroponic garden filling the courtyard was the housing complex's pride and joy – it grew vegetables all year round, maintained by volunteers from throughout the building. The management didn't mind, because the landlord who lived on the almost-palatial top floor grew herbal teas in the garden for his wife – it made her happy, which made him happy. Since the combined rents easily covered the cost of the 'ponics lights, and the added allure meant that empty rooms only stayed that way for as long as it took him to advertise, it was a very welcome addition to his property.

It made for a welcoming sight when you got home, too. The cramped alleys and neon-encrusted streets outside in the

Copper Corridor, one of the less affluent sectors of November, contrasted quite starkly with the softly lit green utopia nestled here. When the plants weren't being mist-watered, the small preschool on the third storey would regularly bring its students down into the garden to read and play. It was as close to some kind of idyll as you'd likely get, outside parks or upcity.

"Tomatoes are coming on nicely, Rimah!" Ryan called out to a man perched on a ladder, changing a bulb above one of the vegetable racks.

"That they are! Want me to set some aside for you?"

"I'll love you unendingly. Want anything from Henderson?"

The man paused a moment, tapping his chin exaggeratedly.

"There's that stall usually sells manure for fertilising herb gardens, if you could pick me up a dozen bags, I'd-"

He cut off as he saw Ryan's eyes narrow.

"Christ girl I'm kidding, come on now. See if there's any seeds what we haven't got growing here already. Alright?"

"You're on thin ice, Rim."

The man's laughter followed her out into the street.

The raucous noise of the Henderson market made itself known long before Ryan actually reached the plaza – mostly the sound of chatter, of shouting vendormen advertising their wares, but also the sounds of flickerdrives in motion, cars and vans moving into and out of the plaza's airspace.

The next tell was the streets themselves – the buildings became that little bit fancier and more decorative, the roads that little bit better taken care of. They were busier, too, with people streaming to and from the market. Ryan melted into the flow of people, flicking her link's display active for a moment to check the time – she was cutting it close. Syke wouldn't mind if she were late, but he'd tease her about being punctual; that was far worse.

She hurried her pace, and stepped out into Henderson Plaza market, the cacophony reaching its crescendo of overlapping voices and languages. As always, it was packed to bursting all through the western end of the plaza – that's where all the food stalls were, and that's where the majority of the day's shopping was: fresh fruit and vegetables grown out of a hundred small privately-run hydroponics domes dotted around the edges of the city.

Ryan pushed her way through the crowds around the fast-food stalls, working towards the fruits sellers – if there were pears to be found today, they'd be there. Trying to find the right stall amongst the many was hard, especially with people bustling all over, but eventually she found it. The small stall was run by an equally small man, who seemed far out of his depth. Shy and unassuming, he simply sat with a serene smile whilst people tried to argue his wares down. Ryan didn't know him all that well, but she knew better than to bother begging a lower price; he was iron. So she grabbed a bag of six pears, and handed him the requisite coin without argument, earning a smile and pleased nod from him before he went right back into the attempted negotiations of the rest.

Gripping her spoils tightly, Ryan made her way out into the less-busy aisles and lanes of the market. They'd pick up as the day wore on, but the morning belonged to the grocers.

She briefly considered eating one of the pears but, annoying as the kids from down the hall could be at times, pears were their favourite treat. She fought down the urge and tapped her link active again. She briefly berated herself for the fact that she still hadn't fixed the battery – leaving it active constantly wasn't a luxury it could handle at the moment – but she kept just not quite finding the time.

As, she realised, she had done now – she was late. God only knows where that twenty minutes had gone, but she was late. Her pace picked up and she made her way into the electronics stalls where she knew Syke would be waiting for her, breaking through the crowds and finally reaching the almost quiet electrics lanes. She checked them one after the other, and finally turned a corner, to see him standing at the other end of a short run of stalls.

"Ryan? Damn girl, you're early."

"Early? But it's–" she broke off mid sentence. Syke smiled.

"You still haven't fixed your link, huh?"

Ryan sighed and rolled her eyes. Now it was running fast. *Great.*

Syke made his way slowly up the lane towards her, and she saw something strange in his eyes. She couldn't place it.

She was still trying to work it out when he spoke again, a couple of metres from her.

"Want a peppermint?"

Immediately, every muscle in Ryan's body tensed and she fought to not let it show. Why was he using the warning? What was wrong?

Suddenly her link's HUD display flared white and fizzled out, and computer tech along the lane sparked and died. Panic erupted across the stalls as vendors tried to save their wares.

Syke reached her.

"Sorry, I had to do it. They bugged me and I had to blow it. We don't have much time."

"The fuck man? Who bugged you, what's wrong?"

"The Seven."

Ryan's blood ran cold.

"That stuff in the Redstone vault?" he continued, rushing his words, "Most of it was theirs. Front businesses all. Nix should've checked closer, stupid bastard. Word gets around fast, Ryan. They know it was us."

She tried to say something, but he held a hand up.

"Sorry girl there's no time. They caught me on the way over here. They don't know where you live, but they intercepted my message. They're here to get you and they're doing it through me. They might've already got Nix and Jace, I don't know about the others. And fuck knows about Kay. They can't hear us talking now, but they had men going up into that building at the end of the lane. They had a sniper."

"Jesus, Syke, what do we do?"

She finally recognised what was in his eyes. Sadness. Regret. Why was there no anger?

"If we leave here alive, they'll kill my family."

She froze. They wouldn't, would they? Yes, she decided, of course they would.

"You... you have to kill me Rye. You have to do it now, and then run. Down that alley, away, back to your place. Load up and disappear. Find the others if you can, but run."

"What? You know I can't do that! We'll get out of it, we'll get your family and – "

"No, we can't. They have men with my family already. If you kill me here they'll think I did what they wanted and you gunned me down. Take my link too, I have the details from the vault in here and they know it – they'll think you're just after the money."

"Syke, I can't do this, I..."

"You have to and you know it. I have a gun in my hip holster. Make it quick, Rye."

Syke reached around Ryan and pulled her close, hugging her tighter than he ever had in the decade they'd been friends.

"And tell Lizzy and the kids that I love them, okay?"

He choked the words out, trying not to let tears out with them.

Ryan had no such compunction; tears slipped down her cheeks as she held him tight for a moment. Her hand slipped down to his hip. There it was. His favourite gun.

She slowly drew it out and brought it around between them.

"Do it Ryan."

"Syke..."

"Do it!"

Ryan pulled back, gun in hand aimed directly for Syke's forehead.

"I'm sorry, Johnathan."

The gun kicked madly in her hand, the loud report ringing louder in the close quarters between the electronics stalls. Syke's body sagged, its strings cut, and he crumpled downwards. Ryan grabbed him, trying to bite down on the wracking sobs fighting to come out, and reached down to slip his link off his wrist. She shoved it deep into her jacket pocket, Syke's pistol alongside it. She stood, taking in the horrified expressions of the vendors around her – those who hadn't immediately run and ducked for cover when she drew the gun, at least. She looked up at the building overlooking the lane's end, and saw a window on the third storey slide open. The man behind wore an upcity suit and an undercity expression. He fumbled as he wrestled a rifle up to the window and aimed down at her.

A suddenly jerking motion took control and she part fell, part ran to the opposite end of the lane, slipping around the corner on the wet pavings and running for all she was worth towards the alley Syke had indicated. A bullet cracked off the ground behind her, blistering through the space she'd have occupied if she'd gone on straight. Three more tore through the cloth awning of the stall she was hidden behind, sparking off metal struts and stone floor. A fourth was stopped by the unlucky stallholder, who fell into and ripped through the fabric, holding his arm and screaming.

Ryan ran for all she was worth.

The alley opened up before her and she disappeared into it, past horrified pedestrians and a parked flickercar. A droplet flew through the air behind her, blown from her cheek. It splashed down into a puddle lying undisturbed on the ground. As Ryan dashed around the cornering alleyway, the salt water mingled and disappeared into the oiled rainwater and the sun continued to rise on a beautiful day for awful things.

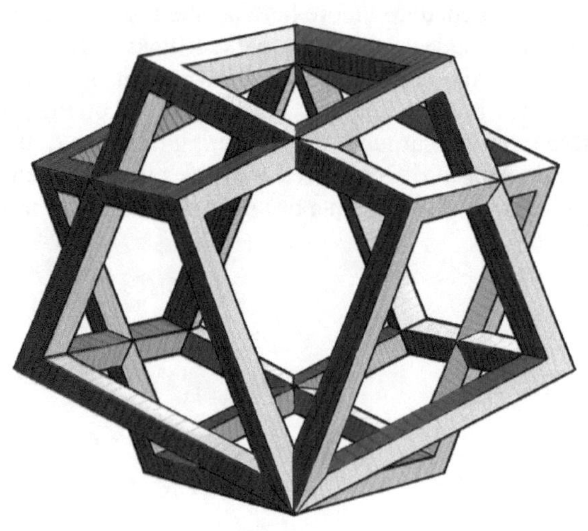

Bird Brains

by
Douglas Thompson

Douglas Thompson's short stories have appeared in a wide range of magazines and anthologies, most recently *Albedo One*, *Ambit*, *Postscripts*, *New Writing Scotland* and *The Speculative Book*. He won the Grolsch/Herald Question of Style Award in 1989 and second prize in the Neil Gunn Writing Competition in 2007. His first book, *Ultrameta*, was published in August 2009, nominated for the Edge Hill Prize, and shortlisted for the BFS Best Newcomer Award, and since then he has published further novels, *Sylvow* (Eibonvale, 2010), *Apoidea* (The Exaggerated Press, 2011), *Mechagnosis* (Dog Horn, 2012), *Entanglement* (Elsewhen Press, 2012), *The Brahan Seer* (Acair Publishing, 2014), *Volwys and other stories* (Dog Horn, 2014), *The Rhymer, an Heredyssey* (Elsewhen Press, 2014) and *The Sleep Corporation* (The Exaggerated Press, 2015).

I

I used to be a particle physicist you know. No, really, I'm not shitting you. But of course these days I'm just a drunk. Most drunks drink to forget, but I drink to forget something that hasn't happened yet. Confused? You, as they say, will be. I'll just cut to the chase right now then, shall I? I'm not a tease. The Large Hadron Collider will soon create an event which has only happened once before in Earth's history. On that occasion, it was an accident caused by a meteor strike. Yes, the same one that wiped out the dinosaurs. But it didn't just wipe out them and other life forms, it reversed the polarity of the Earth's magnetic field and thereby reversed the arrow of time on this planet. Now, I know you'll be starting to struggle with the implications of that, so did I at first. *At first*, now what was it at first that put me on to this idea? -This idea that grew into my head until it became on obsession and then as I progressively confirmed it with one test and experiment after another: a terrifying fact. Am I talking too fast for you?

Dinosaurs. This is so obvious that you're going to kick yourself when you hear it. They had feathers. Archaeologists and scientists have been progressively accepting this over the last twenty years as more fossils confirming it have come to light. Nobody seemed bothered by this except for me. But feathers make no sense on dinosaurs. They are hollow under a microscope, a highly evolved adaptation to combine incredible lightness with the ability to give uplift in flight. A large heavy flightless carnivore would have no need for them. *Unless*, unless. Unless time has reversed, and dinosaurs are going to evolve from the birds we have now, here in our present, and their feathers are just leftover traces from that. Why would they evolve like that? They would do it if there was a catastrophic event which wiped out all large mammals and left birds as the dominant and ascendant species on earth. They would do that if that same event reversed the direction of time.

If you think this is crazy then I'll give you ten minutes to go away and look up time reversal on your beloved internet and then come back to me. It's accepted as completely possible at the level of particle physics, and only questionable at our macro level due to the inherently entropic nature of organic life. Entropy: energy is constantly being lost, things decay and die, shit happens. A reverse-direction universe would be anti-entropic, energy would be being created all the time. Sounds rather joyous actually. Something for nothing, things appearing out of thin air. Gravity, interestingly, is a time-neutral event. Think about it. Toss a ball up in the air and it come down to earth, or the ball fires itself off the ground and loops down into your hand which then lowers it back down to earth again. Perfect symmetry. Something organic, like baking a cake or gunning down thirty unarmed civilians, on the other hand, looks pretty different depending on time direction. Cake made from ingredients, people turned into worm food: cake turned into flour, living people made out of soil. Quite a magic trick.

If only the damned birds didn't exist. I know we all love their songs and their pretty colours, me as much as the next guy, but their mere existence tells us that a time-reversal event is due soon in order to start turning them back into dinosaurs. If they weren't here, we could conclude that only one time-reversal event occurred in Earth's history and it's been going forward ever since, and was going backwards all the time before. You making sense of this? I'm thirsty, man. That old bag over there behind the counter doesn't serve me anymore. I've got money. You buy me a couple of bottles of whisky with this cash and I'll come back and tell you some more of this next week, give you time to get your head around it. We got ourselves a deal?

*

You looked me up, really? Wow, I'm impressed and flattered. You believe me now, I really did work at CERN. I was drummed out for alcohol problems? Well, they would say that, wouldn't they? To discredit me, of course, as a scientific heretic. They're worse than the Spanish Inquisition these days, the scientific community. Cruelly intolerant of all forms of dissent. Take it from me, man, I got their sharp end right up my jacksy. You want more proof of my theories? Another couple of bottles first please. I might even show you my laboratory, if you're nice to me.

*

Bit of a mess this place, sorry. My wife Marie left me six months ago. Understandable really, I don't blame her. It was all the dead birds that got to her I think, and the glass chambers and the electrical wires. You want a drink, my friend? Really? You sure? I think you're going to need one when you see this shit. Here, mind your feet there, just step over the transformer and compressor… that's liquid nitrogen that tube, don't want to freak you, but be careful, you bust that one and you'll know all about it. Right, follow me, just up a couple of ladders now, into the attic. You're not claustrophobic or anything are you? Good. No terror of birds either? Terror of birds in confined spaces? Good, you're cut out for this job. You sure you're not a reporter, mister? You do seem ideal for this.

I know, I know. Now you know where I've been putting all the empty bottles. Nothing goes to waste in this household. Nor in this garden. The suburbs still supply a fine selection of bird species, despite mankind's ravages of the erstwhile biological diversity of the Belgian countryside through pollution and over-development. Yeah, just shift those notebooks out the way, make yourself a seat there, get comfortable. You sure you don't want a drink? This will take a while at first until the equipment heats up, until your eyes adjust to the hazy atmosphere. Chemicals, drugs? No man, a bit of formaldehyde here and there, a few free radicals and ionised trace elements, argon and helium: nothing harmful.

*

I'm glad you took a drink in the end. I knew you'd change your attitude. I can see I've gone and blown your mind, you poor bastard. Here, would you like me to let one out to play on your lap? He won't bite too hard, their teeth are still quite delicate when they're first coming in. Ha ha! Look at the little critter go! I'll set a few more out and we can see them play with each other. Little monsters, make human children look well behaved, I can tell you. This little guy here, the orange one, I call him Hubert, I made him out of a chaffinch who I reversed half a million times, took me three years. Three years of setting the chamber going, stopping, starting again, making him into an egg then watching his parents appear then ringing the neck of the male and setting the female going again. Poor old men, we really are history's janitors, the dogsbodies, while women do all the important work in evolutionary terms.

Could I do that to a human? What a sick frigging idea, mate. I'd need a lot bigger glass chambers for a kick-off, which would be higher technology than I can lay my hands on here in suburban Antwerp. And Christ, watching two real live adult human beings appear out of nothing then knowing you have to kill one of them? That would be a real horror movie. You want another drink? Hell, this is just me playing around with some poor rodents, sky rats. You'll forgive me if I don't display quite the sentimentality for the little flying feckers that my fellow men and women do, but maybe that's because I know they're going to take over the planet. The meek shall inherit the Earth it says in the bible, and it's rarely wrong, about that or anything else. The birds are going to inherit the sky, actually, then everything.

*

Hello again. Good to see you, mate. You don't look so good, I tell you. Grey about the eyes, a tad unshaven, if I might say so. Not that I'm entitled by any means to regard myself as a paragon of good health and sartorial elegance, but hey I'm just a wino, remember, not married with a good job and stuff? Really? Man, I'm sorry to hear that, you sound like you could do with a friend to talk to, a good drink. Say, you got some money on you? Let's treat ourselves to a couple of crates each and make a weekend of it, what do you say?

*

Well, now you've nearly seen it all, eh, Adam? I know that's not your real name, but I'm going to rename you, the first man you see, the first man other than me of course, to set eyes upon this stuff. I don't count because I'm not a man anymore. I'm a god, because I can create life and destroy it, because I've seen the true hidden meaning of life, understood it and mastered it and put it to use. Maybe that's all gods are, people who've found out the real way of things and learned to rise above it all. That blackbird and those two starlings are coming on nicely, aren't they? We might let them out later. Things get really interesting when the booze runs out and you start to sober up on the third day. You've not been through that stage, so this will be your first time. Usually in the middle of the night, I find I'll wake up and all the wee critters will be oozing out of the plasterboard ceiling and the sarking boards, running all over your skin and pecking at you. It makes you panic at first, the first couple of times, then I learned to just laugh about it. Wave after wave of avian invasion washing over you, a little foretaste of all that's to come for the rest of humanity.

I picked up a copy of *Le Monde* from a waste paper basket the other day and saw that those raving lunatics at CERN are going ahead with that experiment soon, the one I warned them about. The end is nigh, my friend, want another drink of this bottle? Still a little left, before we have to settle in for the thaw-out and the shakes. Delirium Tremens is the correct Latin medical term for the effect, I believe. Hallucinations. Cold Turkey is the druggie's version. Cold chicken for us maybe, eh? Get it? Squawk squawk, flap flap. It gets better every time. Last weekend the west gable dissolved, just slid away like a magic carpet and their leader, the bird god Loplop fluttered in to visit me. The surrealist artist Max Ernst used to do collages about him. About four feet high, red plumage and nasty looking talons but wearing a gentleman's waistcoat and top hat and talking in a kind of metallic croaking tone of voice like a crow. He sang me a song that changed all the colours in the sky, which turned my fingers into the fine green fronds of a primordial palm waving in a swamp breeze. I got real hot and my mouth filled with sand, sweating tropical rivers. Man, I was suddenly so dried up and gagging, I got up and followed him out and tripped then flew across the suburban rooftops, flew down a few chimneys together until we found ourselves outside the supermarket. The local MP was doing the rounds in his black suit, shaking hands and kissing babies in the lead-up to the next elections. But me and Loplop rumbled him, we saw the feathers sticking out of his shirt, the beak concealed under his five-o'clock shadow.

We liberated the headless frozen chickens in the meat counter and led them all a merry dance like the pied piper, up and down the aisles and out into the street where they terrified the old ladies. How we laughed. The birds are coming back to life. Even your eggs and your omelettes aren't safe. You've been murdering birds for years, centuries, millennia. But they won't stand for it much longer. If you can't beat them, join them. Beat them, eggbeater, get it? I'm with the birds, and we're coming to get you. Drink eases the pain of knowing I'm a traitor, and it helps me to fly, fly like they do, and to see it all from above from where everything looks so small, so arbitrary, so fragile. You all think you're in charge, but you're nothing, an accident of history because the tide went your way for a while. But what does tide do? It goes out again, and reveals all the flapping fish suffocating, the washed up crabs and stones and fossils. And then it washes all your footprints away until there's nothing. Nothing but a few cryptic clues that everybody misses. Look at me. Like I said, I used to be a particle physicist, but now I'm just a drunk.

II

Monsieur Oiseau is just the nickname the children of La Chapelle call him. Rumour has it he is actually a form of bipedal dinosaur, approximately man-height, the result of some grotesque experiment undertaken by the missing and discredited mad Belgian scientist Henri Vermeulen, who lost his job under mysterious circumstances at CERN in 2012. No authenticated photographs have yet emerged of Oiseau, despite numerous, supposed, sightings and ongoing investigations by Swiss, Belgian, and French undercover police agencies. Paris is a big place. Sightings have also been reported in the 18th arrondissement. Monsieur Oiseau seems to emerge only at night in poorly lit areas, usually in overcast conditions when even moonlight is limited. He wears a long dark grey raincoat and hat and strangely shaped boots which have been adapted to hold his talons, some of which have been seen to protrude through the leather in places. Oiseau's movements appear odd, even at a distance, resembling human walking only superficially. His progress is generally slow and furtive, but on occasions when he has been challenged by ill-intentioned adolescents he has been seen to move off at a phenomenal speed, sometime removing his ungainly footwear in order to do so. A video on YouTube, unauthenticated and possibly a fake, purports to show a shady figure sprinting down Rue d'Orsel at a speed in excess of seventy miles an hour, far in excess of human capability. This might provide a clue as to why the creature has so far proven so elusive and evaded capture. A spate of stray dog carcasses found in 2013 was connected for a while with the Oiseau rumours, as was an unusual number of disappearances of homeless men and drug-addicts last winter, followed by accusations that the Gendarmerie had been implicated in a cover-up in order to reduce the risk of panic among the wider Parisian population. The impression that Oiseau seems to limit his appearances to the poorer immigrant areas of the capital has fuelled social discontent and the suspicion that not enough has been done to address the danger. Some sceptics maintain that this bird-man is an urban myth, a projection of social division and simmering racial tensions in city where far-right politics and large ethnic populations sit uncomfortably side by side.

III

The shouting children and ragged street people scare her. Her creator, or her father (as she thinks of him) Professor Vermeulen named her Sappho, and this is the name with which she thinks of herself. She wants only to be left alone but, paradoxically, the dense chaotic streets of a major European city are actually the safest hiding place she has been able to devise. She needs a ready food source, and the poor and the homeless seem to her to have been discarded by the wider populace, pushed aside like the unfinished dirty dinner plates of overfed aristocrats. Vermeulen showed her films of human history. She understands a great deal of it, insofar as any rational being can, or at least all she needs to. Her large green eyes, slit vertically and merciless as a hawk's are generally enough to paralyse any would-be assailant at close quarters, through sheer shock. Her powerful prehensile tale is also extremely useful and unexpected in any contretemps with mammalian bipeds.

Of course she is a female. This is how it works, the Matryoshka Doll principle as Vermeulen explained it. She is the product of a localised time-reversal experiment, and so her metabolism and development is anti-entropic. She is getting slowly younger in other words, and in several years' time will finally have to seek out a safe and secluded hide-away in which to regress to the size of a helpless chick and synthesise finally into a beautiful turquoise egg the size of a basketball. Then the most mysterious and miraculous thing of all will happen: both her adult parents will spontaneously emerge out of the ether as the egg deliquesces into its component parts. Without the professor on hand for the first time, of course, nobody will be able to supervise the destruction of the unnecessary male, and so the danger will emerge of the population starting to grow and expand over time from that point forward. Starting out as fully grown intelligent adults, will present this new reptilian race with a distinct evolutionary advantage over its human counterparts. If they can stay undetected and breed and expand in covert locations dispersed across Europe, then in time they may present a real threat to the current human dominance of the planet.

For now Sappho enjoys her evening walk by the Seine, walks down the narrow streets of the Île Saint-Louis wrapped in the perceptual scarf of winter fog, and gazes in the windows of the antique shops. On the next corner, she spies a fine lady's hat with peacock feathers in it. On a whim, her claw smashes the glass and she struts in to seize it. Two blocks on, a police car pulls up at a crossroads, blocking the street, and she regrets having been so foolhardy to have ventured for the first time this close to the city centre and the middle-class areas. The two uniformed guards getting out either side of the vehicle ahead look better fed than her usual choice of dinner partner. She surmises that they are probably more likely to be missed too, stitched in to the whole wider fabric of human society, social pack animals that they are. Foregoing the chance to taste their flesh, she instead simply scrambles vertically straight up the four-storey façade of the Haussmann tenement immediately to her right and scuttles and flutters away across the rooftops.

Later she makes her way to one of towers of the west façade of Notre Dame, a nice flat lead roof on which she can feast on a Korean tourist with a side salad of Algerian pickpocket, both plucked from the richly-stocked streets below. Her short vestigial feathers are quite adequate to keep her warm, even at this altitude in the chill easterly breeze of oncoming winter, and her wings, though short and ineffectual, will certainly suffice to help her glide back down in due course, should a rapid descent be necessary to evade capture before daybreak.

The way home does not prove as inconsequential as she has hoped. Driven down into the Métro to escape the pursuit of three police cars with irritating flashing lights and wailing sirens, she takes a wrong turning, failing to find the sewer entrance where she thought she remembered one, arriving instead at a busy train platform packed with opera-goers in furs and shawls, preparing to head home to their elegant well-to-do suburbs. She is their worst nightmare, the ultimate immigrant, a refugee not just from another country but from another time. The humans don't realise it, but one of their most unwittingly effective weapons against her is their screaming when they are panicked, since it causes intense pain and disturbance to her vastly superior hearing system, evolved to let her detect herds of prey moving up to twenty-five miles away across the great plains of central Asia.

Forced onto a Métro train in confusion, she bounds through all six carriages at speed leaving dazzled and petrified passengers in her wake before smashing her way out of the front cabin and into the darkness of the tunnel beyond, swiftly taking the driver's yelling head off, as much to silence him as by way of a snack. She finds an entrance from the Métro tunnels to the sewer system at last, which she usually knows and remembers well, but after a few miles a new section blocks her way unexpectedly so that, knowing daybreak is dangerously near, she has to take the ultimate last resort and rise up through a street gully on Rue Saint-Denis. A gypsy beggar, playing an accordion cross-legged on the pavement next to her point of emergence, looks up at her in awe as his polka grinds down to a sagging halt in his disbelieving arms. Too full to eat any more, but resourceful enough never to give up, she hold her talons out towards him and lets her long tongue salivate over his face until he parts with his coat, hat and instrument as invited and runs off gibbering.

The streets are not yet busy enough for anyone to have witnessed the truth before she completes her new disguise and kneels down over the accordion and begins to puzzle over how to coax passable human music from the instrument. The sun is up now, so this seems as reasonable a strategy as any for a place to hide until the next nightfall. Wrapped under old blankets, doubtless passers-by will just mistake her for the tragic victim of some disfiguring disease. In this shady corner by a train station, who will attempt to look past the overhanging brim of her hat or the folds of her tattered old coat? Whoever wants to meet the eyes of a beggar anyway? But if they do they will doubtless be rendered magically speechless and unable thereafter to be believed.

IV

For the benefit of the tape, this interview is between Henri Vermeulen and Officers Bertrand and DeBeer, of Interpol. A consultant scientist and psychologist, Professor Mousavi and Doctor Brezinka, are also in attendance.

Q: We thought you were dead, Monsieur Vermeulen. Where have you been hiding and why have you decided to re-emerge in plain sight after so long?

*A: It's **Professor** Vermeulen to you, actually. Brussels is a big place. I began to realise I was missing a relative of mine in Paris so I decided to come through and visit her here at last. You may have heard of her: six feet tall with* *feathers and a beak and talons.*

Q: Your inappropriately joking reference is, we presume to the so called Monsieur Oiseau phenomenon. Can you tell us please of the whereabouts of this creature and its true nature?

A: As her only guardian in the world I had a moral duty to protector her from you people for as long as possible. Her name was Sappho by the way, she was female and she was as intelligent as you are, possible more so in your particular case.

Q: We notice you are talking of her in the past tense, Monsieur Vermeulen.

A: Quite so. She finally deliquesced into an egg a month ago after a six month period of vulnerable childhood during which period I watched over and cared for her. She has now been replaced by her two adult parents. Ha. I see that got your attention. No, I won't be telling you their whereabouts any time soon. Then again, I don't need to. Have any of you got the exact time on you?

Q: We're asking the questions, but it's about five minutes to noon. Why?

A: Then I suggest you get your televisions and internet fired up and get ready for a very interesting news story which will be breaking.

Q: We are on guard for your notorious pranks and hallucinations, Monsieur Vermeulen. Your file describes in detail your sorry record as a hopeless alcoholic and social misfit.

A: Oh, but I thawed out years ago. Woke up and smelt the coffee, as those damned Americans say with their invasion of Franglais. I kicked the bottle the day my little dino-birds started getting sentient and calling me daddy.

Fatherhood brings out the best in even the worst of us, wouldn't you say? I'll take that as a yes. Since you seem intent in persisting in acting like complete dullards with your line of questioning, perhaps I should just start imparting the relevant and required scientific information, shall I? Your two so-called experts sitting there may at least understand some of it, even if you don't.

Q: Mister Vermeulen. Henri...

A: Ever heard of T-symmetry? The theoretical reversal of the vector of time at the quantum level? Good. One of you at least. I've tried warning CERN about this and they won't listen, which is why I have been driven to this, this campaign of avian terror, if you want to think of it that way. According to my estimates and calculations and the latest scientific papers I've been able to get my hands on: CERN will undertake the T-symmetry experiment some time around summer 2020. We don't have much time left therefore, quite literally. We have to stop them from doing that. It will set a series of events in motion that will reverse the direction of time and humanity will begin moving backwards, de-evolving, generation by generation. Nobody will even be aware of this of course, because they will be trapped within their own biological framework from which everything will appear indistinguishable from normal. The net effect however will be that this planet's future will have been aborted, we will be heading back towards the dinosaur age when creatures like my friends Castor and Pollux ruled the earth, and were probably doing rather a good job of it before a meteor struck the Yucatan peninsula.

Q: You're losing all of us, Professor. Castor and Pollux?

A: Sappho's parents. Have you any idea how rare fossils are? To become one, you have to be very stupid and lie down to wait to die on a river bed. Ninety-nine percent of the species that have been and gone upon this world would never have been so daft or so unfortunate. I know, too mind-blowing to think about, isn't it? Which may be why most people don't. We therefore know almost nothing of the vast arrays of species, including intelligent dinosaurs, and intelligent forbears of modern birds, that once lived on Earth. Sappho's parents are examples of such. She and I prepared films and books to teach them about our world when they arrived and to explain that they should treat me as their parent, the one human being they could trust, the exception that proves the rule. I saddled up Castor last night and flew here on his back, an exhilarating nocturnal journey across the rooftops of Paris, I can tell you. Sappho used to pluck her feathers so that she could conceal herself in human clothes, but her parents are not going to be so shy. We've decided to start a sort of public information campaign, and my turning myself in was just the start of it. When people see the evidence splashed across their screens, they're finally going to start believing all the 'crank' stories I've been leaking onto the internet for the last ten years. I'm not the mad scientist, CERN are, and they need to be stopped. Like I say, turn on your television. By now I estimate that the French President should be as besieged as a pile of pumpkin seeds in his offices, by a giant bird pecking all the glass out of his windows, and the custodians of a certain famous tourist landmark should be starting to regret all those vindictive anti-pigeon measures....

V

The Eiffel Tower was only supposed to be a temporary building. The thought is always buried in the back of the mind of every visitor, Parisienne and foreigner alike. Those lifts bounce to a worrying degree as they stop at each floor. Today the effect is heightened by the unexpected arrival of a two metre tall bird – with vibrant red and orange plumage, savage green eyes and vicious beak – alighting on the top of the lift car and attempting to bite its way through the cables. For weeks, nervous local jokes have been used to mask the Parisiens' growing disquiet at proliferating rumours of the wing beats of huge birds being heard flapping over the rooftops on dark nights, and of disturbingly loud thumps heard on flat roofs overhead, as if something monstrous is strutting about up there.

Bored with the lift carriages, whose emergency brakes would in any case prevent catastrophic descent even after the cables are severed, Pollux makes her way up to the viewing platform itself, which the proud city fathers had so wisely enclosed in a decorative cage to prevent suicides many decades beforehand. The mesh is mostly dense enough to prevent her beak penetrating too far, although a few appendages are lost proving the issue, but she still causes several strokes and heart attacks. The point, as ever in our brave new media-savvy world, is publicity. The footage of sixty terrified men, women and children being pecked at, hounded and tormented by a giant bird with vicious talons and a particularly blood-curdling screech, three hundred and twenty metres above Paris, will certainly burn its way indelibly into the public retina. Pollux is also actually quite a gentle and intellectual creature at other times, but has been told to play up stereotypical expectations for the cameras. As a cynical man once said, nobody ever lost a fortune underestimating the public intelligence. She will fly off before the army helicopters and fighter jets get here, or maybe bring a few down on the way for her amusement. The tourists will be mostly rescued and unharmed, led away in single file down the seldom-used escape stairs. But the point will have been made: in the complacent minds of all the self-satisfied bourgeois French and in the soiled underpants of their president. Shout the news from the rooftops. History is attacking us, fuelled by our blind ignorance of it, on which it feeds. The threat is here, it is upon us. Not from foreign immigrants and terrorists but from ourselves. Not from elsewhere, but elsewhen.

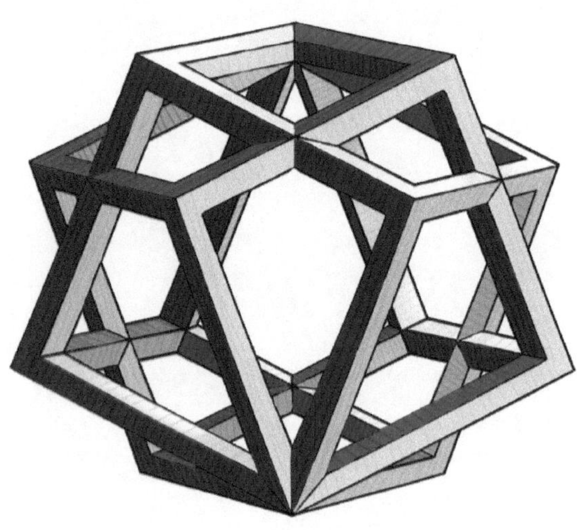

The Last Days

by

Tej Turner

Tej Turner has just begun branching out as a writer and been published in anthologies, including *Impossible Spaces* (Hic Dragones Press) and *The Bestiarum Vocabulum* (Western Legends). In 2015 Elsewhen Press published *The Janus Cycle,* his first novel. He is currently engaged in writing an epic fantasy series.

His parents moved around a bit while he was growing up so he doesn't have any particular place he calls "home", but most of his developing years were spent in the West country of England. He went on to Trinity College in Carmarthen to study Film and Creative Writing, and then later to complete an MA at The University of Wales, Lampeter, where he minored in ancient history but mostly focused on sharpening his writing skills.

Tej recently returned from backpacking his way across Asia, keeping a travelblog (http://tejturner.wordpress.com) to let his friends and fans follow him on his adventures as he gallivanted around Burma, Indonesia, the Philippines, and Nepal. When he is not trekking through jungles or exploring temples, reefs, and caves he is usually based in Cardiff, where he works by day, writes by moonlight, and squeezes in the occasional trip to roam around megalithic sites and the British countryside. The next time he has enough money he will be flying off on another adventure.

"There is no easy way to tell you this, Mr Morecombe... but there are some things you must know before I let you see your wife," he said, as I sat myself down.

I have always liked Dr Hammond. Throughout every ordeal we have endured since this nightmare began he has somehow known the correct way to compose himself, however good or bad the news he was about to deliver. But this time, even Dr Hammond was struggling. He couldn't look me in the eyes.

"The tumours have grown again, and last night she had a seizure... we managed to get it under control," he hurriedly added. "She's still alive, but we have not managed to get any response from her. The areas of her brain which were damaged during the seizure were where the sensory–"

He went into doctor talk. A tidalwave of words which sounded like they were lifted straight out of an encyclopaedia. I stopped listening half way through, not much of it made sense to me apart from one crucial point.

"So she can't... see or hear?" I whispered, as I felt the blood drain from my face.

He nodded gravely. "I think it is time... I mean..." he scratched his head and looked at the ceiling. "When the cancer metastasised we told you that the chances were small... but now I think we have reached a point where the best we can do is make her comfortable. I'm truly sorry, Mr Morecombe."

A few minutes later, I was finally allowed to step into the room and I saw her. She was lying under white sheets, with sterile, colourless walls around her and several plastic tubes spiralling out from her arms and her neck, connecting her to the grey machines that were keeping her alive.

I stood in the doorway for a while: I was too scared to approach her at first. Which was silly because I knew she couldn't hear or see me. I was scared of doing the wrong thing. What was the *right* thing to do?

She was thinner, again. How could that have happened in a mere few hours?

When the cancer first began I was amazed at how healthy she still looked – it made it almost hard to believe what the doctors claimed was going on inside her. Now, she truly looked ill. Her face was gaunt. I could see the bones of her cheeks through the thin layer of her cracked skin. The flesh around her eyes was blue.

And the shocking thing was that she was still beautiful, and if anything I loved her even more. The nature of some of that love had changed, though – some of it had been replaced by the kind of emotion you feel when you encounter an abandoned puppy or a starving child. The type of love which makes people drop everything and sprint across a busy road, or a predatory animal take another creature which is usually their prey into their paws and lick their wounds.

"Alica," I said, as I approached her. I knew it was useless saying her name. The doctors had already told me that she couldn't hear me. Or see. She was trapped in a world of mute darkness. Did she even know what was going on?

I took her hand. She smiled faintly when I first touched her – was it because she knew it was me?

I traced eight letters onto her palm.

I love you

I remember the first time I met you.

I had just finished University and was staying at my parents. I was enjoying that last summer everyone has just after they graduate. They live in their old bedrooms, see their old friends, and live rent-free just before they venture off into the 'real' world. I went to the fete. That fete that so many villages in the West Country have, every summer. And then to the party in the evening. The sort which happens after every fete. In the same field, every year. The ones where bales of hay are stacked around as seats, and the normal rules of behaviour are eased. Even some of the kids are drinking cider. A folk band is playing, and everyone is dancing. Most of them don't even like that kind of music, usually.

You were there. You were the girl who turned up because you were visiting some distant family or an old friend. The one that every guy tried to flirt with because you were new. Including me. I hovered around you, and tried to make it look like an accident. When I finally caught your attention I asked you where you were from.

"Around," you said, smiling as you drank from that plastic cup which was probably filled with wine. You gave me that look. The one which said; 'I know you're trying to flirt with me, and I don't mind'. "I've moved around a bit."

You were always like that – a bit mysterious. Even now, after three years of being together, there are so many things I don't know about you.

"I remember that night too," she said.

I jumped in my seat, startled. Her lips were moving. She was talking.

It was as if she knew what I had been thinking. How was that possible?

"I noticed you long before you even spoke to me," she said. "Did I ever tell you that? Well, I'm telling you now. I even asked my friend about you."

"Alica," I said, prodding her shoulder. "Can you hear me?"

No response. Of course she couldn't hear me.

But how did she know what I was thinking?

Maybe it was just a coincidence.

Or maybe not; I decided to try something.

I took her hand again and ran the tip of my finger across her palm. The same words.

I love you

When I met you I was ready to start a career and settle down. I was applying for jobs in offices and banks. I was set upon a path which led towards financial stability.

I can see now that such a banausic existence would have been meaningless. You pulled me off the treadmill and dragged me to the window. You pointed to the hills, and I realised that there was a whole wonderful world out there. You taught me that there was so much more to living.

"Do you want to come to work in a hotel in Scotland with me?" you asked one evening. "It's on an island.... and, oh Joshua – it's beautiful! Look!"

You showed me a picture on the screen. It truly was beautiful, but I was more mesmerised by the smile it brought to your face. We had only been seeing each other for a few weeks at that point, but we had become almost inseparable.

The summer was almost over, and none of the applications I had filled, or interviews I had attended, had come to anything.

I said yes. It was spontaneous, not the sort of thing I would usually do, but I am so glad I did. The pay was crap, it was cold, and isolated, but we were given a free room and the people were very friendly. We ended up living there for an entire year.

"I was so nervous when I asked you," she said. Her lips were moving again. "I didn't think you would say yes, but it was one of the happiest moments of my life when you did. Maybe I should be laid to rest there... would you do that for me? Scatter my ashes around that tree we used to sit by. I think that is where I belong."

Tears spilled from my eyes, uncontrollably. I had to pull my hand away from hers to catch them.

I didn't want to think about that. Not yet. How could she be so frank and accepting of what was happening to her when it was tearing me apart?

It should have been me being the strong one, not her. She was the one who was dying. She was entering the unknown. For my entire life I had thought of myself as a believer, maybe not in a Christian god, but I had always been convinced that there was something beyond this material world. That everyone had an essence – a soul, if you will – which could never cease to exist.

But now, as I was watching Alica fade away, I suddenly realised how uncertain I was. What if there really was nothing beyond this life? What if this was it?

What if when Alica went, she was truly gone?

My thoughts were interrupted by the door opening. Footsteps echoed across the floor, but I didn't care enough to turn around and find out whose they were.

"Mr Morecombe," a voice said. It was Dr Hammond, with a nurse standing beside him. "Do you mind? We've just come to–"

"She's talking to me..." I whispered.

"You have managed to get a response?" he said, looking at her. "That's... good. I am glad she–"

"Doctor," I said, turning to him. "There's something weird going on. Every time I touch her she knows what I am thinking. Look."

I held her hand again.

Alica, Dr Hammond has come to check up on you, I said with my inner voice.

I had doubts. I was not just doing it to prove it to him, but also to myself. I wanted to make sure it wasn't just my imagination playing tricks on me. I have heard that people often go crazy in times of grief.

"Dr Hammond," she whispered, dispelling my fears and making my heart surge with joy for the briefest of moments. "I want to thank you... for all that you've done for me. I know you tried... I..." she winced, finally letting some of her pain show. "I'm grateful."

There was a long silence which followed her words. A little tear ran down the side of her face so I dabbed it with a tissue.

"It's good that you've found a way to communicate," Dr Hammond eventually said. "Many people under similar circumstances don't–"

"No," I shook my head. "You don't understand. All I have been doing is writing 'I love you' on her hand. But somehow she knows what I am thinking. Don't you think it's strange? How does she know *you* are here?"

"There are many subtleties about communication... not all of which we understand," Dr Hammond said, shaking his head. "I am sorry, Joshua, but I think this is just–"

"But it's similar to what Ben–" the nurse beside him interjected.

"*No!*" Dr Hammond cut her off. "This is not the time for any of your old wives' tales."

His face contorted irritably, and hers went red. She turned her eyes to the floor.

"Anyway, Mr Morecombe," he then said, turning back to me. "I am sorry, but there are things which must be tended to concerning your wife. May I suggest you come back in a few minutes? Maybe you could go and get some lunch or a coffee..."

I didn't eat any lunch. I sat in the nearest chair to her room and watched the door. Dr Hammond wasn't in there for very long. In fact, as I watched him step out of the room only a few minutes later, it made me feel angry. Was that all the time he could spare for my wife now that she was dying? He had always had plenty of time for her before.

I went back inside. The nurse was still there, dutifully replacing one of the see-through bags of liquid which was being pumped into my wife by the tubes.

"Mr Morecombe?" the nurse said. She paused from what she was doing and stared at me.

"Yes."

"I just wanted to talk to you... about what you said...." she hesitated. "About your wife."

"What is it?"

"Is she psychic?" she asked.

My kneejerk reaction was to say 'no'. But then I looked at Alica, and realised that it wasn't necessarily true. I took her hand again.

I love you

The more I think about it, the more I realise that there has always been something enigmatic about you.

I remember that terrible day my father left. When it came to light that he had been having an affair with that slut from down the road.

Before I even found out about it, you ran into my study. "Ring your mother!" you said. It was unusual, because the two of you didn't even get on very well. I asked you why, but you just shook your head. "Ring her now! She needs you!"

I rang her, and she was in tears. She did need me.

Somehow, you knew.

*Or that time you made us cancel our plans to visit my friends. "No!" you said. You actually **looked** terrified. "We can't go!"*

I thought it was because you were just nervous about meeting them. We had a massive argument that day, but you won in the end.

Later I found out about that pileup on the motorway. It was on the news.

When we were living on that island in Scotland, every

morning you used to cast your eyes out of the window and tell me if it was going to rain or not. Your predictions were often different from the official forecast, but you were always right.

There are so many examples... I can't even remember them all...

I have never thought of you as psychic, though. The word 'psychic' brings to mind images of tarot cards, staring into tea leaves, speaking in tongues, and swinging pendulums around. You didn't do any of that. You just always had this mysterious knowingness about you. You weren't showy with it. You carried it with you as naturally as breathing. You wore it with such a congenial grace that I never properly acknowledged it. It became so ingrained into my day-to-day life, I took it for granted.

There are many things about you that I took for granted.

"I guess she is... in a way," I replied, turning back to the nurse. "Why?"

"Something similar happened to another patient we had once," she said. "He was a medium; talked to ghosts and all of that stuff... when the tumours spread, strange things happened... he couldn't speak to the spirits anymore, but he could do other things..."

"It's just... your wife... it got me thinking..." she said. "Did you know that many people in her condition experience symptoms of synaesthesia... I–" she then blushed and turned her eyes to the floor self-consciously. "I'm sorry. I forgot myself. Please, forgive me... many of the doctors and other nurses think me silly... I didn't mean to–"

"No," I shook my head. "It's okay... what you were saying was interesting. Please..."

"It's just that I had this theory..." she mused. "If the five normal senses can be affected by synaesthesia, then maybe the extra ones that some people have can too... anyway, I should go now," she said, gathering her things. "Please let us know if there is anything we can do."

I nodded, and she left the room. Alica and I were alone again.

Did you hear that? I wondered, as I held her hand. *That*

nurse... she thinks that you have some sort of psychic synaesthesia... Do you think that is why you can talk to me? I tried to explain to Dr Hammond but he wouldn't listen. How can I get him to believe us?

"Why is it important for others believe?" she asked.

"Because this is a miracle!" I said it out loud as well as thought it. "We have to show people because... because...."

I trailed off, realising that I didn't actually know why.

She twitched her head, weakly. "I am dying, Joshua. What difference does it make if people believe this? I don't want fuss, or strangers in the room, or tests, or anything like that. I just want *you*. I want you to be here for me."

I inhaled deeply. She was right – as usual. I had let myself get so swept away by the wonder of this phenomenon, that I drifted from the grim reality. It was just a distraction.

This was the wrong kind of miracle. It didn't change the fact that she was dying.

"How is Flossy?" she asked.

I immediately drew my hands away, breaking the contact so she wouldn't sense my guilty thoughts.

That damn cat. I got her the bloody thing because I read on some webpage that the comfort of an animal can help console people who are undergoing chemotherapy.

She fell in love with that kitten. She adored it. She held it in her arms throughout all of the nausea, the headaches, the pain, the loss of her hair. I thought it would help, but it broke her heart when she had to return to the hospital and the cat wasn't allowed to come with her. 'Too many germs', they said.

Looking back, it was a stupid idea, but I was desperate. I felt so helpless.

Now that bloody creature was just a hindrance. Alica insisted that I go home at least twice a day to feed it. Every time I entered the house it plodded over to me and made a pathetic whining sound. I think it missed her, but I hated the damn thing. I hated that I had to keep wasting precious moments I should have been spending with Alica tending to it. I wished I could just get rid of it, but I knew that Alica would never have forgiven me if I had. I locked it in the conservatory most of the time, but, even then, it just made a terrible screeching sound and scratched at the door.

"Where have you gone?" Alica cried out. She clawed her hands around, blindly. "Joshua!"

"I'm here!" I said, taking her arm and stroking it. She calmed down then and pressed her cheek onto the back of my hand. I took her palm again. Traced the words.

I love you

I'm sorry Alica. I know it must be scary there when you are alone. I am here now. Think of nice things.

Think of when we bought that campervan and toured around Europe. All the things we saw. Calabria. The Tatra Mountains. That beach in Brittany we only meant to stop at overnight, but you fell in love with the place so we stayed there for a whole week. Or even that time we broke down in Poland and couldn't get a signal and nobody spoke English. I was so stressed about it, but you were always calm. Remember that kind man who picked us up? He drove us to his home and let us stay there and eat with his family. They never let us pay them any money.

Remember the happiest day of my life: when we decided to get married. My mother was so pissed off that we didn't go for a big wedding, but we weren't bothered by that. We were just certain by then that we wanted to be together for the rest of our lives, and we didn't have any savings left. We blew it all on that trip.

We were happy, weren't we? I mean we were only together for three years, but it felt so much longer and we did so many things...

*I'm sorry. I should only be thinking of happy things, shouldn't I. I am trying. I am trying really hard, but I can't help but to keep thinking about **this**.*

Are you feeling better now, Alica?

Alica...

She didn't say anything, but the machines were still ticking away with their usual noises. Her eyes were closed, and her breathing was soft and steady. I guessed that she must have fallen asleep.

I kissed her on her forehead, and then I finally let myself cry. Unashamedly.

My mother came to visit her the next day, which was surprising. It took me a while to explain to her that Alica could only hear what you were saying if you were holding her hand.

They wanted some time alone, so I left the room for a while. Eventually my mother came back out with tears streaming from her eyes.

Alica never told me exactly how their conversation went, but I sensed that a lot of the bad tension between them had been lifted. My mother rang me every day from then, and the first thing she would say when I answered was; 'How is Alica?' It had never been 'Alica' before, it had always been '*her*', or '*she*', or '*your wife*'.

Even my father came to visit, a few days later. It was the first time I had seen him since he left, and I was still very angry with him for what he did, but I held it all back. Him leaving my mother had once been the most devastating event of my life, but now it seemed like such a small affair. Alica was surprisingly pleasant to him. He cried when he left as well, and the two of us even shared a stiff embrace.

That nurse – it turned out her name was Naomi – became a frequent visitor and friend. She came to see us every day, either at the beginning or end of her shift, but she never stayed for too long, and I think it was because she guessed that I wanted Alica to myself most of the time. Always very understanding, was Naomi.

Many other friends came, too, and some of the more inquisitive ones noticed that there was something peculiar about the way Alica was still able to communicate with us. I tried to play it down as much as I could because I didn't want them to make a fuss, and eventually they all dropped the subject. They were all very supportive.

Throughout all of it Alica was brave. She never broke down in front of the others. Only occasionally when she knew it was only me there. She got thinner each day. Her voice got weaker. So did her coughing.

One evening, when I had just popped home to feed the cat and have a shower I received a phone call. It was from Naomi.

"Hello, Joshua," she said, sombrely. "It's Alica. She's almost..."

"Okay," I said, shocked by how calm and controlled my voice was. I reached for my coat and went to the car.

When I entered the room Naomi was leaning over the bed, holding Alica's hand. She turned around as soon as she heard the door open.

"I best leave," she said, getting up. "I'm actually on duty.... if I stay here too long I might..." her voice trailed off as she brushed the side of her eye. "I will leave you with her..."

I stared at the bed for a few moments. I knew that something must have happened since I was away because the assortment of machines behind her bed had been rearranged. I sat beside her and took her hand.

"Alica?" I said, while tracing *I love you* onto her palm. Despite the fact that she could hear my thoughts, I had never gotten out of that habit.

I didn't get any response from her at first, but eventually she stirred and her eyes opened. They were unfocussed, staring into nothing, but it meant that she was at least awake.

"Josh," she said, smiling weakly. "I'm glad you made it."

Yes, I'm here now Alica. I... I...

I staggered even for thoughts. I didn't know what to think that would help her through this.

I don't want you to die.

I don't want you to go.

How would thoughts like that help her through this moment? What could I do to help her?

"Just hold my hand, Joshua," she said. "That is all I want you to do. I don't want to be alone."

I held her hand and traced *I love you*. Again and again.

"It doesn't hurt anymore," she said. "The pain is all gone. I don't know if it is because the doctors gave me drugs, or just my body is... I don't know. But I am actually feeling quite good, now. Everything was dark before, but now I can see lights. They are getting closer. Joshua!" her eyes widened. "It's just like–"

She trailed off, and one of the machines started beeping. I just carried on running my finger over her palm.

I love you
I love you
I love you
I love you
I love you
I love you

I didn't cry. Not when she died. Nor when the doctors finally noticed and ran into the room. Eventually one of them coaxed me away from her. In the movies when someone interferes like that, the newly bereaved man goes into a rage and has to be restrained – but I didn't do that. I just silently got up, and left.

I didn't cry when I was in the car, either. When I reached my house I pushed my keys into the lock and swung the door open. I went straight into the living room and sat on the couch.

The cat wandered in. I didn't know if it was because it somehow knew what had just happened or it could just sense something about me, but the creature was especially pathetic that day. It let out a small wail, and approached me, cautiously.

I tried to ignore her, but she jumped onto my lap and nuzzled my neck.

I looked down at her furry face and those large green eyes with blackened ovals in the centre. She meowed, again, and I suddenly felt this heavy feeling in my chest. I put my hand on her head, and ran my fingers through her fur.

"It's just me and you now, Flossy," I said.

She settled onto my lap, and I held her against me as the tears finally came.

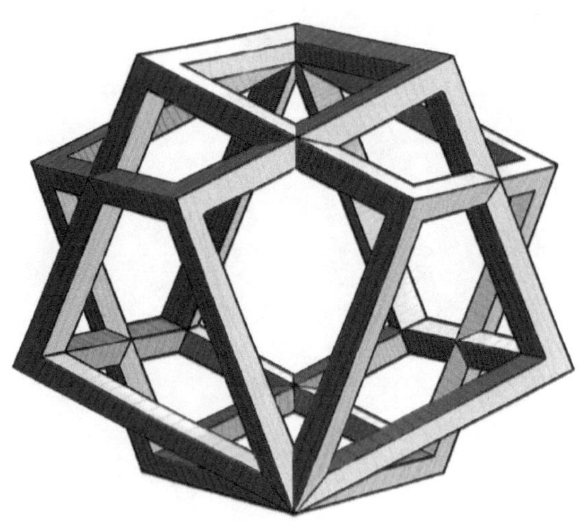

The Copy

by

Dave Weaver

Ever since, as a boy, Dave Weaver first watched invading Daleks trundle across London Bridge in grainy BBC monochrome, thrilled to Professor Quatermass' discovery of Martian corpses buried deep in the London Underground and read about mankind's tenuous grip on existence being almost wiped out by marauding Triffids, he has loved science fiction, particularly the British variety.

A graphic designer by day, Dave has been writing by night for over a decade. With numerous short stories published in anthologies and webzines, he has had three novels published by Elsewhen Press. Although much of his writing hovers on the shifting borders between fantasy and reality, science fiction has never been far away. After years of creating his own future-scapes of flawed space exploration, dystopian visions and time-warped analogies, Dave has his own tales to tell of future worlds and fantastic revelations. He firmly believes that the seeds of the future are all around us; it's not as far away or different as we might like to think.

She'd been with the host family for almost the full week. They had to give her a week by law, the whole seven days. Some gave slightly more, most didn't. It was better for all concerned to stick to the Government guidelines. No false hopes or misunderstandings.

The company told her the rules on day one; two hours after she awoke in the growth pod, an hour after they told her she wasn't who she thought she was. Wasn't anything like in fact; she was a Copy.

"No, you're wrong, you're crazy... let me out of here...call my parents, I want to go home, now!"

When the screaming and crying and swearing and frustrated anger had finally died down (all these violent new emotions that had come out of nowhere) they showed her the proof; the charts and x-rays, the pictures of her rapid growth in the pod, pictures of the host family watching as the fluids pumped into the tiny body did their work. That had been six months ago, they'd told her; today was her birth-day, today she was ready for them to start the procedure. But first she had one week.

While she sat shaking, staring into her incredibly finite future, the role was carefully, explicitly, explained to her. 'Time is of the essence now, if you agree', they told her. 'We must have your agreement by law'. The alternative of course was... well basically there wasn't one. Once she finally understood that, she listened.

Rule one: Don't talk to your host family unless they initiate the discussion.

Rule two: Don't go out on your own, or in fact anywhere from the home area unless accompanied by one or both host parents.

Rule three: Don't make personal contact with the Recipient unless a host parent is present.

Rule four: Even though you will share duplicate memories, even though you are a carbon copy of your Recipient please remember that your position is ephemeral; you are merely borrowing these traits for a short period of time. Any emotions felt, however fleetingly, will be yours and yours alone; this is how you will be paid for your co-operation, for your... usage.

Rule five: Don't try to reason, plead with or threaten your host family.

Rule six: Don't try to escape. There is a chip already implanted in your brain that will kill you if we deem you to be a 'runaway'. Don't make us do that to you; it will be far more painful than your decommissioning.

Rule seven: The most important rule of all: do not attempt to make an ally of your Recipient. They are in a physically and emotionally vulnerable state that can only be worsened by pressure from you. This is undesirable for all concerned.

If you are caught attempting to break any of these rules termination will occur immediately, despite the cost to the company, despite the upset for the host family, despite the valuable loss of time in the procedure. In summary, any discrepancy between your contractual agreement and performance thereof will not be tolerated.

You are being given one week of sentient life under these, and only these, conditions. Good luck and thank-you for agreeing to take part in this programme.

Please sign here. And state chosen name for this period.

She didn't care about that of course; she signed, and chose Anna. For 'analogue' you see, like a machine; a sense of humour must have survived along with the memories. Was that what they called irony?

One or other of the host family had taken her on sightseeing trips around their local neighbourhood. It was the accepted thing to do for your Copy; the experience of some kind of life, however brief, was inherent in the agreement.

The Recipient, their daughter, didn't come with them on their little jaunts to the park, or the zoo, or the swimming pool. Her condition forbade physical exertion but it was more than that. To be seen in public, side-by-side would have been awkward, embarrassing even, for both the daughter and the host parents. The girl white-faced and shaky, the Copy strong and glowing with health; nobody wanted to see that spectacle. That frightening glimpse of their own mortality...

So Anna had done all these things that week, the one precious week allotted to her, and in a way been grateful. It couldn't have been easy for them; to silently, guiltily, take her to these places, the ones their own child's memory had reminded Anna they'd all visited together before. She could still see herself at nine riding on the donkey at the petting zoo, her parents proudly filming her wide grin as she hung on tight. But of course it wasn't *her* grin, *her* memory, or *her* parents; they belonged to the girl in the bed back at the house. Soon the needle would be pushed into Anna's healthy skin, the drug that would still her brain but keep her young heart pumping for a while would be administered and all this, whatever 'this' was, would be over. The daughter would grow well again while she would be discarded and forgotten, become nothing more than an unpleasant family memory. An unfortunate but unavoidable 'procedure'...

So she made as much of it as she could; eating an ice cream they'd bought for her, the heat of the sun on her face, the breeze gently ruffling her hair, the water in the pool coolly caressing her skin with phantom fingertips, the carefree laughter of the children playing in the park, the smell and the touch of the animals at the zoo. She picked up a purring cat and felt another, wilder, heart beating next to her own; a heart that would beat on long after hers was eventually stilled in the hospital's cold antiseptic chamber of dismemberment and brain-death. Would she dream? she wondered. The company doctor had said no. Her brainwaves would virtually cease right after that one decisive injection of fluid into her bloodstream. She would no longer be aware, be sentient. This brief time was all she would ever have, these smells and sounds; that touch, this taste...

They all ate together on her last night, for the first time. Until then she'd been taken meals in her bedroom, away from the mother and father who ate together silently at the kitchen table (she opened the door to bring her plate down and saw the father head bowed over his untouched pasta whilst the mother stared past his head out of the window, seemingly at nothing). The daughter also ate in her room, the thin wall between them allowing the occasional clink of spoon against plate to be heard. It was almost the only sound she ever made, apart from the groans of pain that would wake Anna in the middle of the night, and the mother's frantic soothing.

But that last evening she was called downstairs to find all

three of them seated around a dining table spread with a little of everything they'd given her, plus other things she'd never tried. Some looked and smelt exotic; she knew the names, had eaten them before in the other's memory but to Anna their taste was still a beguiling mystery.

The daughter was propped-up by cushions, on a chair between the two adults. She raised her dark-ringed eyes to Anna as the mother clutched her hand.

"I'm sorry I haven't been in to see you before." It was the first time Anna had actually heard her speak; the voice was a cracked husky version of her own. She stopped to cough into a tissue then continued shakily. "I'm sorry for everything. I know you don't want to hear this from me right now..." more coughs, "but I have to say it while I still can. Thank-you... Thank-you for giving me the chance to live; I promise you I'll make the most of it. I won't forget you, or what you've done for me. I'll remember you for the rest of my life, however long that is."

Anna fought down the anger surging inside, 'however long that is' would still be a damn sight longer than hers.

She looked at the deathly pale imitation of herself; simpering pointless apologies next to the parents who'd paid their life savings to create Anna, use her up then destroy her. 'You're the Copy' she thought, 'you're the fake, not me. You're sick, I'm well, you're using me but I'd never do something like that. I'd rather die first.' But would she if in another world it ever came to that, if the positions were reversed; she the original about to lose everything, the other girl the Copy instead? Would she...?

In the car as they all drove to the company's medical centre that final morning, she tried to process all she could see, all she could feel, of the bright summer day. She opened the window for the breeze to flow through her hair, for the sun's warmth to find her upturned face, for the thousand and one subliminal sounds of this world to leave their trace on her mind. Once she was through those doors it would all be over; no more sensations left, bar fear of the lonely slide into oblivion.

Her attuned senses picked up a noise above the rest, high-pitched and discordant, monotonous. Looking out across the park they drove beside, the one visited on her first day, she realised what the sound was. "Stop the car please..."

"Anna, we haven't time. The appointment..."

But the father put his hand on his wife's and pulled over. "Don't go far, you've got five minutes. And please..." His face clouded with embarrassment.

"Don't worry; I won't try to run away."

She opened the door and walked slowly across the newly mown grass to the wailing child. She crouched down beside him. "What's the matter, have you lost your mummy?" The boy nodded, nose snotty, hand in his eye failing to stem the flow of tears. "It's alright, I'm sure she's here somewhere, looking for you. I'll stay until she finds you ok?" He nodded again, then clumsily put his short stubby arms around her neck. Anna squeezed the little body to her. She saw a flustered, panicky-looking woman rushing from one group of picnickers to another. Anna called out to her and waved. The woman stopped and looked her way, then began to run across the gap between them; halfway there, the run turned to a stiff walk as she collected herself.

"Oh thank-you, I'm so sorry, thank-you so much. I was... it's so kind of you..." She picked the child up and he clung to her. As she was walking away he turned to look over her shoulder and wave at Anna.

Lying on the bed as they were about to prepare her for surgery the company representative visited her again. "Thank-you for your co-operation Anna. We feel the experience has been mutually beneficial for all parties concerned and..."

"I want to change my name please." Anna cut him off.

He looked surprised. "I'm afraid that's highly irregular, the documentation involved..."

"I've read all the small-print; I know I have the right."

The company representative sighed. "Very well then, I'll make a note." He must have seen her doubtful expression as, surprisingly, he smiled. "You can trust me, it's the least we can do for your kind. What name did you have in mind?"

She thought of the child waving happily back at her, of the mother's wiped-away tears of relief, of the gentle breeze in her hair and the sun's warmth on her face. She thought of the terrible fragility of life itself, and the moment she'd shared that fragility with another.

She understood what it was to lose it and how other Recipients to come must realise this; that she was more, much more, than just an unfortunate procedure.

"Joy," she told him, "I want to be remembered as Joy."

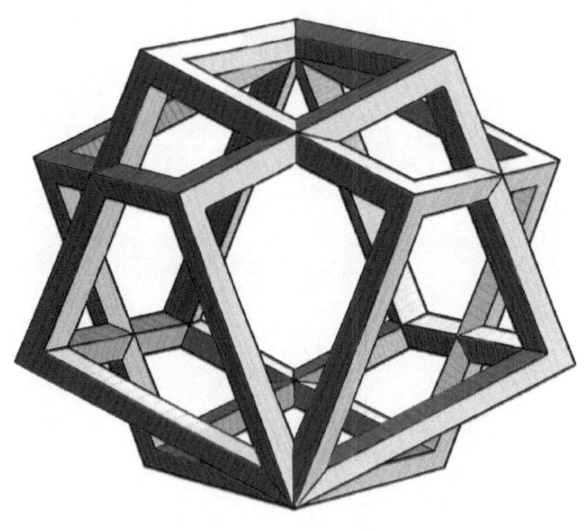

Murder in M-23

by

Peter Wolfe

Peter Wolfe lives the life of a hermit, desperately trying to avoid the mysterious and terrifying 'Real World', preferring instead the varying realities that inhabit his bookshelf and his mind.

Peter lives in Leeds with his fiancée and their cat, who has the joint function of being Emperor of the Known Universe and Chief Editor. His Lordship seems to disapprove of Peter's writing, forever stealing his pens and or leaving indecipherable comments by walking across the keyboard.

Peter's first published story was in *[Re]Awakenings* (Elsewhen Press, 2011). On a more personal note Peter finds writing about himself in the third person quite peculiar and fears that if he doesn't stop soon he might do a Jack Torrance. After all, All Work and No Play...

My name is Marcus Raines, disgraced naval officer, failed husband and alcoholic. When I woke up this morning my mouth was dry and my head was splitting. I rolled onto my side and vomited all over the deck plating. Spitting the sour taste from my mouth, I tried to pull myself up. It didn't work so well and instead I dropped back to the floor with a heavy (and very painful) thud. Unfortunately that set my head spinning and it took a few seconds before I could even see again. That's when I noticed something strange, I wasn't in my bed. Hell, it wasn't even my room.

I grabbed hold of the cargo pallet I was leaning against and dragged myself shakily to my feet. OK, cargo pallets, that probably meant I was in a cargo bay. That only helped a little though, the station had more than a hundred cargo bays ranging from some that were just a few metres square to the main bays which were more than half a mile long. I rubbed at my eyes and could just about make out a large M-23 painted on the wall. Well that explained which bay at least. It seemed familiar for some reason. Hadn't I been working there yesterday? Had I gone home? Hell, had I even made it to the end of my shift?

M-23 was one of the station's mid-sized cargo bays, almost three hundred metres long with dull grey walls and stacked high with cargo crates. The label beside me showed that the crates were filled with food packs bound for one of the colonies. Even thinking about the less than appetising food packs sent a wave of nausea flowing through me. It ended with what was left of the contents of my stomach spewing all over the floor and splashing up my boots. Slowly my head began to clear a little and I realised I could hear the distant murmuring of voices coming from the far side of the cavernous room.

I sobered up in an instant. It was against station regulations to be in one of the cargo bays out of hours. At best I'd lose my job, at worst get locked up by Station Security and accused of stealing or smuggling. As quietly as I could I meandered my way through the maze of crates until I came to a dead end. The voices were clearer now and coming from more than one location, inspection teams maybe. Rather than double back and risk bumping into someone, I clambered up one of the stacks, using the mag-grabs on my newly stained, station-issued boots to help. Using my new altitude to help me, I took a guess at which direction would lead me to the door and began crawling along the tops of the crates.

I almost made it. I was even close enough to see the access door, but a group of heavy looking guys in civilian clothes were standing around, guarding the entrance. Civilians weren't allowed in the cargo bays so in my mind there was no doubt who these guys were. They were smugglers.

Most people have a romanticised idea of smugglers. Ruggedly handsome rogues who bend the law, cheat the taxman and fight for the poor. None of that is true, not around here anyway. Smugglers are not nice. They are certainly not modern day Robin Hoods. They are just killers. When they aren't killing to help or hide their crimes, then they're killing with their contraband. Most of the time what they smuggle is illegal for a reason whether it be weapons, drugs or, if the smugglers are the lowest form of scumbag, people.

I watched from my perch, hoping that they might move off long enough for me to sneak past. I considered trying to make my way to the huge cargo bay doors at the far end of the room but decided against it. There was too great a chance of me bumping into some of the smugglers' friends and besides, I felt like crap. So I lay there and watched. Minutes passed and my already stiff body began to ache even more. Finally another group of rough looking men emerged from the stacks and stopped by the door. One of them was out of place and, unfortunately, I recognised the bastard.

James Franklin had been my supervisor on the docks for the past six years, ever since I'd been booted out of the service and left marooned on this godforsaken station. He'd always seemed like a good guy, stern but fair and usually willing to look the other way it if I turned up for a shift a little late, hungover or both. He was even nice enough to buy all the guys a round if he saw us while we were on a night out.

I watched as Franklin opened one of the crates and removed a small, cylindrical metal container that looked a lot like a cigar tube. It wasn't a cigar though. It was A.S.H.,

Adrenal Stimulant H, the new 'in' drug that let you run faster and further, lift more than you ever could normally and of course fuck for longer. But if you took it you were hooked for life. Literally. If you stopped taking, you died. My respect for Franklin dropped dramatically, but as I watched what happened next it went forever.

Franklin and two of the others grabbed hold of the crate and slid it forward revealing a grey cargo container hidden behind it. The door was a three metre square but, hidden inside the crates, I couldn't see how far back it went. Franklin placed a thumb on the keypad and the door slid open to reveal the cargo inside. Men and women dressed in plain grey jumpsuits were chained up inside. Men and women who were probably kidnapped from their beds, from their homes. Men and women who were chained and beaten and who were bound for frontier colonies where they would be used as labour until they died from exhaustion. Men and women made into slaves. Suddenly, I hated Franklin.

Even if slavery wasn't totally immoral and depraved, there is no need for slaves anymore. Clone servitors were created centuries ago for the express purpose of doing all menial tasks so humans never had to. But when did humans ever need a reason to do something that would hurt someone?

One of the smugglers said something to Franklin that made him laugh and me want to jump down there and pound his face in. I restrained myself though, being outnumbered eight-to-one helped. Franklin turned back to the crate, preparing to close the door and reseal the slaves in darkness. As he did so, the smuggler who made him laugh raised his arm, a gun held in his hand and fired a round into the back of Franklin's head. Ten minutes ago I would have been upset at Franklin's death, not anymore. The blood sprayed over the slaves who all began to scream. Even from where I lay I heard the thud as Franklin's head hit the deck, then watched as the man I had now mentally nicknamed 'Joker' fired three more rounds into his body.

Normally the sight of blood doesn't bother me but I wasn't feeling too good and unfortunately my body chose this moment to puke again. The vomit hadn't had time to fall to the deck plates below before the smugglers opened fire on me, bullets ricocheting off the crates and ceiling alike. I rolled left and dropped off the pile of crates and onto the floor with a heavy bang. It hurt like hell but I didn't wait. I scrambled to my feet and set off at a sprint through the labyrinth of crates, heading in what I hoped was the direction of the cargo bay doors. Behind me I heard shouts and the thundering of feet as the heavies near the door began to give chase. Luckily I had a head start, they needed to make their way around the crates. Even so, I'd better not waste it.

I careened around a corner and saw two confused looking smugglers ahead of me. I hadn't seen them near the door so they probably didn't know what was going on. I decided not to give them a chance and shoulder-barged one of them into a crate while ramming my elbow into the throat of the other. Both dropped to the floor, the one I'd elbowed gasping for air through his crushed throat. I gave the other a quick kick to the gut before bracing myself against the crate. I was already breathing heavily and my body was nowhere near recovered from the previous night's binge. I couldn't pause though. Panting, I started to run again, weaving around crates and hoping to hell that I didn't run into any more smugglers or dead ends. I paused at a cross roads of crates, desperate for a chance to catch my breath, as I decided on a direction.

No luck though, I heard noises behind me, a shout then a gunshot and a bullet ricocheted off a crate beside me, grazing my right thigh as it passed. I let out an involuntary noise, somewhere between a yell and a (manly) scream, and limped forward, leg stinging, but not wasting time looking back. I took a left, another left, a right, ran straight on then took another right and found myself staring at the huge doors. I gave thanks to whichever gods were looking after me and put on another burst of speed. I collapsed against the door console and fumbled my station key card from my uniform pocket. I swiped the card and heard a huge 'THUNK' as the doors unlocked and began to slowly inch open. I dived towards the opening and began to squeeze through the gap.

There was another shout and bullets bounced off the door around me. I forced my way through the widening gap and reached for the console on the other side, slamming my hand on the large, red button on the surface, the one titled

'EMERGENCY OVERRIDE'. Slowly the doors ground to a halt and reversed their path, grinding shut. At the same time red lights began to flash and a siren sounded, warning people not to get their stupid asses crushed by the big doors. Finally the doors shut completely, the huge bolts locking into place. I fell to my knees, legs turned to jelly, chest heaving and body trying to vomit up contents that just weren't there. My head was pounding and my vision fading. My body just couldn't handle the mix of hangover, detox and adrenaline. I needed to find a place to lick my wounds and recover. Fortunately I knew a place nearby. I stumbled across empty F-24 to the main door where I carefully peered out making sure the coast was clear. Then, taking a right I jogged along the corridor, seeing no one except the occasional diminutive servitor as I went. It must have been early, the docks on this side of the station were always busy with the exception of the scheduled morning maintenance. Eventually I came to an elevator and pushed the keypad for J deck. I slumped against the wall as the lift whirred into motion and began to drop down through the mid-levels of the station.

30 seconds later the lift came to a stop and I staggered out, almost bumping into a servitor. The short grey skinned creature bowed its bulbous head as I emerged from the lift, its large lidless eyes fixed firmly on the ground. Stepping around it, I began to move along the corridor for a few metres until I found the door I was looking for. Supply Closet J-154 hadn't been used by anyone except me (and servitors) in the six years I'd been on the station and I'd passed out there drunk more than once. It should be safe. I opened the door with my thumb print and staggered inside. It was deserted as always and I was unconscious in the corner only seconds after the door slid shut.

When I woke again I felt slightly better. Don't get me wrong, my head still hurt, my body ached and now the pain in my leg added to it all. Somehow, while asleep, I'd cocooned myself in the handful of blankets I'd left here as a makeshift bed. Untangling myself, I noticed the blood on the sheets and paused to inspect my leg. The bleeding seemed to have stopped but the gash still hurt like a bitch. Dragging myself up, I began to hop my way over to the small sink in the opposite corner. Underneath I found the stash of medical supplies I'd left there, fished out a med-patch and slapped it onto my leg. Almost instantly I felt the pain lessen as the nano-whatsits got to work on the wound. Letting out a sigh, I turned on the tap and began gulping down the cold water. I splashed some on my face and glanced in the mirror. It wasn't a pretty sight. My eyes were red and bloodshot, my skin a few shades too pale, my hair greasy and plastered to my skull. Between that and the stubble on my chin I looked like hell.

In the corner of the mirror a flashing light caught my eye. Stretching out a hand I tapped it and the mirror changed to show a different version of my face, though this one wasn't much prettier. Now I had two black eyes, broken nose and busted lip. I looked more than a little drunk. Under my face were words which made my blood freeze: 'WARNING! MARCUS RAINES – WANTED FOR MURDER. DO NOT APPROACH. MAY BE ARMED. IF YOU SEE THIS MAN CONTACT STATION SECURITY IMMEDIATELY.' They were using the mug shot from the last time I had been picked up by the station's security forces for drinking and brawling. Below the wanted poster a newsfeed was playing and, as I tapped it, it grew to fill the screen as one of the stations many bottom-feeding press officers reported on the bullshit story.

"Dockworker Marcus Raines is wanted by Station Security in relation to the murder of supervisor James Franklin earlier this morning. The office of the Security Chief has refused to comment but sources inside the department report that Raines key card was used shortly after the murder and that his DNA was found near the body. He is considered armed and danger–" I tapped the display and shut the bitch off mid-sentence. Shit. Note to self, don't vomit at crime scenes. This changed things, no way could I go to Security now. They'd never believe me. I was royally screwed! Murderous smugglers hunting me on one side and trigger-happy Station Security on the other. What the hell was I going to do?

I flopped onto a box of cleaning supplies and considered what to do next. I had to get away from both factions and off the station. First stop would have to be my quarters though, I had my old service pistol stashed there. I stripped off the stained work clothes leaving my key card in the pocket (it would only get me caught now anyway) and tugged on a spare pair of trousers and a battered brown jacket (both left behind from previous stays).

Emerging from the closet I found the corridor empty and set off back to the lift. Arriving without incident, I hit the button for P deck where I slipped onto one of the mag-trains bound for the residential district. The entire journey I just sat, eyes fixed on the floor, expecting to be spotted at any second. I guess I just looked like any drunk heading home though because no one approached me or raised the alarm. When the train reached my stop I hopped off but didn't head straight home. Security were sure to be watching so I had to be sneaky. Luckily I knew a way.

Like the docking area (and everywhere else on the station), the walls of the residential area were a dull grey but this area seemed much more lived in, with the walls being scuffed, dirty and even covered in graffiti. It was also much more cramped here, the corridors were barely wide enough for two people, the lights were dim and even the ceilings were lower. I'm 6'2" and the top of my head almost scraped the roof. Behind one of the adjacent dorm blocks, I found what I was looking for: a maintenance shaft which took me up into the crawlspace between decks. It would be a tight squeeze and take me almost fifteen minutes to wriggle across to my quarters but it was safer than using the front door.

The space between decks was incredibly tight, barely half a metre high, and, with no lights, felt a lot like being trapped in a coffin. Moving through it wasn't easy either, my clothes and boots kept catching on exposed bolts and I banged by head more than a few times. The only saving grace were the numbers on the ceiling tiles to indicate which room lay below, numbers which I unfortunately had to read by the meagre light of my comm unit. Those fifteen minutes were some of the longest of my life.

When I finally arrived, I carefully unscrewed the ceiling tile and peeked into the room below. The whisky bottle next to the toothbrush told me I had the right bathroom and from what I could see the coast was clear. I dropped down as quietly as I could and slotted the tile back into place. I looked longingly at the whisky bottle wishing I could take a drink. I knew it would make me feel better, hair of the dog and all that, but I also knew I'd end up finishing the bottle and I needed my wits about me if I was going to survive.

Trying my best to ignore the bottle I tapped the keypad and opened the door to my main living space. What I found there was chaos. I'm not the neatest of people but this mess was not mine. Everything had been turned over. Books had been tossed from their shelves, clothes ripped from drawers and dumped on the floor, bed stripped and turned over and the biggest surprise, two hulking guys stood in the centre of the maelstrom of mess.

There was a moment where I just stood there, not sure what to do next. To be fair one of the men looked just as shocked as I did, the other just looked angry. He had good reason to be pissed though, the last time we had met I'd barged him into a bulkhead and kicked him in the stomach. He let out an almost bestial roar and charged at me. Thinking quickly, I stepped back into the bathroom and stuck out a leg. Childish I know, but it worked. Beast man tripped over my leg and went head first into the wall, his big bald head making a sickening crack as it collided with the solid steel. Leaping forward, I tackled his friend before he could react and heard an 'Umph' as the breath was driven from his lungs and my momentum carried us both to the floor. My opponent recovered quickly and drove a fist into my stomach causing the air to explode from my own lungs and making me want to retch again.

I fought down the need to vomit and struggled to catch my breath. Unfortunately the smuggler wasn't willing to give me the chance. Twisting his body round he sat astride my chest and began to pummel me around the face. He was strong, seriously strong, and his blows felt like sledgehammers. I raised my arms, trying to deflect the blows and protect my face as best I could. Wriggling and trying to throw him off me did nothing, the bastard was just too damn heavy so I resorted to cheating.

Punching someone (especially over and over) isn't as easy

as most people think. In fact it's damn exhausting so I did my best to keep blocking, waiting for an opening. The moment his onslaught slowed, I struck. I swung both arms up as hard and fast as I could, cupping my hands as I did, and slapping them onto the smuggler's ears with all the force I could muster. He gave a scream and clapped his hands to his ears. Using the distraction I jerked my hips once more and this time managed to throw him off. I glanced around for something I could use and saw an empty whisky bottle half under the bed. Grabbing it by the neck, I brought it smashing down on the smuggler's face. He grunted as I raised the bottle again and again and again until finally he was quiet and I let the bloody bottle drop to the floor.

I had just made it back to my feet when I heard another shout and turned to see Beast man staggering out from the bathroom. There was a large cut on his head but the worrying thing was that it was already healing. He was an ASH user which meant he was not going to be as 'easy' to take down as his friend.

I dived for the bloody bottle on the floor hoping I could stun Beast with it but as I swung it at his head he easily caught my hand. He gave a squeeze sending pain shooting up my arm and causing me to drop the bottle. Still holding my wrist he backhanded me across the face.

I could only have been out for a second because when the world came back into focus I was still on my feet held in Beast's vicelike grip. I needed to get free. This guy could kill me without breaking a sweat if he wanted to, and by now he definitely wanted to. Time to cheat again. I know it's not honourable but fuck honour, as far as I see it if you're in a fight, you do anything you can to survive. So with that thought I kicked him as hard as I could in the balls.

It didn't do much good though. I was hoping he'd end up curled up on the floor whimpering but he barely flinched, just grunted. His grip did loosen a little though, just enough for me to twist free. I staggered backwards, legs still weak. Before I had a chance to recover and regroup Beast lunged at me, one massive fist swinging at my head. I ducked under the blow and dodged around him, managing to trip over the upturned mattress and fall into the bathroom. As I fell to the floor I grabbed for anything I could use but when I finally landed all I found in my hand was my toothbrush.

Suddenly Beast was towering over me and reached down to grab the front of my jacket. Desperate, I gripped the toothbrush as hard as I could and jammed it into his left eye. This time he reacted. Beast let out a deafening bellow and staggered backwards giving me a chance to get back to my feet. What I wanted now was my gun but it was stashed on the far side of the room, behind Beast. Even wounded the guy was a monster. His punches, if they connected, were probably lethal. Since I couldn't get to my gun I decided to improvise. While he was distracted I crept closer and acted quickly. I hooked my left hand behind his head to brace it while, with my right, I punched the toothbrush as hard as I could driving it deeper into Beast's eye socket. Instantly Beast stopped struggling and silence fell in my quarters.

Beast's enormous body slumped to the floor just as dead as his partner. I let out a sigh of relief, collapsing down next to them. I didn't care, I just let my body relax: felt the utter exhaustion and the shaking that came with the adrenaline leaving my system. As soon as I could, I got back to my feet and headed to my small wardrobe. Most of the clothes I kept there were currently decorating the floor but they weren't what I was after. I was in luck, the loose floorplate was still in place and my gun, along with the three spare magazines, were all where I'd left them.

I carefully tucked the pistol into my waistband and slipped the clips into my pocket then I stripped off the jacket and shirt which were now covered in blood and snatched a cleanish jacket and one of my old navy shirts from the floor. Donning them quickly I ducked into the now quite trashed bathroom and splashed water on my face in an attempt to wash off the worst of the blood. Then, bracing my foot on the sink, I climbed back into the ceiling, not relishing the prospect of the claustrophobic crawl back to the maintenance shaft.

Sandy's Bar was a fixture on the promenade, at least to anyone who lived on or around P deck. I'm sure the fancy upper levels had their own posh bars with champagne and caviar and the lower decks had their dive bars, but Sandy's was ours.

Sandy's was a nice, clean place styled after an Old Earth English pub. Lots of synthetic wood and beer on tap. He also had a good supply of whiskies which he got from a freighter captain he knew. Despite all that had happened to me since first waking, it was still early in the day and not quite lunchtime. Samuel Sandy didn't bother opening until late afternoon. He always said it was because he was a busy guy, but I thought it was just so he could sleep in. Sam usually helped himself to a decent amount of his own stock each night and it was a common sight to see him as drunk as any of his patrons.

I dropped into the bar through the ceiling tiles just as I had into my quarters. The drop was a bit further here, but I managed to turn my landing into a roll, narrowly avoiding a couple of stools. Climbing to my feet, I clutched at my right side. As I'd been crawling through the maintenance passage away from my quarters I had become aware of the pain. Either Beast or his friend had broken a rib or two sometime during the fight. At first I thought the bar was empty but, after a quick inspection behind the bar (I was making sure the place was secure and certainly not checking out the whisky bottles!), I discovered Sam, camped out on a bed of blankets. From the stains on the blankets this probably wasn't the first time he'd crashed here either.

"Sam!" It took a fair bit of shouting and shaking to rouse the bartender before I sat him down on a stool with a bottle of water and a promise not to shout anymore. Sam was somewhere in his forties but you wouldn't know it from looking at him, he was solidly built and in great shape. He could have passed for twenty if not for the long grey hair that he had pulled back into a ponytail.

"Marcus, you know you're always welcome here but I have to ask, what the hell are you doing here so early? And how'd you even get in?"

I considered what to tell him. I knew Sam pretty well, hell I'd spent more time in his bar in the last six years than I ever spent with my wife. An unfortunate fact that pretty much explained why my marriage failed. No, I trusted Sam. He was a friend and I needed his help. Perching on a stool, I began to tell him everything: where I'd woken up, what I'd witnessed, the chase, the fight in my quarters, even the news broadcast I'd seen. By the end Sam looked stunned and almost sober.

"Damn. You don't come in for one night and look at the trouble you get into. Wait here." Sam got up and crossed to the till behind the bar before tapping a few buttons. The drawer popped out and Sam paused for a second. After a moment he pulled out a stack of credits and tossed them to me, "Here, these'll help. And you're in luck, todays the day my whisky shipment comes in. Docking Bay 17. The captain's name is Spencer Morgan. I'll let him know you're coming and he'll give you a lift off the station."

I shook my head, "This is too much," I waved the stack of credits at him, "I've no way to pay you back."

"I know you'll find a way. Send it by courier ship if you have to." Sam checked his watch. "Spencer's ship should be arriving in about an hour. You'd best get to the docking ring." He made his way around the bar and towards the door, "I'll go first and make sure Security aren't watching the place. Give it two minutes then head for the docks and for god's sake, use the door."

Sam did his job well. When I left the bar there was no sign of him or any security forces and I managed to make it all the way to the station's docking ring without incident. Oddly the docking bay I was headed to wasn't far from M-23. This worried me, Station Security or even the smugglers could still be lurking around. Because of this I crept along the corridors and checked every corner before rounding it. I'm sure I looked damn suspicious but, apart from servitors scurrying around on their various tasks, the hallways were curiously empty. Maybe the murder had scared people away.

I arrived early and ducked into the bay. The docking chamber was very similar to the cargo bay, except for the enormous air lock which opened out into space, and a cargo crane in the corner which would be used to aid unloading. The space door was still sealed, meaning Captain Morgan's freighter had yet to arrive so I paused, wondering what to do. I didn't want to wait around, in case someone came in and recognised me but I also didn't want to leave, in case I got delayed and missed my ride. That just left hiding.

I crossed to the cargo crane ladder, passing dozens of crates stacked chest high near the wall, and climbed up into the cab near the roof. I was barely settled when the hallway door opened and six heavily armed smugglers burst inside, automatic rifles sweeping the room. By some stroke of luck none of them thought to look up. Had they followed me or were they checking everywhere nearby? I got my answer when the six of them finished their sweep and took up position at the door clearly waiting for someone. They were definitely there for me.

Quietly as I could, I slipped my pistol from my waistband and checked the safety was off. Something told me I was going to need it. I didn't have to wait long. After just a few minutes the door opened again and two familiar figures stepped through it: Joker and Sam. I began to panic. Somehow they'd got hold of Sam and it was all my fault. He'd been trying to help and now he might get hurt because of me. That was when I got my second shock.

Sitting up in the crane's cab, I was too far away to hear anything going on below me but I could see just fine. Sam began gesturing angrily but instead of seeming pissed off the smugglers appeared to be doing whatever it was he was telling them to do. He was part of this, one of them. Hell, from the way they were acting he might be in charge!

My former friend, the traitorous scumbag, didn't stay long. After about a minute he turned and left the way he'd come, leaving Joker and his men watching the door. Well, I was back to square one: trapped on this damn station with no way off. As I pondered what to do, the doors opened once more but instead of Sam, it was a pair of security officers. Down below me everyone froze. Then one of the officers went for his gun but, before he could even get it out of his holster, he and his partner died in a hail of bullets.

This was my chance, using the distraction I climbed from the crane's cab and slid down the ladder using my mag-grabs to stop my descent just short of the deck. I ducked behind the crates and made my way swiftly along the edge of the room. I peeked around the corner and found I was barely twenty metres from the smugglers and most of them even had their backs to me. I wasn't going to get a better chance than this. I levelled my gun and quickly squeezed off the whole clip.

By this point my dishonourable discharge from the navy had been more than six years earlier and, with guns being banned on the station, I hadn't practiced since. I was a tad rusty and the shakes didn't help either. Still, I did manage to hit four of them and they quickly dropped to the floor – not that I stayed to watch. I ducked back behind the crate, already ejecting the empty magazine and fumbling a fresh one into the slot. Behind me I could feel the crate shaking as the three remaining smugglers fired round after round into it. When they paused to reload I leant back out and fired off a pair of shots. My aim was improving. One of them took a bullet in the head and dropped to the deck.

When the Joker and his friend opened fire again, I crept back along the row of crates a few metres before popping back up to fire off another round. Joker's pal span to shoot at me as soon as I emerged from behind the crates, his hail of bullets throwing off my aim so that, instead of getting another kill, the gunshot went through his leg. There was a scream and the sounds of gunfire stopped. I turned and, still hunched over, ran the length of the room and back to the base of the crane. I turned the corner and waited, wondering what Joker would do. Would he continue to hunt me? Or help his friend and maybe fall back?

I got my answer when I heard the sound of a single gunshot and the screaming stopped. Joker was one heartless bastard. I peeked around the corner once more and my chest exploded with pain. It was so extreme that I blacked out again.

This time I was out for more than a second. When I came to I was struggling to breathe and Joker was standing near me, his back turned. He'd assumed I was dead. To be honest normally when you hit someone in the chest with an automatic weapon that's a safe assumption. Normally they aren't wearing a naval issue nano-weave shirt though. The shirt, while able to stop the bullet, couldn't stop the force of the impact. It had felt like being hit by a shuttle and would leave a hell of a bruise. Still, better than being dead I suppose.

I wasn't going to give Joker the chance to realise his mistake. I reached for the pistol lying beside me, raised it and emptied the remainder of the magazine into his back. Yeah, yeah, I know it was a low blow but you already know my opinion on fighting fair. Anyway it was the exact same chance he'd given Franklin. Lying on the ground I pulled up my shirt to check the damage. Slap bang in the centre of my chest was a nasty looking red welt. If I hadn't been wearing a bullet-proof shirt I'd be dead for sure.

Very carefully and very, very slowly I rolled onto my side and climbed to my feet, wincing and groaning most of the way. Putting weight on my right leg, it almost gave way and I discovered that the med-patch had come loose, ripping open my earlier cut as it did. I gave a sigh. This was turning out to be a very long day. Then, grumbling to myself, I began to limp for the door.

The lights were off in Sandy's when I dropped from the ceiling for what felt like the hundredth time that day. This time had been worse than the others, not only did I have to contend with the tight spaces but also the pain in my chest. In the end I'd had to give up and slide my way along on my back. My landing was less than elegant as well, my leg instantly gave way and I collapsed to the ground with a crash and a great deal of swearing.

As I lay on the ground, I waited for Sam or one of his goons to come running in with their guns drawn but, even after a few seconds, the bar remained silent. Somehow I had made it back before Sam. I dragged myself up using a table, and drew my gun, checking around before settling myself in the darkest corner, facing the door. I was tempted again to help myself to a bottle of whisky behind the bar but all the action had me exhausted and the brief respite from violence gave me a chance to rest and (rather unwisely) fall asleep.

I jerked awake when I heard the bar door opening and the sound of someone talking on their comm unit. I pressed myself as far into the shadows as I could and tightened my grip on my pistol.

"No, it's being dealt with. Has the shipment been moved? Good." I heard the door shut and the voice moved deeper into the dark room. "I'll let you know when I know. I've got to go, the bar needs opening. Business has to go on as usual." I heard a beep as the call cut out and after some fumbling around the lights flared on. "Shit!" Sam, it seemed, was surprised to find a gun pointed at his head, "What, err, what are you doing here Marcus? Shouldn't you be at the docks?"

I got slowly to my feet, "You know what I'm doing here Sam. Thought maybe you'd want a chance to kill me yourself instead of having your heavies do it, you son of a bitch."

To his credit Sam dropped the act pretty quickly, the bastard even smiled. "How'd you catch me? Something I said?"

"No, I saw you. I was in the docking bay when you arrived. I watched you tell those dicks to kill me. Oh, and they won't be doing business with you anymore. They're all dead."

Sam's smile didn't falter but he did take a step backwards, "There are always more smugglers, I'm sure I'll find someone else to do business with. What is it you want Marcus? A ship? I've got a shuttle stashed away down on V. It can be all yours if you just leave."

"Don't worry I'm going, but first I have a few questions," I watched as Sam took another step backwards. "Why slaves? I can understand the drugs even if I do think you're a scumbag son of a bitch, but why people? Were you just not destroying enough lives?"

"Just business Marcus, just business." He took another step backwards so he was leaning against the bar.

Now it was my turn to smile, "You really are scum Sam. I trusted you, thought you were a friend but you're just scum." Sam edged towards the till. "Don't bother Sam. I've already taken the gun from the till. Why didn't you just shoot me earlier?" His only answer was a shrug but at last that arrogant smile was gone. "I take it from your call that the slaves are already off the station?" Silence. "I'm going to find them. You've made sure I can't stay here so I'm going to find them and free them." I strode over to Sam and grabbed him by the shirt, "Care to make it easy and tell me where they are?" His poker face was unreadable. "I thought not." I gave Sam a shove and he collapsed onto one of the bars many chairs. I walked round to stand behind him, "Goodbye Sam."

The gunshot seem thunderous in the otherwise silent bar then there was a moment of silence before, THUD, Sam's body hit the floor. He died just as Franklin had, just like they both deserved. Two people I thought I knew had turned out to be slave trading trash. My ability to judge people was seriously messed up. Somehow I didn't think I'd ever be so quick to trust again.

Elsewhen Press
an independent publisher specialising in Speculative Fiction

Visit the Elsewhen Press website at elsewhen.press for the latest information on all of our titles, authors and events; to read our blog; find out where to buy our books and ebooks; or to place an order.

J.A. Christy

SmartYellow™

SmartYellow™ is the story of a young girl, Katrina Williams, who finds herself on the wrong side of social services. After becoming pregnant with only a slight notion of the father's identity, she is disowned by her parents and goes to live on a social housing estate. Before long she is being bullied by a gang involved in criminal activity and anti-social behaviour. Seeking help from the authorities she is persuaded to return to the estate to work as part of Operation Schrödinger, alongside a surveillance specialist. But she soon realises that Operation Schrödinger is not what it seems.

Exploring themes of social inequity and scientific responsibility, J.A. Christy's first speculative fiction novel leads her heroine Katrina to understand how probability, hope and empathy play a huge part in the flow of life and are absent in the stagnation of mere survival. As readers we also start to question how we would know if the power of the State to support and care for the weak had become corrupted into the oppression of all those who do not fit society's norms.

SmartYellow™ offers a worryingly plausible and chilling glimpse into an alternate Britain. For the sake of order and for the benefit of more fortunate members of society, those seen as socially undesirable are marked with SmartYellow™, making it easier for them to be controlled and maintained in a state of fruitless inactivity. Writer, J.A. Christy, turns an understanding and honest eye not only onto the weak, who have failed to cope with life, but also onto those who ruthlessly exploit them for their own ends. At times tense and threatening, at times tender and insightful, *SmartYellow*™ is a rewarding and thought-provoking read.

ISBN: 9781908168788 (epub, kindle) / 9781908168689 (320pp paperback)
Visit bit.ly/SmartYellow

Peter R. Ellis

Evil Above the Stars

This thrilling fantasy series appeals to readers, of all ages, of fantasy or science fiction, especially fans of JRR Tolkien and Stephen Donaldson. If old theories are correct until a new idea comes along, does the universe change with our perception of it? Were the ideas embodied in alchemy ever right? What realities were the basis of Celtic mythology?

Volume 1: Seventh Child

September Weekes discovers a stone that takes her to *Gwlad*, where she is hailed as the one with the power to defend them against the evil known as the Malevolence. September meets the leader and bearers of metals linked to the seven 'planets' that give them special powers to resist the elemental manifestations of the Malevolence. She returns home, but a fortnight later, is drawn back to find that two years have passed and there have been more attacks. She must help defend *Gwlad* against the Malevolence.

ISBN: 9781908168702 (epub, kindle) / 9781908168603 (256pp paperback)

Volume 2: The Power of Seven

September with the Council of *Gwlad* must plan the defence of the Land. The time of the next Conjunction will soon be at hand. The planets, the Sun and the Moon will all be together in the sky. At that point the protection of the heavenly bodies will be at its weakest and *Gwlad* will be more dependent than ever on September. But now it seems that she must defeat Malice, the guiding force behind the Malevolence, if she is to save the Land and all its people. Will she be strong enough; and, if not, to whom can she turn for help?

ISBN: 9781908168719 (epub, kindle) / 9781908168610 (288pp paperback)

Volume 3: Unity of Seven

September is back home and it is still the night of her birthday, despite having spent over three months in *Gwlad* battling the Malevolence. Back to facing the bullies at school she worries about the people of *Gwlad*. She must discover a way to return to the universe of *Gwlad* and the answer seems to lie in her family history. The five *Cludydds* before September and her mother were her ancestors. The clues take her on a journey in time and space which reveals that while in great danger she is also the key to the survival of all the universes. September must overcome her own fears, accept an extraordinary future and, once again, face the evil above the stars.

ISBN: 9781908168917 (epub, kindle) / 9781908168818 (256pp paperback)

Visit bit.ly/EvilAbove

STEVE HARRISON

TimeStorm

In 1795 a convict ship leaves England for New South Wales in Australia. Nearing its destination, it encounters a savage storm but, miraculously, the battered ship stays afloat and limps into Sydney Harbour. The convicts rebel, overpower the crew and make their escape, destroying the ship in the process. Fleeing the sinking vessel with only the clothes on their backs, the survivors struggle ashore.

Among the escaped convicts, seething resentments fuel an appetite for brutal revenge against their former captors, while the crew attempts to track down and kill or recapture the escapees. However, it soon becomes apparent that both convicts and crew have more to concern them than shipwreck and a ruthless fight for survival; they have arrived in Sydney in 2017.

TimeStorm is a thrilling epic adventure story of revenge, survival and honour. In the literary footsteps of Hornblower, comes Lieutenant Christopher 'Kit' Blaney, an old-fashioned hero, a man of honour, duty and principle. But dragged into the 21st century... literally.

A great fan of the grand seafaring adventure fiction of CS Forester, Patrick O'Brien and Alexander Kent and modern action thriller writers like Lee Child, Steve Harrison combines several genres in his fast-paced debut novel as a group of desperate men from the 1700s clash in modern-day Sydney.

ISBN: 9781908168542 (epub, kindle) / 9781908168443 (368pp paperback)
Visit bit.ly/TimeStorm

Ira Nayman

**A series of novels attempting to document the trials and tribulations
of the Transdimensional Authority**

If there were Alternate Realities, and in each there was a version of Earth (very similar, but perhaps significantly different in one particular regard, or divergent since one particular point in history) then imagine the problems that could be caused if someone, somewhere, managed to work out how to travel between them. Those problems would be ideal fodder for a News Service that could also span all the realities. Now you understand the reasoning behind the Alternate Reality News Service (ARNS). But you aren't the first. In fact, Canadian satirist and author Ira Nayman got there before you and has been the conduit for ARNS into our Reality for some years now, thanks to his website *Les Pages aux Folles*.

But also consider that if there were problems being caused by unregulated travel between realities, it's not just news but a perfect ~~excuse~~ reason to establish an Authority to oversee such travel and make sure that it is regulated. You probably thought jurisdictional issues are bad enough between competing national agencies of dubious acronym and even more dubious motivation, let alone between agencies from different nations. So imagine how each of them would cope with an Authority that has jurisdiction across the realities in different dimensions. Now, you understand the challenges for the investigators who work for the Transdimensional Authority (TA). But, perhaps more importantly, you can see the potential for humour. Again, Ira beat you to it.

Welcome to the Multiverse*
*** Sorry for the inconvenience**
Being the first
ISBN: 9781908168191 (epub, kindle) / 9781908168092 (336pp paperback)

You Can't Kill the Multiverse*
*** But You Can Mess With its Head**
Being the second
ISBN: 9781908168399 (epub, kindle) / 9781908168290 (320pp paperback)

Random Dingoes
Being the third
ISBN: 9781908168795 (epub, kindle) / 9781908168696 (288pp paperback)

Visit bit.ly/TransdimensionalAuthority

Christopher G. Nuttall

Royal Sorceress series

Book I: The Royal Sorceress

In an alternate history, the principles of magic, discovered in the 1770s, saw Britain win the American War of Independence. Master Thomas, the King's aged Royal Sorcerer, needs a successor with mastery of all magical powers. The only candidate, untrained & unacknowledged, is perfect in every way but one: the Royal College of Sorcerers has never admitted a girl before.

But even before Lady Gwendolyn Crichton can begin her training, London is plunged into chaos by a campaign of terrorist attacks co-ordinated by Jack, a powerful and rebellious magician.

ISBN: 9781908168184 (epub, kindle) / 9781908168085 (400pp, paperback)
Visit bit.ly/TheRoyalSorceress

Book II: The Great Game

After the uprising in London, Lady Gwendolyn Crichton is settling into her new position as Royal Sorceress and fighting the prejudice against her gender and age that seeks to prevent her from fulfilling her responsibilities. But when a senior magician is murdered in a locked room and Gwen is charged with finding the culprit, her inquiries lead her into a web of intrigue that combines international politics, widespread aristocratic blackmail, gambling dens and personal vendettas... and some of her discoveries hit dangerously close to home.

ISBN: 9781908168375 (epub, kindle) / 9781908168276 (400pp, paperback)
Visit bit.ly/TheGreatGame

Book III: Necropolis

The British Empire is teetering on the brink of a war with France that may, for the first time, see magicians in the ranks on both sides. As Royal Sorceress, Gwen will be responsible for the Empire's magical resources when the time comes. But her adopted daughter Olivia, the only known living necromancer, has been kidnapped. Intelligence soon establishes that it was Russian agents who took Olivia, so an incognito Gwen joins a British diplomatic mission to St Petersburg.

ISBN: 9781908168726 (epub, kindle) / 9781908168627 (416pp, paperback)
Visit bit.ly/RSNecropolis

Sanem Ozdural

LiGa series

A thought-provoking series of books in an essentially contemporary setting, with elements of both science fiction and fantasy.

LiGa™
Book I

Literary science fiction, LiGa™ tells of a game in which the players are, literally, gambling with their lives. In the near-future a secretive organisation has developed technology to transfer the regenerative power of a body's cells from one person to another, conferring extended or even indefinite life expectancy. As a means of controlling who benefits from the technology, access is obtained by winning a tournament of chess or bridge to which only a select few are invited. At its core, the game is a test of a person's integrity, ability and resilience. Sanem's novel provides a fascinating insight into the motivation both of those characters who win and thus have the possibility of virtual immortality and of those who will effectively lose some of their life expectancy.

ISBN: 9781908168160 (epub, kindle) / 9781908168061 (400pp paperback)
Visit bit.ly/BookLiGa

THE DARK SHALL DO WHAT LIGHT CANNOT
Book II

We find out more about the organisation behind LiGa as we travel with some of them to Pera, a place which lies beyond the Light Veil on the other side of reality. There are light trees there that eat sunlight and bear fruit that, in turn, lights up and energises (literally) the community of Pera. There are light birds that glitter in the night because they have eaten the seed of the lightberry. The House of Light and Dark, which is the domain of the Sun and her brother, Twilight, welcomes all creatures living in Pera. But in the midst of all the glitter, laughter and the songs, it must be remembered that the lightberry is poisonous to the non-Pera born, and the Land is afraid when the Sun retreats, for it is then that Twilight walks the streets…

ISBN: 9781908168740 (epub, kindle) / 9781908168641 (480pp paperback)
Visit bit.ly/Darkshalldo

DOUGLAS THOMPSON

ENTANGLEMENT

FINALLY, TRAVEL TO THE STARS IS HERE

In 2180, travel to neighbouring star systems has been mastered thanks to quantum teleportation using the 'entanglement' of sub-atomic matter; astronauts on earth can be duplicated on a remote world once the dupliport chamber has arrived there. In this way a variety of worlds can be explored, but what humanity discovers is both surprising and disturbing, enlightening and shocking. Each alternative to mankind that the astronauts find, sheds light on human shortcomings and potential while offering fresh perspectives of life on Earth. Meanwhile, at home, the lives of the astronauts and those in charge of the missions will never be the same again.

Best described as philosophical science fiction, *Entanglement* explores our assumptions about such constants as death, birth, sex and conflict, as the characters in the story explore distant worlds and the intelligent life that lives there. It is simultaneously a novel and a series of short stories: multiple worlds, each explored in a separate chapter, a separate story; every one another step on mankind's journey outwards to the stars and inwards to our own psyche. Yet the whole is much greater than the sum of the parts; the synergy of the episodes results in an overarching story arc that ultimately tells us more about ourselves than about the rest of the universe.

ISBN: 9781908168153 (epub, kindle) / 9781908168054 (336pp paperback)
Visit bit.ly/EntanglementBook

THE RHYMER
an Heredyssey

The Rhymer, an Heredyssey defies classification in any one literary genre. A satire on contemporary society, particularly the art world, it is also a comic-poetic meditation on the nature of life, death and morality. Nadith, a wanderer who appears to be an amnesiac or possibly brain-damaged tramp, is on a journey through the satellite towns and suburbs of a city called Urbis. With spiteful intentions, he is seeking his brother Zenir, a successful artist, who is always two steps ahead of him. But as his brother's fortunes wane, his own seem to be on the increase. When Nadith finally catches up with Zenir, what will they make of each other? Told entirely in the first person in a rhythmic stream of lyricism, Nadith's story reads like Shakespeare on acid, leaving the reader to guess at the truth that lies behind his madness. Is Nadith a mental health patient or a conman? ... Or as he himself comes to believe, the reincarnation of the thirteenth century Scottish seer True Thomas The Rhymer, a man who never lied nor died but disappeared one day to return to the realm of the faeries who had first given him his clairvoyant gifts?

ISBN: 9781908168511 (epub, kindle) / 9781908168412 (192pp paperback)
Visit bit.ly/TheRhymer-Heredyssey

Tej Turner

The Janus Cycle

The Janus Cycle can best be described as gritty, surreal, urban fantasy. The over-arching story revolves around a nightclub called Janus, which is not merely a location but virtually a character in its own right. On the surface it appears to be a subcultural hub where the strange and disillusioned who feel alienated and oppressed by society escape to be free from convention; but underneath that façade is a surreal space in time where the very foundations of reality are twisted and distorted. But the special unique vibe of Janus is hijacked by a bandwagon of people who choose to conform to alternative lifestyles simply because it has become fashionable to be "different", and this causes many of its original occupants to feel lost and disenchanted. We see the story of Janus unfold through the eyes of seven narrators, each with their own perspective and their own personal journey. A story in which the nightclub itself goes on a journey. But throughout, one character, a strange girl, briefly appears and reappears warning the narrators that their individual journeys are going to collide in a cataclysmic event. Is she just another one of the nightclub's denizens, a cynical mischief-maker out to create havoc or a time-traveller trying to prevent an impending disaster?

ISBN: 9781908168566 (epub, kindle) / 9781908168467 (224pp paperback)
Visit bit.ly/JanusCycle

Dave Weaver

Jacey's Kingdom

Jacey's Kingdom is an enthralling tale revolving around a startlingly desperate reality: Jacey Jackson, a talented student destined for Cambridge, collapses with a brain tumour during her final history exam at school. In her mind she struggles through a quasi-historical sixth century dreamscape whilst the surgeons fight to save her life.

Jacey is helped by a stranger called George, who finds himself trapped in her nightmare after a terrible car accident. There are quests, battles, and a love story ahead of them, before we find out if Jacey will awake from her coma or perish on the operating table. And who, or what, is George? In this book, Dave Weaver questions our perception of reality and the redemptive power of dreams; are our experiences of fear, conflict, friendship and love any less real or meaningful when they take place in the mind rather than the 'real' physical world?

ISBN: 9781908168313 (epub, kindle) / 9781908168214 (272pp paperback)

Visit bit.ly/JaceysKingdom

Japanese Daisy Chain

In *Japanese Daisy Chain*, Dave Weaver takes us on a very individualistic journey around contemporary Japan through the eyes of the participants in a series of apparently unrelated incidents. Events that, to an outsider may seem a little strange or hard to explain, but to which we are given an exclusive insight – enabling us to see the consequence of contact with the paranormal, fantastic or downright weird. As each episode unfurls and our journey progresses, we alone can see the invisible thread that connects these events, albeit tenuously. A participant on each occasion, a minor character if you will, becomes the main protagonist in the next, creating a human daisy-chain. Just like a daisy-chain, what goes around comes around. The chain is completed and we finally understand karma.

ISBN: 9781908168504 (epub, kindle) / 9781908168405 (240pp paperback)

Visit bit.ly/JapaneseDaisyChain

THE BLACK HOLE BAR

Simon, a traveller with time to kill, enters an inn on the outskirts of London. Inside he meets a motley crew competing to tell tales for their own amusement. So starts Dave Weaver's new novel, *The Black Hole Bar*, which has already been compared to Chaucer's *Canterbury Tales* and Boccaccio's *Decameron*.

Simon has stumbled into what was supposed to be a closed session for the Black Hole Bar Writers' Group, their monthly short story competition. Simon writes stories too and begrudgingly they let him participate. The stories begin, and Simon starts taking the competition far more seriously than he intended.

Each of them tells two stories, variously strange, amusing and occasionally downright scary. The writers' own histories, come tumbling out one by one into the cramped room. As they do so, we learn more about the background of this world. A world recognisable as our possible future but also chilling in its recent past.

ISBN: 9781908168597 (epub, kindle) / 9781908168498 (256pp paperback)

Visit bit.ly/BlackHoleBar

www.ingramcontent.com/pod-product-compliance
Lightning Source LLC
Chambersburg PA
CBHW030801200726
48285CB00013B/390